Solitude

Cecile Czobitko

ISBN 978-1-64458-259-6 (paperback)
ISBN 978-1-64458-260-2 (digital)

Christian Faith Publishing, Inc.
832 Park Avenue
Meadville, PA 16335
www.christianfaithpublishing.com

Printed in the United States of America

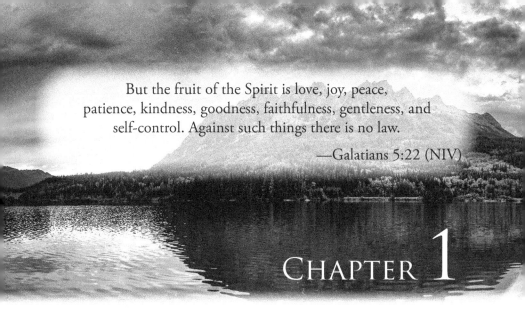

But the fruit of the Spirit is love, joy, peace,
patience, kindness, goodness, faithfulness, gentleness, and
self-control. Against such things there is no law.

—Galatians 5:22 (NIV)

CHAPTER 1

The phone kept ringing and ringing then went to voice mail. A short time later, it rang again then went to voice mail. This happened for a while. Daniel could hear the phone, but it seemed like his body was not letting him respond. Finally, Daniel moved his left arm and reached for the phone. He saw that it was his dad who was calling him.

"Hey, Dad, what's up?" he mumbled in the phone.

"Daniel, are you okay? You sound a hundred miles away," his father said.

"Dad, I'm alright. I had to face a very hard incident last night. Why did you call?" he asked.

"Daniel, your sister went into labor this morning. She asked me to call you to ask if you could go be with her. Ted is with her, but she says you promised her you would be there when the time came."

"Yes, Dad, tell her I'll be there as soon as I can."

Daniel pressed the off button on his phone and rolled out of bed. So, Lilly was having her baby today. He found it hard to believe that his twin sister would soon be a mother. No one believed that they were twins. Lilly was petite, with dark brown hair and brown eyes, while Daniel was nearly six feet in height and had blondish red hair and blue eyes. She was the picture of their mother and Daniel the picture of their dad.

Growing up, Daniel and Lilly had a very close brother-sister relationship, and in adulthood that had not changed. Even after Lilly had married Ted two years ago, they had remained close. Lilly always took comfort in her brother. Lilly had fallen for Ted, a guy that reminded Daniel of Tom Cruise—handsome but too short. Ted was a nice enough guy. He had a lot of confidence in himself and knew what he wanted unlike Daniel who always questioned all the decisions he ever made. Ted owned a restaurant and was a professional cook. People sought him out to have him cater or barbeque for their functions. He was reputed to be an excellent chef.

Daniel hurried to take a shower. It brought him out of the drowsiness he felt. After last night, he wasn't sure if he wanted to face a new day. In his eight years as a police officer, he had never witnessed such wickedness. He got dressed, found his truck keys and was off to the hospital. When he got there, he was shown to his sister's room. Lilly was sitting on the bed and looked relaxed. Ted was by her side holding her hand. Pregnancy suited her. Daniel had made fun of her big belly as it became bigger, telling her she had swallowed a pumpkin seed and now there was a pumpkin growing in her.

"Oh, Daniel am I ever so glad to see you. I don't know that I can do this but now that my two favorite guys are here, I know I'll be alright." She rubbed her big belly and said to the baby, "Uncle Daniel is here now; you can come out now." She just finished saying that when a pain gripped her. She squeezed Ted's hand and cried, "I… I… I… I think the pain is getting worse! Can you get the nurse?"

The nurse examined Lilly and told her she was progressing just fine, that it would not be long now. Ted and Daniel took turns holding her hand, putting ice on her lips and encouraging her with every moment of pain.

In the late afternoon, Lilly and Ted's little daughter was born. Daniel was happy to see her sister safely through the birth of his niece. After the birth, he went to meet his father in the waiting room. His father did not like to see people in pain so he had opted not to be in the delivery room.

"Lilly is alright, she did really good. You are now a grandpa to a beautiful little girl. Grandpa Ken! That sounds okay, I suppose," Daniel teased then added, "The nurse said we can visit for a short time."

When they got to Lilly's room, Lilly was sitting in bed holding her baby daughter. Ken went to stand by her and said, "Hello, my girl. How are you doing? Let me see this new baby. You just made me a grandpa, but I can't say that I mind." He gave his daughter a kiss on the forehead, he said, "She looks just like a little angel."

"Would you like to hold her, dad?" Lilly asked. He carefully took the baby from Lilly and took a closer look at her. He saw that she had long, perfect little fingers and a head full of dark hair. *She looks just like her mom*, he thought.

"She is lovely, Lilly. Congratulations. You must be tired, so we better go and let you get some rest," Ken said as he handed the baby back to Lilly. He shook hands with Ted and said, "Congratulations, Ted! You are now the father of a precious little girl. We'll leave you two so you can get to know her."

After Daniel had congratulated Lilly and Ted, he left with his dad.

As they left the hospital, Ken asked, "Want to go for a bite to eat?" Daniel's father—Ken Erikson—was a lawyer. He could read people very well. He knew that something was bothering Daniel. They had a close relationship, and sharing a meal was a good way to get Daniel to talk.

"Sure, I'm a little hungry. I don't think I had anything to eat all day. Let's go to Ed's Place. He makes a good hamburger," Daniel said as they drove to the restaurant.

After they ordered their food, his dad asked, "Daniel were you at that accident last night? I heard that two little kids died." Daniel did not say anything for a moment. He was not sure he wanted to talk about it.

"Dad, if you don't mind, I can't talk about it just now. Let's talk about something else." Ken knew not to push so they talked about the weather and how little Lilly's baby was. They got their food and after Daniel had taken a few bites of his burger, he looked

5

at his dad, shook his head and said, "Yeah, two kids died." He took another bite of his burger, but did not say anything more until he had finished eating his meal. What he had seen at the accident had disturbed him. He looked at his dad, took a breath and said, "The evidence showed that the car in which the children had been was in the wrong. It showed that the dad ran a red light, and a semi plowed right in the car. The entire back side of the car was pushed in. The kids had no chance of surviving, but the dad walked away with minor injuries. It's just not fair," Daniel shook his head, and took a sip of his coffee.

"The dad was drunk. He was sitting on the gurney complaining that his back hurt. He did not seem too concerned that his kids were dead. When I went to interview him, I could smell the liquor. He admitted that he killed his kids so his ex would not have them. In all the years I've been a cop, I have never seen such a low life. It took all my self-control not to knock the daylights out of him. It's a good thing Rodney, the EMT, was there." Daniel shook his head again and continued, "When I see this type of cruelty, it makes me want to yell 'Stop this world I want to get off!'"

Daniel could not go on. Ken could see his son was shaken by what he had witnessed. He reached out and touched his sons hand. He looked in his sons eyes and said, "You have to take some time off, son. If you don't, you'll burn yourself out."

"Yes, I know. The chief already told me that. I'm thinking of going on a road trip, maybe go see Charlie on the farm. I know Charlie would put me to work. Could be just what I need."

Charlie was Daniel's older cousin by a year. They had grown up together. They had spent their summers on their grandpa's farm, the farm Charlie now owned. Their grandfather had willed the farm to Charlie because Charlie was the only one that had loved the farm as much as he did. The farm was still a place the family went to, a getaway from the busy life they led.

"When will you be going?" Ken asked.

"I have to finish off the report for that accident, then the chief said I had three weeks off. So, I think I'll pack up and be gone by tomorrow night."

"Make sure you stop by to say goodbye to your sister. If you don't, that's all I'll hear from her," Ken said as Daniel drove him to his car.

"Yeah, I will," Daniel replied.

After he finish the police reports, Daniel went to the hardware store to buy supplies and to the grocery store for the food he would need for his trip. In the morning, he would slip by Lilly's to say good-bye, then he would be on his own, free to do what he wanted.

I love those who love me,
and those who seek me find me.

—Proverb 8:17 (NIV)

CHAPTER 2

As Daniel drove, he could feel his spirit rising. After what he had seen as a policeman, he needed to see something that would make him feel right again. Everyday in his work, he saw the worst in people. He was starting to believe that evil prevailed in this world. Where was the goodness?

He had been raised in a loving family. His father lived by strong moral beliefs and had instilled this in him. Daniel had joined the police force to help people. He thought by being a police officer he could make a difference, do some good in the world he lived in— but now he wondered if the work he did was all worth it. When he thought like that, he knew it was time he had a break or work would do him in.

He had never taken a road trip on his own. He headed for the mountains in the hopes he would find a secluded place, maybe by a lake. After driving for a few hours, he came to a rest stop. He got out of the truck and stretched his legs. The scenery in the distance was stunning with mountains surrounding an opal green lake, their slopes covered by tall evergreen trees. As he leaned against his truck, eating his lunch, he decided to drive to the lake to find a campsite.

When he got to the lake, he found a camp-ground and was surprised to find that there was no one else camping. He pitched his tent near the beach, where there was a fire pit and a picnic table. He went to get an armful of chopped wood from the wood pile the campground provided, thankful that this campground provided wood for their campers. He unloaded his supplies and took his kayak off the roof rack. He was now set to have a good camping experience.

The water in the lake was crystal clear and very inviting for a swim, but Daniel quickly changed his mind about a swim when he found the water too cold to swim in. It made his feet cramp up. Since swimming was out of the picture, he decided a tour on the lake with his kayak would be lovely. At first the wind was light and the water smooth, but after a half-hour of paddling, the wind suddenly picked up, making the lake very rough. Daniel turned toward shore and went back to camp.

After walking on the beach for a while and throwing a few rocks in the water, he found that he was a little bored. This was not going like he had expected. It was too early for supper so he decided to go for a drive up the road that went past the camp site. As Daniel drove, the road became very rough, just like a washboard. He had to be careful not to drive into one of the many potholes. *This must have been a logging road; not very well maintained*, he thought. On the left side of the road, there was a new growth of trees where it had been logged years ago. On the right side, the trees were tall evergreens.

Daniel was thinking of turning back when he noticed something white in the distance. When he got closer he saw it was a "For Sale" sign. He parked by the gate and started walking up the driveway. Both sides of the driveway were lined by tall fir trees creating a canopy overhead. As he walked, he wondered who would live in a place like this. After a short while, a house and a shop came into view. When he got closer to the house, he saw there was a large deck in the front. A short distance away, there was a vegetable garden with small plants growing. He walked on the deck and went to check the door. It was locked. The house faced the lake, overlooking a low bluff. Daniel took in the wonderful view of the mountains reflecting on the lake, and the surrounding trees edging the water making it appear dark green.

Again, he wondered who the lucky person was who owned the place. He walked off the deck and went to the edge of the bluff to see if he could go to the lake shore, but he found that it was to steep to walk down. The bluff rose about five feet up from the shore. He walked along the edge of the bluff until he came to a ravine where he found a path that led down to the shore. He could hear water flowing but could not see it because of the undergrowth.

As he walked down the path, he found that it became rather steep, but with some care he made it to the shore. Daniel was surprised to see a narrow, gravelly beach—no sand just round pebbly rocks. He took in the view and got his iPhone to take a few pictures of the view from shore. As he walked back to the house, he took a picture of it and of the surrounding yard.

Once at the house, Daniel walked to the back and saw a large grassy field surrounded by trees. At the edge of the clearing, the terrain sloped down where Daniel found a swift running creek. With difficulty, because of the undergrowth, he followed it past the house and to a small waterfall just before it drained into the lake.

As he walked to the front of the house, he noticed solar panels on the roof. *This place must be off the grid. Looks like it has been built to be self-sufficient*, he thought. He went back up the deck and sat for a while. *I wonder how much a place like this would cost? It would be interesting to live away from everything and everyone. Sure would be different from the life I have now.* He shook his head, and decided to return to his truck. He copied down the realtors number and drove back to his camp.

When he got to his camp, he built a fire and cooked his supper of hotdogs and beans. As he ate, he kept thinking of the place he had seen. *I can see myself living in a place like that. The scenery is just stunning. Can you imagine waking up to those mountains every morning! It would be incredible. What a place to live in! And that log house, it would be living like a pioneer. It might be just the change I need. I wonder?* The more he thought about it, the more it seemed like the thing to do. All night he churned the thought in his mind.

After two days camping, Daniel packed up his gear and decided to drive to Charlie's farm. He had to discuss his plan with his cousin. He was sure Charlie would laugh him off the planet.

Charlie's farm was a few hours away. When Daniel got there, Charlie was surprised but very happy to see his cousin. Charlie was on his way to do some seeding, so he told Daniel to make himself handy by helping Carol, his wife. Charlie had met Carol on a holiday to Florida. They had married after knowing each other for only a month. Now after six years of marriage, they had two beautiful boys. Carol had such an infectious smile. Daniel could see why Charlie had married her. She looked like a Polynesian princess with her light brown skin and dark eyes and hair. Charlie was definitely a lucky man.

He spent the day doing chores and helping Carol with the boys. When Charlie returned in the late afternoon, he found Daniel turning over the dirt in Carol's garden. Charlie went in the house to wash up while Daniel finished with the garden. They met on the porch and sat in their grandparents' old chairs.

"How have you been? You haven't been here in over a year. Would you like a beer?" He had just finished saying the words when Carol showed up with two beers.

"Ah, thanks, sweetheart, you always know what I want. Where are the boys?" He took the beers, opened one and handed it to Daniel. Daniel took a swallow. He found the beer was very cold and tasted so good.

"They're helping me with supper. They wanted to make something special for Uncle Daniel," she said with a huge smile on her face. She gave Charlie a kiss on the cheek and went back in the house.

"You sure are a lucky man, Charlie, you have such a wonderful wife and family. I can't say the same. In the eight years since we graduated, you have a place and a family. You have built something for yourself. I don't really have anything. I think I am burnt-out. I don't think I can do this police thing anymore."

"Ah, Daniel, is it that bad? Are you thinking of leaving the force?"

"I don't know yet. I'm thinking of buying a place. I saw this place for sale. It's in the mountains, away from everything. It's off the grid. Here, do you want to see the pictures I took?" Daniel said as he retrieved the pictures off his phone.

Charlie looked at the pictures but did not say anything for a while. He finished his beer, looked at the bottle, and said, "Daniel, the pictures certainly look very intriguing. If you want me to go see the place with you, I'll do that. You call that realtor and set up a viewing. Try to make it for Sunday. We could make it a family outing."

"Charlie really? You would do that for me? I thought that you would have yourself a good laugh. Tell me what you really think," Daniel said a little surprised by Charlie's response.

"Daniel, before I can say anything, I have to see the place. Then maybe I'll have my laugh. I think supper is ready. Let's go in." Daniel felt so good to be here with this family.

After supper, Daniel called the realtor and set a viewing for Sunday afternoon. So early on Sunday morning, all the family and Daniel piled in Charlie's Suburban to go see the property.

It was a beautiful day. The traffic was light. *Just right for a family outing*, Daniel thought. He sat in the front and as they drove, he and Charlie reminisced about the times they spent together when they were younger. Charlie's boys—Liam, five and Dennis, four—loved to hear stories of their dad. Daniel had been the prankster, putting fake snakes and mice in Charlie's bed. Once Daniel put a little kitten in Charlie's sock drawer, and went to tell Charlie that he had seen a rat in it. Charlie did not like rats and he would not open that drawer. He had asked Daniel to open it to let the rat out but Daniel had refused, saying that it was not his drawer. After some coaxing, Charlie finally opened the drawer and when he saw the kitten move, he screamed very loud. Daniel laughed so hard his sides hurt. Even now it made him laugh.

"We did have a lot of fun those days. We were always doing something. Life was really nice on Grandpa's farm," Daniel said. "I wish that those summer days had never ended." Charlie nodded his head in agreement. When Daniel had gone to the Police Academy, everything changed. It was like Daniel could not separate the policeman from his personal life—like he was always on duty.

"How much longer 'til we get to this place?" Charlie asked.

"We just passed the lake. It's not to far now, but the road gets really rough."

"It sure is off the beaten path, that's for sure. But very scenic," Carol said from the backseat.

The boys had fallen asleep so they went on without speaking until they got to the gate of the property. The gate was opened so they continued until they reached the house where they were greeted by two men. One had white hair and was hunched over a little. He looked very old. The other was a burly, middle-aged man wearing a suit. He introduced himself as Larry, the realtor, and the older man as Zeb, the owner of the place. Zeb was very friendly and looked genuinely happy to see them. He shook everyone's hands as they were introduced, including the boys. Daniel introduced himself as the one interested in the property. Zeb welcomed everyone in the house and offered them some tea.

"So, you want to see the place?" Zeb asked Daniel. "Before we do that, I have a little something I want to say. This is part of the deal. I'm not going to change my mind on this so I'm putting it right up front. The deal is I'll only sell if you agree to let me stay here 'til I die. If you buy the place and stay with me 'til I die, I'm going to put you in my will. It'll state that you'll get back the full amount you paid for the place."

"That is a very unusual request. Why would you want to do something like that? Don't you have anyone to care for you?" Daniel asked.

"I'm a very old man. The doctors say I don't have long to live. My daughter wants to put me in a nursing home. I would not survive a day in that kind of place. No, I want to end my days here. The thing is they will not let me live here by myself. I need a little help sometimes. So, if I could get someone to make this agreement, it would work just right," Zeb said in a sad voice.

Daniel could not believe what he heard. The old man was giving away the place. All he had to do was take care of him until he died.

"Can we have a look around the property before I agree to your condition?" Daniel asked.

"Sure, Larry will take you around," Zeb said. Larry took them outside, and Zeb stayed in the house. Larry first took them to the workshop and opened the large doors. It was empty. When Daniel looked in, he was pleased to see that it would be large enough to park a truck inside. Larry told them the workshop had a wooden frame and a metal roof.

Next, they looked around the house. Larry told them that the house was built with cinder blocks. The blocks were covered by log type siding making the house look like it was a log house. The roof had a high pitch and was covered with solar panels. In the front of the house there were large windows taking advantage of the southern exposure. There was a large deck that surrounded the southern and eastern side of the house. Just off the southern deck was a small green house in which grew what looked like to be tomato plants. Larry explained how the solar panels and the batteries worked, and continued to explain how the water and electrical systems functioned. Daniel thought that all of it was a little too complicated. He never considered that these features would be a part of living here. Once they had gone over most of the property, they went inside the house and found Zeb asleep in his chair. He was instantly awoken by the sound of their voices.

"Well, what do you think young man? Taking my deal? I'm not asking for much money, twenty thousand would be a fair price," Zeb asked.

"Zeb, you drive a hard bargain. I'll have to think it over. I did not think when I bought a place, it would come with an old man. I'm not saying no. I like the place. I can see myself living here. I just don't know if I can take care of you. That's a big responsibility. Can you give me a few days to get back to you?"

"Take care of me? There's not much to that. I need help with cooking and cleaning. Let me put your mind at ease. I still go to the bathroom by myself, and I can wash on my own. Maybe I'd need help with filling the tub for my bath occasionally, but it would not be too hard to care for me. You'd have to remind me to take my medicine too. I forget sometimes," Zeb said with a smile on his face.

"Okay, Zeb, I have to think about it. It was very nice to meet you. I'll call Larry when I make my decision."

After they finished the tea Zeb had placed in front of them, they said goodbye to Zeb and Larry.

On the way back home, they discussed the offer. To Daniel's surprise, Charlie was not laughing but was supporting him with the idea of buying the place. The only thing was the old man—could he move in and live with this old guy? "There maybe something good about having the old guy around. He could show you how the place works and teach you how to live off the grid. There's that big garden; would you know what to do with all that the garden produces? He could show you what he does. I think he would be very resourceful and beneficial for you. It would be interesting to live like that," Charlie said.

"I was thinking the very same, Charlie. Zeb seems like a good sort. He does have a lot of know-how. The place looks like it has been well maintained. The house looks like it was well-built; built with cinder blocks. I don't know how that water system works, though. Did you get all the things Larry said?" Daniel asked.

"No, it sounded a bit complicated. See, there is another thing the old guy could show you."

"Yeah, you're right. Having the old man there would make things easier. He would help me get to know how to work the place, and I would help him with his needs," Daniel replied.

It was a long drive home. Daniel volunteered to drive so Charlie went to sit in the back and cuddled with his wife and kids. Daniel was left alone with his thoughts. *If I bought the place, I would have to leave the police force. Is that what I want? I just don't know.* He considered that for a while. Then he thought, *I could study law in that place and be uninterrupted. It sure would be quiet. Life would be simple there. There'd be no orders to follow, no conflicts, no one asking me to do things I did not want to do. I would not have to see all the suffering people inflicted on themselves. I've seen enough misery and grief to last me a life time.* Just thinking of living there gave him relief from the heaviness he felt in his heart. But was that enough to leave his work and go live in the bush? He wondered. He knew he was not in a good frame of mind. Maybe he needed to wait before deciding. He formulated a plan. He would wait until he went back to work and then see how he felt. If he still could not shake this heaviness he felt, then he would consider leaving the force.

He mulled it over and over in his mind as he drove. Another thought came to mind. *I'll have to talk this over with Dad and Lilly. I wonder what they would say about me moving there. Maybe the chief could give me some advice. I'll go talk to him. I should call Larry to tell him to give me a month to decide.* By the time he got to Charlie's place, he knew what he had to do to make his decision.

Daniel stayed with Charlie for the rest of the week. He found the physical work on the farm very therapeutic for him. He loved the slower pace of life; he liked the tranquility. With only one more week of vacation, he said goodbye to Charlie and went to see his father and sister to tell them about his situation. He decided he would go speak to the chief once he was back to work.

His dad was about to leave his office after a long day's work when Daniel walked in.

"Hi, Dad, how are things?" Daniel asked.

"Hello, Daniel, you looked well-rested. By the color in your face, I'd say you spent a lot of time in the sun. How are you doing?" Ken asked.

"I'm better. It was great to get away. Charlie says hi. Dad, I have something I want to go over with you," Daniel said as he sat in the chair in front of his dad's desk.

"Sure, Daniel, what is it?" Ken inquired.

"I'm thinking of making a change in my life. I went to see this place, and I'm considering buying it. I don't know if you'd approve of it, though," Daniel said.

"Why would I not approve? Is it condemned?" asked his dad.

Daniel was a little reluctant about telling his dad. The place was way out in the bush with no power, no telephone and no one around—not something everyone would want.

"No, it's not condemned. It's a little isolated," he said. He went on to describe the place and the old guy he would live with. Daniel looked at his dad for his reaction. Ken did not say anything for a long time. So Daniel continued saying what Charlie's reaction had been.

"Charlie went to see the place with you?" Ken asked, a bit surprised.

"Yes, he thinks it's an interesting place," Still his dad kept quiet. Daniel could see that he was thinking this over. Ken was a man that would consider the options before he would voice an opinion.

"Daniel, I know you are struggling with police work. The case you had before you went on holidays disturbed you. If you want a different way to live, it's up to you. It's your life and you should live it the way that suits you. It's your decision, son. I'll support you in whatever decision you make," Ken assured him.

"Thanks, Dad, I'm glad to hear that. Now, I must go talk to Lilly. She might have a problem with me moving away. How is she doing with the baby? What did she name her?"

"The last time I was there she looked very happy. Ted took time off work to be home. They are quite taken by that little princess. Lilly named her after your mother, Elizabeth. They call her Beth. She'll love to see you. I'm going there for supper tonight. I'm sure she will love having you too. Ted is barbequing."

"Okay, Dad, I'll see you there. Sounds good. I should go home and unload my truck. Maybe I could do with a shower and a shave. It has been good to be off work. I wish I had another three weeks. Bye for now."

Daniel went back to his apartment. As he unloaded the truck, he thought about the name Lilly had given her baby, his mother's name. Their mother had died when they were young teenagers. The first years without her had been very hard on them. Ken had not taken her death well and had buried himself in his work, leaving Lilly and Daniel to look after each other. That was when Lilly had started to rely on him more and more. They had always been close but with their mother gone they became even closer. It was in those years Daniel and Lilly had gone to spend all their summer months on their grandpa's farm. In their last year of high school, their dad had become active in their lives again.

After putting all his camping gear away, Daniel cleaned up, then drove to his sister's place. He was a little apprehensive about telling Lilly what his plans were. But on the other hand, she would be his voice of reason. It seemed like she had a solution to all his problems. He was curious to see what she thought.

When he got to her house, Lilly was sitting on the porch swing with the baby. He ran up the steps and went to give her a kiss on the cheek, and said, "Hey there, sis, how are you and the little one doing?"

"We are just the best. I've missed you. Seems like you were gone a long time. Tell me where you have been," Lilly said, as she fussed with the baby's blanket.

Daniel told her about the farm and the camping, and he ended with the place he went to see and was thinking of buying. He could see that Lilly was not too pleased.

"You have got to be kidding me, Daniel Erikson," Lilly said loudly. "You can't be thinking of leaving me. You have always been there for me. I don't think I could live without you." She was just about in tears. Ted heard her voice and came to the porch to see what was happening.

"What is it, love?" Ted asked, surprised to see Daniel there.

"He's leaving us, Ted. He's going to buy this place and go live in the bush. You have to talk him out of it, Ted," Lilly took the baby and went in the house. Big tears were running down her cheeks. Daniel was a little surprised by Lilly's reaction. *Maybe that would not be the right move after all,* he thought.

"Are you thinking of moving, Daniel? It sure has upset Lilly. Want to tell me what you're planning?" Ted asked. He was fond of Lilly's brother, but he sometimes thought that Lilly relied more on Daniel instead of him.

"Go be with Lilly, I think she needs you now. I'll tell you later," Daniel said sorry that he had upset his sister.

Ted went in the house and found Lilly in the baby's room, putting the baby in her crib.

"Come, Lilly, let's talk about this." Ted led Lilly to their bedroom. He had her sit on the bed and said, "Lilly, you have to let Daniel to lead his life the way he wants. We should support him in what he wants to do. He supported us when we got married. He didn't tell you that you could not marry me. You have me now to rely on. That's what a husband is for. Have I ever let you down?"

"No, Ted, you have been really good, a great husband and great daddy to the baby. It's just that Daniel has been there for me all my life. It's hard to let go of that. You know how emotional I can get. You're right, I should lean on you more and let Daniel go live his life like he wants. I was a little hard on him, wasn't I?"

"Why don't you lie down and rest a while? I'll go talk to Daniel and see how serious he is about leaving us," Ted said, covering Lilly up.

"Okay, I am tired. I'll rest until Beth wakes up. She should be hungry in an hour or so," Lilly replied.

Lilly awoke when she heard her baby and went to her. After feeding her, she went to find her husband and brother. She found them and her dad on the patio getting ready to barbeque.

"Have a good rest, Lilly?" Daniel asked. "You still upset with me?"

"Daniel, I'm sorry I reacted like I did. I should be more supportive. I'm just a bundle of emotions these days. I was upset but I've calmed down. I'd like to see that place. Would you have any pictures of it?" After Daniel showed the pictures, Lilly said, "These pictures look very beautiful, Daniel. I can see why you would want to live there. How serious are you in buying this place?"

"I have not decided to buy the place. I don't know what I'm going to do yet. I'll decide that after I've gone back to work and see how that goes. Let's talk about something else now." Daniel felt sorry he had ever mentioned what he was planning.

For the rest of the evening, they talked about the baby, how Charlie and his family were doing, and how long it had been since they all had been there together. The meal that Ted cooked for them was superb.

The next Monday, Daniel reported back for work. The minute he stepped in the station, he felt a heavy feeling come upon him. After he sat through the debriefing, he joined his partner in their cruiser. Today they were charged to patrol the main highway going north. They wrote a few speeding tickets—nothing major. The week was slow until Friday night when they found a woman on the side of the road. She said there had been a car that was stopped and a guy standing by it, waving for her to stop. The minute she stopped, a guy came to her car, dragged her out and assaulted her. He got in her car and drove off. She said that the car that was stopped had sped off the minute the guy came to her car.

Daniel could tell she had been badly beaten up so he called for an ambulance. As they waited for the ambulance, they questioned her but she could not describe the guys. It was dark and it had happened so fast. Once the woman was safe in the ambulance, Daniel and his partner continued up the same road. A few miles on, they came upon a car in the ditch. They called the plates in and discovered the car belonged to the woman they had rescued.

It was late in the night when they returned to the station. What Daniel had witnessed that night brought back all the bad sensations he had felt before he had gone on holidays. He could not imagine why a guy would do such a thing to a woman. Why? What a senseless act. He took these acts personally now. The heaviness he felt was becoming to much for him to bear. He could not see himself doing this for much longer. He had to talk to the chief.

When Daniel returned to work the next day, he learned that they had found fingerprints in the car and a guy had been picked up. At the beginning of the interrogation, the guy admitted taking the car. He said the car belonged to his girlfriend. He was driving back to her place when he had swerved to miss hitting a deer and ended in the ditch. When asked who his girlfriend was, he did not want to say. In the end, he finally admitted to beating up the woman and leaving her on the road. Said she deserved it because she had made fun of him at a bar and belittled him in front of his buds.

The guy's story made Daniel's blood boil. If he met this guy on the street, he was sure he would not be able to control himself. Daniel knew that this was not a normal reaction. He had to get away from these incidents. When he got to the station, he walked straight to the chief's office and sat down. The chief had an open-door policy. If one of his officers wanted to talk to him, he was available at any time. Everyone knew him as Chief but his name was Barry Davidson. Barry had joined the force in his twenties and over the years, had worked himself to become the chief. He knew how his officers felt so he was not surprised when he saw Daniel come in.

"Hey Daniel, how were your holidays? Did you do anything special?" the chief inquired.

"Yes, the holidays were great but it now feels like I need more time off," Daniel said as he rubbed the side of his head. He had to get a grip. He took a deep breath then continued saying, "I think I'm losing it, Chief. I take everything so personally. I just don't think police work is for me. I'm losing my self-control. I don't know how to cope anymore."

"Sounds like you're stressed out Daniel. You're a good officer but you're right, you tend to take things very personally. It's difficult work dealing with a lot of bad stuff. What do you want to do Daniel?" the chief asked.

"I need time off. A leave of absence," Daniel answered very reluctantly.

"The force gives its officers leaves if they want. You can take a year off and still keep your pension and seniority. You sure that's what you want, Daniel?" the chief asked sympathetically.

"Yes, I think so chief. I can't go on like this. It's eating me up," Daniel pleaded.

The chief nodded his head and said, "When do you want to start this leave?"

"As soon as possible. Today, if it can be arranged," Daniel said sorrowfully.

"Daniel, you sure of this?"

Daniel nodded in the affirmative.

"If that is what you want, I can make the arrangements. We're going to miss you. You've worked hard for this force. I'm going to hate to see you go." He looked to see if Daniel had changed his mind. When Daniel did not say anything, he continued, "Okay, you can take your leave starting today. I'll make the arrangements. Hope you get better, Daniel. You are one of the good guys, remember that." The chief stood up and went to shake Daniel's hand.

Daniel felt so exhausted. He went home and went straight to bed. It was dark outside when he woke up. The clock on the side table showed 4:00 a.m. *What? I slept for twelve hours?* he thought. It had been four in the afternoon when he had laid down. *The power must have gone off,* he thought but the figures on the clock were not flashing. He grabbed his phone and sure enough, it too showed 4 a.m.—he had slept twelve hours straight.

For a minute, he was not sure why he had come home so early. Then he remembered the talk with the chief. He was on leave now. Oh, what had he agreed to? What would his dad say to him? No, this is what he had to do, no second guessing himself. He would call Larry in the morning to tell him he was accepting Zeb's offer. He turned over and went back to sleep.

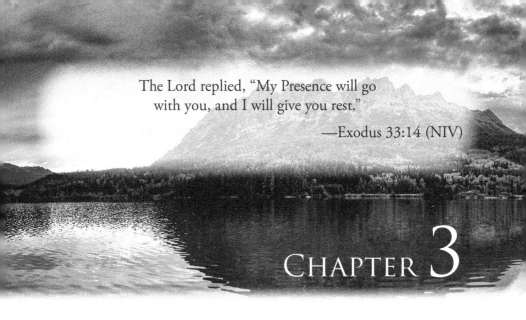

The Lord replied, "My Presence will go
with you, and I will give you rest."

—Exodus 33:14 (NIV)

CHAPTER 3

T he next morning, Daniel met his dad for breakfast. "I did it,
Dad," Daniel said with a big smile.

"You did what Daniel?" his dad asked.

"I finally made the decision to buy the place in the mountains.
I'm on leave from the force. I'm going to call Larry after breakfast
to tell him I'm buying the place." Daniel's mood was light and very
cheerful.

"You're on leave? Daniel what are you saying? You quit the
force?" his dad inquired.

"I took a leave of absence, Dad. For a year. I can't do police work
any longer. You think I'm making a mistake, Dad?" Daniel looked at
his dad for reassurance. It took Ken a few minutes before he replied.

"Son, I told you before, it's your life. You must live it the way
you want. I know you have been thinking of this, I'm just surprised
you made up your mind so quickly. Do you have enough money
to live on for the year? The purchase will set you back some," Ken
questioned.

"Yes, Dad, the way I calculate it, I can live there for half of what
I live on here. I won't have rent or utility bills. Once I've paid for the
place, I'll have enough to live on for two years if I want. I can't wait to

get started." Ken had not seen Daniel that excited for years. He was like a little boy with a new toy.

After Daniel had called Larry to tell him he was taking Zeb's deal, he asked his dad, "Dad, would you come with me? I'll need a lawyer to make sure all is right with my purchase. Larry said he would meet us there tomorrow." It pleased Daniel very much when his dad agreed to accompany him.

Zeb greeted them with a friendly handshake and invited them in for tea. They entered the house by the front door into a large room that contained the living room and kitchen. In the middle of the room was a cookstove with an old couch and chair sitting in front of it. To the left of the stove toward the back was a long counter with a hand pump and a sink. The backdoor was just beside the counter. On the sidewall, there was a window with a table and four chairs under it. To the right of the stove, a staircase led up to a loft and under the stair landing was a door that led into a bedroom.

"Larry tells me that we have a deal. He told me that you'll take over at the beginning of the month. That suits me just fine, the sooner the better. I have to pay for a caregiver now. Money, I don't like to pay," Zeb said as he poured the tea.

"I wanted my dad to see the place. Thanks for letting us visit. Last time I was here Larry explained about the solar panel system, but I think I need to know more about how it works, and how much capacity it has."

Zeb had a big smile on his face. He liked it when people asked him about what he had done.

"I'll be happy to show you. After all, it will be all yours in a few days. Come right this way. I'll show you the electrical system first." Zeb got up and went to the back of the house to the table.

"I put a trap door in the floor. Go ahead, open it. There's a light switch just at the bottom of the stairs." Daniel pulled the trap door open and went down the stairs. He found the light switch and turned it on. He stood at the bottom of the stairs and looked around. He was in a room about ten by ten square. The walls of the room were built with cinder blocks. On one side of the room there was wood cribbing that held old potatoes and carrots, and shelves with plastic tubs. On the opposite side, there was a bank of batteries. In the far corner of the room, there was a cylinder with pipes coming out of it going up into the ceiling.

Finally, Zeb made it down. "It's sure hard getting down these stairs. My knees are not so good these days." He walked over to the batteries. "The batteries are charged by the panels on the roof. In summer, there is plenty of power, in winter we must be a little more careful or we can run low on it. The batteries are low maintenance. We just have to monitor the water levels. See that cylinder there in the corner? It's the well. One water pipe is connected to an electric pump and the other is connected to the hand pump up by the sink. I diverted the creek a bit so the water can seep into the well."

"Why two water systems?" Daniel asked.

"In winter, there is just enough power for lights. I like the lights for the long winter nights so by using the hand pump, I conserve power. In summer, the electrical pump transports water to the two water tanks in the loft. One for cold, and one for warm water. There's a small circulation pump on the hot water tank that pumps the water in the pipes on the roof. The sun heats the water in the pipes and the heated water goes back into the tank. The pump keeps it circulating. I have a shower. Would you like to see it?" Zeb said, happy with himself.

"That is interesting, I'd like to see that," Ken said.

"Okay, let's go back up. Daniel make sure you turn the light off," Zeb said as he walked up the stairs.

Once everyone was up, Daniel closed the trap door and followed Zeb out of the backdoor. As they stepped through the door, Daniel and Ken noticed that they were not outside. They were in an enclosed area. The space was a covered patio with a cement floor. The roof was made of clear material giving the space some light. The patio was bordered by what looked like a woodshed and an outdoor toilet. To the right of the door, there were two cement walls that formed a shower stand. It had a cement floor with a drain in it.

Zeb walked to the shower and said, "My wife wanted a shower so I put the shower outside. There was no room for it in the house."

He went over to the taps and turned them on to show Daniel and Ken that the shower did work. "It was kind of drafty so I covered up the space and closed in that side there." Zeb pointed to the other side of the patio. "Makes for a nice outside room. I use the shower in April through to October. After that, it gets too cold and I have to get that washtub out again."

"What is in that building in the corner?" Daniel asked, pointing to the structure that stood right beside the shower wall. "Oh yes. That's the sauna. There's a little stove in there, works like a charm. I use it in winter to wash up sometimes. Go on, take a look."

"There's not much room inside there," Daniel said as he returned from looking inside.

"No, just enough room for two people. It works really well. My wife liked it in there." Next to the sauna Zeb showed them the woodshed and the outdoor toilet. Just to the right of the backdoor was an old fridge and an old wringer washer. Daniel remembered his grandmother had a washer like that. He walked to it and asked, "Zeb does this washer work?"

"It sure does. Way better than washing clothes by hand. It's a gas engine machine. Bit noisy, but it does the job. There's a clothes line just outside the door. Oh, by the way, that fridge works on kerosene."

As they went out of the side door, Daniel noticed a small shed tucked in behind the outdoor toilet. He asked, "What's in there?" Zeb was in front of him. He turned and said, "Oh, that's the electrical shed. There's an old electric generator in there. It hasn't worked for years. I don't really know why but I can't start it. I keep old odds and ends in there now." When Daniel opened the door, he found the shed was filled with all kinds of things: shovels, picks, axes, hoses, snowshoes, old skates, old saws, lanterns, wire, plywood and different lengths of two by fours.

"I never throw anything away. Never know when you might need them," Zeb said as he closed the door and led them back to the front of the house to looked at the vegetable garden. Daniel noticed that the plants had grown quite a bit since he first saw them.

"The garden needs a good weeding, but it's growing well. We had just enough rain. These two trees are apple trees. Looks like we'll have a good crop." Zeb showed them the tiny green apples forming on the trees. "Is there anything else you would like to see?"

"No, I think we have seen all we need to see for now. I'll be seeing you at the beginning of next month, Zeb. Thanks for the tour. Bye and take care," Daniel said as he shook hands with Zeb.

As they drove away, Ken said, "That is certainly a different place. Zeb has invested a lot of money on the place. Those solar panels and batteries are pretty expensive. He sure took a lot of pride in building it." Ken was impressed. He could tell that a good deal of work and thought had been put into it. "Do you know if he has any family?"

"He mentioned a daughter. She wanted to put him in a nursing home," Daniel replied. "I guess they disagree on his care. I can see why he would want to stay here. He has put a lot of himself in it." As they drove, Ken remarked on the beautiful scenery and of the remoteness of it all.

Back home, Daniel prepared for his move. There was so much to do. He rented a moving U-Haul van, purchased supplies he would need to spruce up his new house, and packed up his apartment. He went to see his professor to ask him what he would have to do to finish his studies. His professor gave him the course study for the next semester and the list of books he would need. The day before his move, he went to visit his sister for a barbeque.

"You invited all these people here? I should have known you'd do that. Thanks, sis, it's a really great surprise," Daniel said giving Lilly a kiss on the cheek. Many of Daniel's friends and co-workers were there to say farewell and to wish him well. Daniel was enjoying the party when he spotted Serge—Fred was his real name. Serge was a co-worker that made everything in the office his business. He thought he knew more about police work then anyone. When he had first started working, Fred had voiced his views on how work should be done to a senior officer and that officer had started calling him Serge. The name had stuck. Daniel had many encounters with him. Serge had poked his nose in his files and had tried to make trouble for Daniel and his partner, Jay.

"Why are you here, Serge? We were never friends. Come to put your nose in my life again?" Daniel asked.

"Your sister gave an open invite. It was never personal Daniel, just trying to help," Serge said.

"Not personal? You were helping? You were meddlesome and always tried to make trouble. I don't want you here. Please leave," Daniel said trying to keep it together.

"Yeah, I'll go, Sharpie, just wanted to see you off. I always knew you were never cut out to be a cop. You're just too weak," Serge said as he started for the door. Jay was standing beside Daniel and placed a hand on Daniel to keep him from hitting Serge.

Serge gave everyone a big smile and walked out. Everyone had seen the encounter and were relieved to see him go. There had been an undercurrent of uneasiness when he had showed up.

"Don't let him ruin your party, Daniel. He likes to hurt people. Sometimes I wonder why the force keeps him on," Jay said as they sat together sharing a drink. "Tonight is for friends, so let's forget about him and let's go enjoy ourselves." Daniel agreed with him and went to join the rest of the party. When the evening came to an end, Daniel thanked everyone for coming to see him off and for their best wishes.

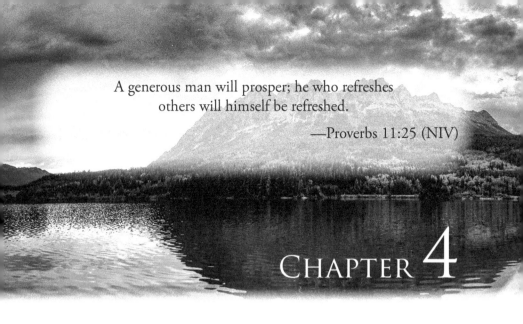

A generous man will prosper; he who refreshes
others will himself be refreshed.

—Proverbs 11:25 (NIV)

CHAPTER 4

Early the next morning, Ted and Ken helped Daniel load up the rented van. With the three of them, the work went fast and by midmorning, all of Daniel's things were loaded up and ready to go.

"Daniel, you take care of yourself. It's going to be so different with you gone. I'll miss you," Lilly said as she gave him a hug. Daniel returned the hug and promised to take care. He got in the van and drove away. Ted followed in Daniel's truck. They were on their way. In a few hours Daniel, would be at his new place to start a new way of life.

The day was clear so they would have an easy drive to Daniel's new place. At first, Daniel was in the lead but Ted did not like driving behind a van, so he passed the van and stayed in the lead until they reached the rest stop overlooking the lake. After a short break, they continued 'til they got to Daniel's new home. When they got to the house, Zeb was sitting on the front deck. Daniel came to a stop in front of the house and Zeb came up to him and asked, "Why did you bring this van here? You're not moving me out of here." Zeb seemed very agitated and a little disorientated.

"Zeb what are you talking about? I'm moving in. You're staying here, remember the deal?" Daniel was a little concerned. He had not seen Zeb confused before so he asked, "Zeb where is your caregiver? Are you alone here?" He helped Zeb back up the deck and sat him in his chair. "Zeb, remember me? I'm Daniel. We have a deal. Do you remember, Zeb?" Zeb looked at Daniel and seemed to come out of a haze.

"Yeah I remember. I'm just a little confused. I told that caregiver to leave. He was so lazy. He told me he was going to tell my daughter to move me to a home. When I saw the van, I thought it was my daughter. I'm very happy to see you, Daniel. Sometimes my mind does not work too fast. Sorry I worried you."

"How long have you been by yourself, Zeb? When is the last time you ate?" Daniel inquired.

"I can't remember, Daniel, but I'm hungry. Would you make me something? Thanks, Daniel." Daniel went in the house and found it a mess. There was clothing all over the living room. The sink was full of dirty dishes. Ted was right behind him. "I sure wonder what happened here. Looks like the caregiver did not do his job." They looked in the cupboard and found some canned soup.

"I'll get my little gas stove and make him some soup," Daniel said. "Ted, would you get Zeb in the house? He might be suffering from the heat. I'll be right back."

When Daniel got back, Zeb and Ted were sitting at the table. Ted had found some crackers and Zeb was now eating one. "What happened in here, Zeb? Looks like a tornado went through," Ted asked.

"That young snip. He was just here to rip me off. After your last visit, he started snooping around my things. He asked me where I kept my money. When I did not tell him, he took the place apart."

"Did he hurt you?" Daniel asked and looked to see if Zeb had any injuries.

"No, he did not touch me. I told him I had no money. What would I do with money living here? I told him to leave, that I could take care of myself. I did not need him. He packed up his things and left. I did not think he could move so fast." Daniel placed a bowl of pea soup in front of Zeb and asked, "Who hired that guy, Zeb? Are you going to press charges against him?"

"My lovely daughter hired him. He was her son's friend, said he needed a job. You're here now, Daniel, everything will be alright from now on. I don't want any trouble," Zeb said.

Daniel and Ted left Zeb eating his soup and went to the living room. "Well, we have to clean this up before we can move you in. Zeb, where do you want us to put all these things?"

"Put them in the bedroom. I'll put them away. I cleaned the loft out, but I just had no energy to do more. Sorry, Daniel," Zeb said from the kitchen.

"Don't fret about it, Zeb. We'll take care of it."

Daniel picked and folded the clothes and put them in Zeb's room. Ted went to the kitchen to clean up the mess there. When the living room was cleaned, Daniel asked, "Zeb, are you thinking of keeping this old couch? It's pretty shabby."

"You can do what you want with that old thing but can I keep my chair? It conforms to me now."

"Zeb if you want your chair, we can keep it. How about the kitchen table? Want to keep that too?"

"You don't have to ask me if I want to keep anything else. You bought the place. It is now yours. I just want to keep my chair," Zeb told Daniel.

"Zeb, it's still your home. You have a say in what you want to keep," Daniel said.

"I'll keep what's in my bedroom and my chair. I put all the things I want to keep in my room already. You can do what you want with the rest. I'm okay with that."

They moved in Daniel's new bed and dresser and placed them up in the loft. Daniel's couch and chair were placed by Zeb's chair in front of the stove. They replaced Zeb's table with Daniel's new one and moved the old table outside in the back of the house. The boxes that contained dishes and other personal belongings were put under the stairs. By late afternoon, the van had been emptied.

The furniture that Zeb did not want to keep, and some other old junk, were loaded in the van to be brought to the dump. All of the time Daniel and Ted worked, Zeb slept in his chair.

"It's getting late, Ted. I think you should stay the night then get an early start tomorrow morning."

"Yeah, I'm pretty bushed. What do you have for supper? I can make it if you want. I'd like to try my hand cooking on a wood stove," Ted said, looking to see if Zeb had woken up. Daniel found the cooler that contained some frozen meat. "I have chicken, steak, pork chops… what do you want to make?"

"Is that chicken breast?" Ted asked as he came over to look in the cooler. "I'll make you the best chicken breast you ever ate. Now I wonder if you have the other ingredients I need?"

After looking for different spices and fixings, Ted had their meal in the oven. "It'll take about an hour before it will be ready. Daniel, I saw some beer in that cooler. How about we have some? Zeb, would you want one?"

"A beer! I have not had a beer in a long time. There was a time I made my own beer, but it never tasted very good so I stopped. Will be nice having one." They all went to sit on the chairs in the front of the house.

"Zeb, what brought you to this place?" Daniel asked.

"I was a bricklayer for forty years. My back and my hands gave up on me. I sold my business, but I was so bored having nothing to do. I needed something to do. I always wanted to live like my grandpa did. So, I called up a realtor and told him to find me a place that was off the grid. He brought me up here and I fell in love with the place at first sight. I was lucky my wife also liked it. So we bought it."

"You had a wife and she lived here with you?" Ted inquired.

"Yes, I had a wife. She loved it here but she was never very healthy. She died ten years ago. She caught the flu one fall and died of pneumonia. My daughter blames me for her death. I guess she could be right, but my wife loved it here. I should have taken her to the hospital sooner. I just did not know how sick she was." Zeb looked sad.

"I'm so sorry, Zeb. Was this place all treed in when you bought it?" Daniel asked.

"Well, this place was a forest fire muster point. The government kept some supplies here in case of fires, and years back there was a watch tower. A fire warden once lived in the shop. This house was the supply shed. The clearing behind the house was where the helicopter landed. When I bought the place, this house was just a square, cinder block building," Zeb said with a touch of pride in his voice.

"You sure did a lot of work to get it like this," Daniel said.

"Yeah, we did. My wife helped a lot. I hired a carpenter to build the peaked roof but my wife and I did everything else. We put the siding on the outside, and once the new roof was in, I demolished the existing roof and built the loft. That was a lot of hard work but we were happy, my wife and I," Zeb said.

"Did you buy this place from the government? How did you ever manage that?" Ted asked.

"It was Larry's doing. He said the government was revising the forest management thing, and they were selling off some of their holdings. When I bought this place, there was talk of opening some lots to sell but they changed their minds. They ended up putting in the campsite instead," Zeb replied. He continued, "They tried to get this place back from me but I said no. They even took me to court, but I knew this judge that owed me a favor. He helped me keep it."

"A judge owed you a favor?" Daniel asked very surprised by what Zeb had said.

"Yeah, I did some brick work for him, and when it came time for him to pay me, he told me he was only going to pay half of the bill. He told me to call him if I ever needed any legal help. I thought I was crazy back then but it turned out good for me. When I got sued, I called him and that's how I kept the place," Zeb said. When Daniel heard that, he became concerned. He would have to ask his dad to look into it.

"Did you put up that fence around the property?" Daniel asked.

"No, it was all fenced when I bought it but I had to redo it some years back. All the pickets were rotten. Was quite the job. You'll have to keep an eye on it. Make sure the "no hunting" signs are up. I've seen hunters come and just cut the wire. They think they own these woods. They're just a bunch of assassins. One time, this guy shot this deer and just took the head and left the rest of the animal there. It made me so mad I complained to the land conservation office, but they did not do anything about it. They finally closed this area off for hunting but there are still the odd few that still come to hunt."

"So, I take it you're not a hunter, Zeb?" Daniel asked.

"No, I like to see animals run free. There are so few of them left here. It's rare to see a deer around here these days," Zeb answered.

"Do you see any other animals? Like bears or wolves?" Daniel asked.

"Oh yes, a few. They sometimes come through here but they never stay for long. I have this shotgun with salt pellets. It makes a really loud noise. They move on once they hear that blast," Zeb replied.

"Well, I best go see to our supper," Ted said and went in the house. He made a salad with lettuce, baby carrots, edible pea pods and green onion from the garden. He checked to see if the chicken was ready and said, "Daniel, would you set the table? I think supper is ready." Once all the food was set on the table, Zeb join Ted and Daniel and they all enjoyed a delicious supper.

As they ate, Daniel asked, "How did you get to town to get supplies?"

Zeb looked around and said, "Two years ago, I still drove my truck. The last time I went to town I got in this big accident. Broke my leg. My daughter made sure my driver's license got taken away. It took a year and a half for my leg to mend. I stayed with her after I got out of the hospital so I could go to rehab. She was adamant I go to a nursing home. That's when I came up with the deal we made. She's okay with me living here just as long as I have some help. She came here to help me with the garden for a day. When she hired the care giver I came back here with him. He was so lazy."

"Zeb, how long were you alone?" Ted asked.

"Well I don't know, there's no calendar here. That bum left a day or so after your last visit," Zeb said.

"You were alone for quite a long-time, Zeb. Did you take your meds?" Daniel asked, a little concerned.

"I took all the medicine that was in the dispenser. I could not open those pill bottles. But I took the pain killers. Those have an easy-to-open cap. I guess I should take my pills now." Zeb got up

34

and went to the cupboard. He returned to the table with a handful of pill bottles.

"Daniel, would you help me? Can you read the label and give me the pills I need? If you fill the dispenser, I can take my pills without any help. Would you do that for me?" He went back to the cupboard and returned with the dispenser.

Once supper was over and the kitchen all cleaned up, Zeb said goodnight and went to bed. Daniel and Ted found sheets and pillows, made up their beds and also retired.

Early the next morning, after a breakfast of rolled oats and strawberries, Daniel said, "Goodbye Ted. Thank you for all your help. Have a safe drive back. Keep care of Lilly."

Ted promised that he would. He gave Daniel a hug, saying, "You take care of yourself." He got in the van and drove away, leaving Daniel at his new home with Zeb.

"Well, Zeb it's just the two of us now. What should we do today?" Daniel asked.

"Daniel, it's your place now. You're the boss," Zeb answered indifferently.

"I know but do you have any advice? I don't really know what I should do first," Daniel said.

"The garden should be weeded if we want to have a good crop. The potatoes need some hilling. I think it would be a good place to start, Daniel," Zeb answered.

"Yes, I think you're right; taking care of food production would be a priority. I'll get the hoe," Daniel said as he started to walk to the garden shed. Daniel spent the rest of the morning weeding and hoeing. By midday, he found it much too warm to work in the garden so he went in the house to get a drink of water. Zeb was quietly snoring in his chair. *He sure sleeps a lot*, Daniel thought.

After he made himself a sandwich, he went up to the loft and made preparations to start to paint. He moved all the things he had to one side of the room, put drop sheets on the floor. After painting the back wall in a beigey colour, he started staining the cedar boards on the ceiling. The next day, he would stain the floorboards of the loft and down the stairs. By the time he finished staining the ceiling, Daniel was famished so he went downstairs and started supper.

Daniel was making chili on his camp stove when Zeb joined him. After they had eaten and the kitchen was tidied up, Daniel found he was exhausted. Zeb had already said goodnight and Daniel was left on his own. He glanced at his watch: only nine thirty. "Who goes to bed this early?" he said to himself. He went to the boxes of books and started placing them on the shelves, but he found he just did not have the energy. He gave in and went to bed.

Daniel got up early the next morning and found Zeb sitting on the deck. When he saw Daniel, Zeb said, "Do you fish? It would be nice having some fish for supper. I'd like that."

"A little, but I've never had much luck at it," Daniel replied.

"You want to give it a try? You'll find a fishing rod in the corner by the washing machine and the tackle box under the sink." As they ate breakfast, Zeb said, "The best place to catch fish is right at the mouth of the creek. Use the yellow and black lure. I caught more fish with that than with any other." So, after eating and cleaning up, Daniel headed for the lake. By noon, Daniel had a couple of six-inch-long lake trout.

Daniel found that everyday brought something new for him to master. He learned how to make sourdough bread, how to make preserves, and dry vegetables in the sun. Daniel would make careful notes on how to do the tasks. On late afternoons, Zeb loved to take short walks. It was on those walks that Zeb showed Daniel where wild raspberries grew and where to find blueberries.

As the summer progressed, Daniel realized that he could survive on his own. He valued Zeb's company and relied on his expertise, but he was the one who made the decisions and did all the work. He now felt good about his life. He worked hard, but this work brought him a satisfaction he never felt while doing police work. He also took time to enjoy his new place. Daniel enjoyed going fishing, going for a quick swim after a hard day's work in the hot sun, and exploring the trails around the lake and mountains. He had appreciated the convenience of city living but now those amenities were not there—he had to rely on his own ability to survive. He noticed that he was becoming a lot more patient in doing things for most of what he did took time.

By the end of summer, they were very busy harvesting their garden. They dug up the potatoes and carrots and put them in the bins in the cellar. Daniel never would have believed it was so much work. By late September, most of the produce in the garden had been harvested.

One September morning, Zeb said, "Let's take the day off from this work. We've worked hard these last few days. Let's go for a walk. I want to show you something."

"Okay, where are we going?" Daniel replied. Zeb started walking across the field behind the house so Daniel followed. When they got to a hollow tree, Zeb said, "There use to be wild honey in there. Take a stick and poke it in that hole there. See if you can get any honey on it." Daniel did what Zeb said to do and when he took the stick out, sure enough there was honey on it. When Zeb saw the honey, he said, "Good we beat the bear to it. Now be very careful not to get stung. Stick your hand in there and get the honey. The bees are very slow now but they can still sting." He saw that Daniel was a little reluctant so he said, "Go on but be careful. Reach your hand in there and bring up the honeycomb. If you go slow, you'll be okay." Daniel had never been afraid of bees but putting his hand in a bee's hive was another thing.

"Zeb, are you serious? There're bees in there, I'll get stung," protested Daniel.

"If you do it very slowly, you'll be okay," Zeb assured him. After some hesitation, Daniel eased his hand in the tree and very slowly brought up the honeycomb. There were bees all around it and on Daniel's hand. "Okay good, now put it in this paper bag. Slowly now," Zeb said as Daniel slipped the comb in the bag. "I'll show you how to get the honey out when we get back to the house."

Daniel's hand was sticky with honey and it amazed him that he did not get stung. When he saw there still were some bees on his hand, he gently brushed them off. Once at the house, Zeb placed the honeycomb over an inverted cup and let the honey drip down into a bowl that held the cup.

37

The next morning, they were having their coffee on the deck enjoying the sunrise when Daniel asked, "Zeb, what do we do with those big cabbage heads?"

"Well, we can make coleslaw or sour cabbage or sauerkraut or cabbage rolls. I could show you how to make cabbage rolls. We still have some rice? The mushrooms we saw on our walk yesterday would taste really good in them." When Daniel nodded yes, Zeb continued, "That would take care of a head. If we start now we could have a batch made for supper."

After Daniel had gone to pick some mushrooms and a big head of cabbage, Zeb instructed Daniel how to clean and cook the mushrooms. Once he had finished with the mushrooms, he took the cabbage head and followed Zeb's directions on how to prepare the leaves to make the rolls. Daniel followed the instructions to a tee. By late afternoon, the cabbage rolls were baking in the oven, filling the house with a delicious aroma. When supper time came, they were not disappointed. Daniel ate half of the batch.

"Daniel, would you heat up some water so I can have a bath? It's too cold for a shower," Zeb asked.

"Sure, Zeb, I'll get right on it. The stove is hot so it shouldn't take to long for the water to get warm," Zeb went to sit in his chair to wait and said, "You have shown such kindness to an old man. Thank you, Daniel."

"Zeb, you're welcome. I like it here. It feels like home," Daniel replied as he cleaned the kitchen and got the tub from outside. When the water was warm, he filled the tub and helped Zeb in it. Zeb sat in the tub enjoying the warm water. It had been so long since he felt warm like this. Once the water cooled down, he washed his hair and got out of the tub. After he had dressed, he asked, "Would you be able to cut my hair, Daniel? Maybe trim my beard? I think I'm a little too shabby."

"I've never cut anyone's hair before but I can try. If I cut yours, you'll have to cut mine. I think I'm a little shabby myself," Daniel replied.

"Okay, it's a deal."

Zeb got the scissors and went to sit on a kitchen chair. Daniel was not at all comfortable cutting Zeb's hair but after a while, he managed to give him a decent do. Now it was Daniel's turn. Zeb was a little shaky. He took his time but when Daniel looked in the mirror, he was impressed that his hair did look fine.

"That's a very good job you did on my hair, Zeb. Thank you," Daniel said.

"I always try to do my best. I'm glad you like it. Now that took a lot out of me, I should find my bed. Good night. See you in the morning."

Daniel said goodnight and went to look at the books he had brought with him. There was a big oak roll top desk on the side of the living room. Daniel had set a book shelf beside it and had placed all his books in it. All summer, Daniel had no energy to look at his books but tonight he thought he would start. He looked over the course study his professor had given him but as he read it over, he found he could not keep his eyes open so he went to bed.

The next day, Daniel asked, "So what will we do with the rest of the cabbages?" Zeb rubbed his chin and said, "I'll show you how to make sour cabbage." When Daniel asked why sour cabbage and not sauerkraut, Zeb said, "Sauerkraut is too much work with chopping the cabbage. No, we'll make sour cabbage. In the basement, there's a five-gallon ceramic crock. Get it and we can get started." Daniel went and brought the crock up, washed it out. He went to the garden to get three of the cabbages. Daniel followed Zeb's instructions and in a short time had the three heads ready to be immersed in the salt water in the crock. Daniel added the spices and carefully added a weight on top of the cabbages to keep them submerged. He placed a cover on the crock and moved it to the corner beside the table. The crock had a spigot at the bottom to let out the liquid. Zed instructed Daniel to empty the salt water and return it to the crock to keep the salt from settling at the bottom. This had to be done every day or the cabbages on top would go rotten.

Daniel cleaned the kitchen and spent the rest of the day chopping wood. Zeb found his chair and fell asleep. When Daniel returned to the house to start supper; Zeb was still asleep. He heated up the rest of the cabbage rolls and went over to wake Zeb.

"Zeb, do you want any supper. I heated the cabbage rolls," Daniel said as he gave Zeb a soft nudge. When Zeb awoke, he was very confused. "Son, what are you doing here? Your mother said you had left us." Daniel was a little taken aback. He nudged Zeb again and said, "Zeb, I'm Daniel, remember? Zeb, are you awake?" Zeb opened his eyes and said, "Of course, I know you're Daniel. You think I forgot? You're my son. Now what's for supper?" Daniel looked at Zeb a little concerned. Maybe a little bit of food in him would bring him around.

"Come, Zeb, let me help you to the table." Zeb got up and slowly walked to the table. Daniel placed a plate of cabbage rolls in front of him and sat down to eat his supper. Zeb took a few bites and said, "I'm not hungry. Would you make me a cup of tea?"

"Okay I'll make you tea. How about a little slice of bread? You haven't eaten very much today." Daniel made him some tea and brought him a slice of bread. Zeb nibbled at the bread and drank his tea.

"Zeb, are you feeling okay? You look a little shaky," Daniel said in an alarmed voice.

"I feel so weak. I feel like I have no strength. Maybe I did too much yesterday. A good night's sleep and I'll be as good as new," Zeb replied with a little smile on his face. "Good night, Daniel." He tried to get up from his chair but fell right back into it. "I think you'll have to help me to bed, son. I don't think I can walk that far."

Daniel helped him to his bedroom, helped him undress and put him in bed.

"Son, it's so good having you with me. I've wanted to have you here for so long. Would you hold my hand 'til I fall asleep?" Daniel was now very worried. He had never seen Zeb in this state before.

"Zeb, are you alright? You're saying strange things," Daniel said as he held Zeb's hand. But Zeb did not reply. He had already fallen asleep.

Daniel left him sleep. *Maybe Zeb had over done yesterday. He'll be okay tomorrow,* he thought. He cleaned the supper dishes and went outside to enjoy the rest of the evening. Once the sun had gone down, Daniel went to his study desk. He found that he could not concentrate on what he was reading so he closed his book and went to bed.

Heavy rain was falling when he got up the next morning. He started a fire in the stove and made coffee and a pot of rolled oats. Zeb usually was up by now so Daniel went to see if he needed help. Zeb was lying in his bed in the same position Daniel had left him the night before.

"Zeb. Zeb, you awake?" Daniel said as he tried to rouse him. But there was no response. Zeb had passed away in his sleep during the night.

"Zeb, now what do I do?" Daniel felt a little panicky. He passed his hands through his hair and said, "Get a grip man, you've been trained to know what to do in situations like this. Now think." He sat on the edge of the bed thinking what the right thing would be to do. Should he leave Zeb here and go get help? Or should he put him in the truck and drive him to town? He decided to take Zeb to town. When he got to town, he'd call Larry and his dad. They would help him. "Yes, that's the best way to care for Zeb," he told himself.

He wrapped Zeb's body in a big blanket, placed him in the back of his truck and closed the cover to the box. The drive to town seemed like an eternity. Daniel decided he would take Zeb to the hospital and call his dad and Larry from there. When he got to the hospital, he was asked a series of questions first by the ER nurse and then by the doctor. Once the doctor determined that Zeb had died of natural causes, he told Daniel he would take care of Zeb's body. Daniel called his dad and Larry to ask them to meet him at the hospital.

"I'm surprised you called and asked to meet you here, Daniel. You hurt?" Ken asked when he saw his son.

"No, I'm okay. Zeb died last night and I drove him down. The doctor said he'd care for him. I called Larry, he should be here any moment. He knows the daughter and he can let her know her dad died," Daniel said. They went to the cafeteria to wait for Larry. They had just about finished their coffee when Larry joined them. "Daniel,

41

how are you? Too bad about Zeb. He knew he was dying. I just did not figure he would go so soon," Larry said as he sat beside Daniel.

"He went in his sleep. I helped him get to bed last night and I found him in the same position this morning. You know the daughter. Would you call her and let her know?" Daniel asked Larry.

"Daniel, don't worry I'll take care of it. I'll call the daughter right away," Larry replied.

"Thanks, Larry. Let me know about the funeral. I'd like to pay my last respects," Daniel said as Larry got up to leave.

"Will do." Larry shook hands with Daniel and Ken, then left.

"So, you'll be sticking around 'til the funeral? It will be good having you around again. What are you planning to do with yourself 'til then?" his dad asked.

"I haven't thought about it. Go see Lilly, maybe go see how my partner is. These last few months have just gone by so fast. I can't believe the summer is already gone. I thought I'd have Zeb around for the winter. Now I'll have to survive on my own."

"You could stay in town for the winter and go back up in the spring," his father suggested.

"No, I'm going to live at my place. That is what I want, to be on my own. Let's go surprise Lilly?" Daniel asked.

"Okay, I'll follow you there," Ken replied.

Lilly could not believe her eyes when she answered the door bell. "Daniel!" she cried and wrapped her arms around his neck. "You're back. It's so good to see you. I've missed you so much." She gave him another hug, stepped back, then greeted her dad.

"Are you here for good? Giving up on living in the bush?" she asked as they all went in the house.

"No, I'm just here for a week or so. I'll be going back home after Zeb's funeral," Daniel said.

"Zeb died? Oh, I'm so sorry. Ted said he was a very nice old man. You must be saddened by his passing. You're still going to live there by yourself? It sure will be lonely, Daniel," Lilly said, trying to get Daniel to change his mind. Daniel sat down at the kitchen table and asked Lilly where her little girl was.

"She's taking a nap. She should be up soon. Want anything to eat?" She said as she showed them a tray of goodies.

"Ted brought these from the restaurant last night. Want some dad?" Ken never refused any sweet treat. He loved Ted's pastries. After Ken helped himself, Daniel did the same. Then Lilly started with the questions. She asked, "Don't you get bored living there with no Wi-Fi or TV?"

Daniel looked at her and said, "I never thought about those things the whole time I was there. There's a lot of work I have to do just to survive. Time-off is a luxury living there."

She gave him a smile and said, "Daniel just wait here I have something for you." Lilly got up and went out to the living room and returned with a big box.

"I was at a garage sale the other day and found these. This box is full of movies on DVD. When I saw them, I thought of you. On some lonely nights, you could pop one of these in your computer and watch a movie. There's a DVD in there about a guy living in the woods. That might interest you."

Daniel was speechless and considered what Lilly had done for him.

"Lilly, that is very lovely… I never considered getting movies but I might just enjoy watching them on some cold evenings. Thank you, sis." He took the box from her and took some DVDs out. He could tell that some were old TV series—*Gun Smoke, Bonanza, James Bond.* "Some of these are pretty old but I think it will be interesting. Thanks again." Daniel was putting the DVDs back in the box when he heard the baby crying.

"Oh, there's Beth. I better go get her." When Lilly got up, Daniel followed her to the baby's room. When little Beth saw him, she stopped crying and looked at him with a curious face.

"Hi, little Beth, you sure grew big since I last saw you," Daniel said. At first, little Beth gave him a smile. She looked at her mother and started to cry. Lilly picked her up and reassured her that everything was alright.

"This is your Uncle Daniel, Beth. He is a very nice guy. You'll like him if you got to know him."

"She'll get to know me, I'll be around. Don't be so negative," Daniel scolded his sister. When they returned to the living room, Ken was ready to leave and said, "I've got to go back to work but I'll be back for supper. Tell Ted to set a plate for me."

Once Ken had left, Lilly went to sit on the couch and said, "He eats here a lot. He says he does not like to cook for himself. I told him he is welcome here anytime. Ted told him he had an open invite for supper whenever he wants. We have him for supper regularly."

"Good to hear that. Is he still seeing his secretary?" Daniel asked.

"No. She left last month. He told me it was not serious. She was just someone he could go places with. He called her his companion. You know Dad, he likes his freedom just like you do." They talked all afternoon. Daniel told Lilly about his summer, about Zeb's death, and how he felt about losing him. Lilly talked about her little girl and how contented she was being a mom. That took them up to supper time. Supper was like old family-time suppers again with a lot of playful teasing and enjoying one another. Daniel realized how much he missed it.

The next morning, Daniel decided to go pay a visit to his old partner, Jay. He gave him a call and agreed to meet him for lunch.

"Good to see you, Daniel. How have you been?" Jay asked as they sat down to share a beer.

"I'm doing okay, Jay. How are things on the force? Things getting better?" Daniel inquired.

"Yes, things are a little better since Serge got his. Did you hear what he was doing?" Jay replied.

"No, what was he doing? I don't think anything you tell me about him will surprise me," Daniel said.

"He had the biggest number of DUI arrests in the department and all of his arrests were women. He was so smug thinking he was the best. Most of the women said that they had not been drinking, but the result of what they blew showed that they were impaired. Then one night he brings in a young woman. He said that she was very drunk when he stopped her, and the reading of her breath sample was very high. She maintained that she had not even had one drink. She was sitting at his desk and said she wanted to call her dad.

Serge told her she could and so she did. When the chief walked in and she called him dad, you should have seen Serge's face. She told her dad that Serge had charged her with impaired driving. The chief knew she never took a drink, so he believed her. It was then that the chief asked Serge to give a breath sample. Serge was incensed by the request but finally he complied. It turned out that it was Serge who was impaired. The chief fired him on the spot and charged him of falsifying evidence. He's out on bail awaiting his trial. The chief dismissed all of the impaired charges that Serge had filed."

"I knew something was not right with him. I'm glad he's off the street," Daniel said. As they ate, they caught up with each other's lives and promised to keep in touch.

The next day, Daniel drove to Charlie's.

"Surprise, surprise, Daniel! We never know when you're going to show up," Carol said. "Charlie is harvesting grain on the adjacent section. He'll be back later tonight. He wants to take advantage of the nice weather. Come in. Want something to drink or are you hungry?" Daniel went in the house and saw the boys were watching TV.

"Hey there, boys, what are you watching." The boys were surprised to see him and jumped up to greet Daniel. "Why are you not outside?" Daniel asked.

"We were outside all morning helping mom pick carrots in the garden. She promised we could watch a movie if we helped her. Have you seen Spider Man?" Daniel said he had not so he sat and watched the movie with them. Once the movie was over, one of the boys said, "Our dog had puppies. Would you like to see them?"

"Yes, I'd love to," Daniel replied. They went to the barn where the puppies were kept.

"Our dog had four puppies but dad said we could not keep any. They are so cute. I wish we could keep them," Dennis said. They played with the pups until Carol called them in for supper. They had finished eating when Charlie returned to the house.

"Daniel, what a surprise! What brings you here? Are you alright?" Charlie asked when he saw him.

"I'm alright. Zeb passed away and I brought him to town. I'm waiting for the funeral before I go back."

"Oh, that's to bad. Now you'll be on your own. How do you like living there?" Charlie said as he ate his supper.

"I love it out there. I'm so busy, the days just fly by. With Zeb gone, it's going to be a little lonesome, I suppose. He was a very good teacher. He usually just sat there and watched me do the work. If he thought I was doing something wrong, he would tell me how he would do it. He was a good man. I'll miss him," Daniel explained. Charlie finished eating and they both went on the porch to have a beer.

"If you think you're going to be lonesome, you can take one of the pups. They are ready to have their own home. It would keep you company," Charlie said.

"I was thinking of doing that when the boys showed me the pups. I like that little, gray female. The boys call her Misty. I think I'll take her. They told me that they could not keep any of the litter, that one dog was enough. They will be happy to hear that Misty will be with me and that they will be able to see her when they come for a visit. Thanks, Charlie," Daniel said.

"I think she'll make you a fine dog. She'll make a good mountain dog being that she's part husky and shepherd," Charlie added. They talked to the wee hours of the night and went to bed. The next morning after they had breakfast, the boys carried little Misty and put her in Daniel's truck. Misty was so excited she could not keep still. When Daniel got in the truck, she was all over him.

"Down, girl, down!" He rubbed the top of her head and told her to sit. To his surprise, she did. "Who taught you to do that?" he said to the dog. He turned to the boys and asked, "You taught her how to sit?" Both boys nodded their head and Dennis said, "She is very smart. We used these special treats. She will do anything for them. Here, Uncle Daniel, you will need these." Daniel thanked them for the dog and their hospitality, then drove off.

The funeral was a simple affair, a small ceremony held at the cemetery by Zeb's grave. Zeb's daughter, her children and husband were standing by the graveside when Daniel, Ted and Ken arrived. They seemed very sorrowful. Daniel went over and introduced himself saying, "I'm Daniel. I bought your father's place. This is my father Ken and my brother in law Ted." Zeb's daughter was a little surprised to see the three men and said, "Thank you for taking care of my dad. I'm pleased you came to the funeral." Larry and his wife and another couple joined them.

After the ceremony, Daniel said to the daughter, "Zeb had things he left for you. Will you be coming to get them? If not, I could bring them down the next time I come to town and leave them with Larry."

"I'm not coming up there. Would you bring the things to Larry? That would be fine," she said wiping her eyes. Daniel said goodbye to the family and to Larry, then left with his dad and Ted.

"They sure are taking his passing hard," Ken observed. "They must have been a close family."

"I don't know. The way Zeb tells it, she was after his money. He told me that he had given her the bulk of his money after his wife died. She was not happy with him, accused him of killing her mother. I don't know if she ever forgave him. Now that he's gone, she might be sorry for the way she treated him," Daniel replied.

"Are you going to stay for another day, Daniel?" Ken asked when they were back at Ted's place.

"I think I'll leave today. I've been away from the place for ten days. I'd better go back," Daniel answered then added. "Misty is already waiting in the cab for me. I've got a lot to do to get ready for winter." Daniel found his sister and little Beth to say goodbye, and after shaking hands with Ted, he was off.

The drive back was uneventful. He was very happy to see his home and then remembered that Zeb would not be there. It suddenly hit him: he was now really on his own. He looked at the dog and said, "We're home now, Misty, I hope you like it." He got out of the truck, and Misty jumped out right behind him. She followed Daniel to the front door and sat as he unlocked the door.

When Daniel opened the door, he just about lost his breath. The stench in the house was so bad, it made him want to throw up. That's when he remembered: that cabbage stuff. He went to the crock and took it outside to the compost pile. The smell was so bad, he buckled over and threw up. *I can't leave this stuff out in the open.*

47

It'll drive me out, he thought. He went to the shed to get a shovel and dug a deep hole, burying the crock and all its contents. Back at the house, he opened the doors and windows to air out the house, but the stench still lingered. Misty kept rubbing her nose with her paw and kept sneezing.

"I'm sorry, girl. This is not normal. It'll get better in a little while. Come, I'll show you around. Let's go for a walk." He walked her around the clearing in the back of the house and brought her to the beach. When Daniel threw a stick in the water and Misty did not go retrieve it, he was surprised. So he said, "Misty, go get the stick. Here, I'll throw another one for you." He picked up a stick and showed it to her. He tossed it a short way in the water. This time, Misty ran in the water and retrieved the stick, then quickly ran back to Daniel. Daniel threw the stick a little further in deeper water, making Misty swim to get it. But in no time, she returned to Daniel with the stick, wanting him to throw it again. "You sure do have a lot of energy for a little dog. Come, we have to unload the truck before it gets too dark," he said, patting her wet head.

He had just finished unloading his truck when darkness fell. The smell in the house was tolerable but it was still noticeable. He fed Misty and made himself some supper. After supper, he decided to go look at his books and review the material he had studied before Zeb had died. He made Misty a bed by his desk and told her to lie down and stay. She was happy to have a nice place to lay down so she stayed there until Daniel decided it was time to go to bed. He told her to stay but, of course, she did not. The minute he stood up and started walking toward the stairs, she was right behind him.

"Okay, girl, you can sleep upstairs with me but you'll have to stay on your bed. You're not sleeping on my bed. I don't sleep with dogs. You got that?" He went back to get her bed and placed it right beside his bed. Somehow, Misty knew that she was to sleep on her bed and was not allowed on Daniel's bed. "Good girl, Misty, you sleep well," Daniel said as he got in his bed.

> Commit to the Lord whatever you do,
> and your plans will succeed.
>
> —Proverbs 16:3 (NIV)

CHAPTER 5

A week later, early one morning, the sun was just coming over the ridge when Daniel was awoken by Misty barking franticly by the front door. He ran down stairs. "Misty, what is the trouble girl?" Misty wanted to go out. When Daniel looked outside, he saw a massive black bear rooting around the place where he had buried that smelly stuff.

"That's just great. Now there's a bear hanging around here. I don't think you're ready for a huge bear like that. You stay here and I'll get Zeb's big shot gun," Daniel said to Misty as he shut her in the room. He went to get Zeb's shot gun which was hanging on the kitchen side wall. He placed two bullets in the gun, opened the door and shot both barrels over the bear. The bear was so surprised he bolted away so fast—it was like he just disappeared.

He let Misty out of the room saying, "Well with all this excitement, I don't think I could go back to sleep. Might as well make some coffee." Misty thought it was time to play. She went to get the toy rope Daniel had made for her and dropped it by his feet.

"You want to play rope pull?" Misty barked and laid down to wait for Daniel to grab one end of the rope. When he did, she bit into the other end and pulled with all her might.

"Misty, you've got to be the funniest dog, always wanting to play," Daniel said as he pulled the rope. Misty loved that game. She was never the one to call it quits. After a while, Daniel tired of having his arm shaken, dropped the rope and went to make coffee. "Let's take you out while the coffee percolates," he said to the dog. He stepped outside and looked around to see if the bear had returned. No bear. As Daniel walked around, he noticed the apples. *That could have attracted the bear*, he thought.

"We have to pick those apples today, Misty. You get the ladder and I'll get the basket." Misty barked and jumped at him. "What's that you say? You can't get the ladder because you have no thumbs? What kind of a helper are you anyway?" Daniel laughed and went in the house to get his coffee and made breakfast.

After breakfast, he got the ladder and set it under the tree. He picked an apple and bit into it. To his surprise, it was very sweet and juicy. As he ate it, he said to Misty, "These are very good." He offered Misty a piece which she took but dropped it. It was not to her liking. Daniel spent the entire day picking apples and storing them in a bin in the cellar.

A few days later, Daniel was walking by the creek. The underbrush grew so thick along the creek that it made it impossible to get close to it. He thought the yard would look better and he would have easier access to the creek if the undergrowth was gone.

"Come, Misty, we have a big job to do," he said as he walked to the garage to get his axe and long-handle cutters. He decided to start clearing an area of the creek that was close to the house. He started by cutting out the long, red branches that seemed to be entangled with all the other bushes. He pulled them out from the brush and stacked them in a pile in the yard.

Misty was always by his side. When he pulled at a branch, Misty would also take a hold of it and helped. As he continued, he found a big patch of devil's club. The shrub was taller then he was, with leaves a foot across—very beautiful but wickedly prickly. He decided to keep it in place. He cut down the dead willows and dried out twinberry bushes. He kept the rose bushes that were out of the way.

They would be nice when they bloomed, he thought. He also kept a stand of high-bush cranberries.

By the end of the day, he had cleared a ten-foot-wide patch, exposing the elusive creek. He walked to the edge and saw sparkly clear water swiftly running over a bed of small gravel. The creek was about two-feet across but the water did not seem to be to deep. After he had taken a drink of the cold water, he dragged the branches he had cut to the compost near the garden. When he had finished with the last of the branches, he noticed that he was very hungry and the sun had gone down. He went in the house and was astonished to see that it was after seven—he had worked all day.

The next day, Daniel found it hard to move, he was so sore. The back of his legs hurt. He found the small of his back hurt when he sat down, and the top of his shoulders needed a good massage. He knew he had overdone it the day before and had to take it easy, but he decided he had to do something with the pile of branches he had cut. He sorted out the bigger branches and cut them into one-foot length pieces and stored them in the woodshed. *These will make good fire starters when they dry out*, he thought. He cut the smaller ones into even smaller sections and put those in the compost. As he cut the branches, Misty would come to steal some and tried to entice Daniel to come and play with her. As he retrieved the pieces Misty had stolen, he said to her, "Misty, I should have listened to you. All this bending up and down made my back feel worse. I think I'll go for a sauna. Might make my back feel better. I'll take you for a walk after." And as he threw Misty a piece, he added, "Here go get it."

On a rainy day, a month after he had returned, Daniel went into Zeb's room. He looked around the room and decided it was time to clean it out. He emptied everything out of the room and washed it. He painted the walls with what he had left over from when he first moved in. Once he was done, he replaced the bed frame and the old dresser. He also replaced the bookshelf that held Zeb's books. As he went through the books, he noticed most were books he would never read. They must have been Zeb's wife's books because he could not imagine Zeb ever reading them either.

51

He kept the series of books by Jane Austen: *Pride and Prejudice*, *Emma*, and *Sense and Sensibility*. Lilly had read those books in high school. She had loved them, said they were classic. As he continued going through the books, he saw a book about handicrafts and a book about wild flowers. He decided to keep. All the other books he threw out. The old mattress, Zeb's old chair, and other old items were loaded in the truck to be taken to the dump. Zeb's cedar chest that was to go to his daughter was also loaded on the truck. He would leave that with Larry. After cleaning the room and having supper, Daniel felt wiped out. Although it was still early, he decided to go to bed.

The next morning, as the sun cleared the ridge, he set off for town. He drove straight to the dump and dropped off all of Zeb's old possessions. Next, he went to see Larry. He unloaded the cedar chest for Zeb's daughter and was off to the super mart to buy a new mattress and other items for his house. When he had done all his errands, he swung by to see his sister and his dad.

"Daniel, you're back. Is something wrong?" Lilly said, surprised to see him. When she saw Misty she asked, "Misty is with you, she sure has gotten bigger. How is she doing?"

"She's getting to be a pretty good dog. I just came to town to get new things for the house." As they both petted the dog, he went on to tell her what he had done.

"Dad will be here soon. You'll stay for supper?" Lilly asked.

"Yeah, okay, it's getting too late to drive back. Supper with the family will be very nice," Daniel agreed.

It was pouring rain when he left town the next morning. The rain changed into snow the closer he got home, so much so that for a while he thought he would not make it. Finally, after pushing snow for the last mile, he got to the gate.

"Misty, we made it, girl," he said as he got out to open the gate. It wasn't until he unloaded the truck and sat down for a bite to eat that he realized how totally exhausted he was.

It was still snowing the next morning. After coffee and breakfast, he went out and cleared the deck, and shovelled a path around the house. It was mid-afternoon when he unpacked the new things he had bought. He placed the new mattress on the bed frame and laid an area rug by the side of the bed. As soon as the rug was on the floor, Misty came to lay on it. He made up the bed with the new sheets and a thick down filled comforter. He now had a presentable guest room.

Daniel had bought two other area rugs. One he placed in front of the couch. The other upstairs in the loft by his bed. Both times, Misty made herself comfortable on them. He also got a thick, down filled comforter for his bed. *This will keep me nice and warm,* he thought. He liked how the rugs added some warmth to the house.

By December, the snow really came down and isolated him from the rest of the world. Daniel had never seen so much snowfall at one time. With Misty, his buddy, he kept busy shoveling snow to keep from becoming buried. It seemed like it snowed just about every day, and keeping up with it was an everyday job. Chopping wood to keep warm and cooking to keep them fed was also an endless job. But the one job he absolutely disliked was washing clothes. He had washed clothes in the summer, but in winter, it took on a totally new experience. The old washing machine was so noisy and smelly in the enclosed back room. In the summer, Daniel had rolled it outside. The noise and exhaust had not seemed that bad, but now it was just unbearable. He resolved to do as little laundry as he could. He would wash only when he absolutely had to.

On laundry days, the house became a laundromat. Clothes and bedding were draped over every chair to dry, and on the clothes drying frame that hung just to the side of the stove. In the evenings, Daniel would fold the clothes that were dried, and he would hang the ones not yet dried. The one thing he loved about laundry day, though, was having clean sheets on his bed and clean clothes to wear. If not for that, he would never do laundry.

One day, he was starting the fire when he noticed a shape in one of the wood pieces. It reminded him of a king with a crown on his head. As he looked at it, an idea came to mind: why not carve out pieces for a chess set? As a boy, his grandfather had showed him how to whittle. He could use those red branches. They were the right diameter and size to make chess pieces. That afternoon, after all his chores were done, he started with his new project. He got a red branch and cut three inches off. He sat by the table and started to shape it. After a short time, he had formed a pawn. The piece was an inch in height and had a small rounded top. Daniel was pleased with how it had turned out so he set out to make another piece.

It amazed him that the days were going by so fast. He kept busy with the work he did during the day and studied in the evenings. He had no time to feel bored or isolated.

As he marked his calendar, he noticed that Christmas was only days away. It would be the first Christmas he would not be with his family. *Lilly will be so sad*, he thought. *Beth's first Christmas and I won't be there*. That afternoon when he went outside, he heard what could have been a machine. He went to chop wood and noticed the sound getting louder. He went to the front of the house and saw a snowplough driving up clearing the snow away, and right behind it was Charlie's truck. Daniel could not believe what he saw: Charlie and his family getting out of the SUV.

He ran to them and gave them all a hug. "You came for Christmas! I can't believe that you are here! It's so wonderful to see you all!" Daniel exclaimed. Misty was happy to see them too. She barked and ran to everyone to get a pat. The boys were so happy to see her. They gave her huge hugs and threw snowballs for her to fetch.

"We could not let you be by yourself for Christmas," Carol said. "Besides, the boys wanted to do something different for Christmas this year. Charlie suggested we come to see you." As the SUV was unloaded, Daniel said, "What did you do? Buy out the store? You sure have brought a lot of stuff."

"There're no stores around here so we had to bring all we needed. Come, I've got something you will like, I think," Charlie said, opening a big plastic tub. "In this tub, we put all types of frozen meats. We packaged it in individual portions for you. We thought it would make a great gift for someone living here." Daniel would have never thought of giving a gift like that, but he was thankful Charlie had.

"Thank you, Charlie, that is very considerate of you. I never had a meat gift before. I'll eat it all up," Daniel said laughing. They carried the tub to the shed where it would stay frozen.

When they went back in the house, Carol had organized his kitchen. There were all kinds of food items on the counter: the big turkey, meat pies, cookies, tarts, and, of course, Carol's famous Christmas cake. When Daniel noticed how large the turkey was, he said, "I hope this bird will fit in the oven. That stove does not have a regular size oven."

Carol went and opened the oven door and said, "I think it will fit but there will be no room for anything else. Don't you worry, I'll get it done. Just make sure the stove is hot enough to cook it."

"Okay, it's a deal. I'll take care of the stove and you cook the meal. Now come, let's go outside and see what your boys are up to. You have to enjoy yourself too," Daniel said.

When she went outside, Carol found the boys were still playing with Misty. She noticed that the wind had picked up and it had gotten colder, so she called the boys to come into the house.

Charlie and Daniel stocked the wood box so they would have enough wood to last for the evening. As Carol made some chili and biscuits for supper, the boys played with their Uncle Daniel. When supper time came, they were so sleepy from playing that they hardly finished their food. Carol made a bed for them on the floor near the stove, and they happily went to sleep in the cozy sleeping bags they had brought from home. The adults talked for a while then they too decided to go to bed.

The next morning, Daniel was the first up. He rustled the ambers in the stove and got the fire going. The coffee was percolating and filled the house with it's aroma when Charlie came out of the guest room.

"Man, did I ever sleep hard last night. Must be the clean air and the quietness here," Charlie said as he joined Daniel on the couch. "The boys are not up yet? They usually are the first to get up. Carol said it was too cold to get up and she wants coffee in bed." Charlie brought Carol a coffee and when he returned, the boys were sitting in front of the stove playing with Misty. "Daddy we're hungry, where's mommy?" they cried when they saw their dad.

"Mommy is sleeping in. Uncle and I will make breakfast." Daniel found the eggs and when he looked in the cooler a little more, he found some bacon. The bacon was frying and just about ready when Carol made her appearance. "Man, does it ever smell good. That bacon smell made me so hungry I had to get up. Good morning, boys." After she had given her boys a kiss, she asked Daniel, "Can I help?"

"No ma'am, we have everything under control. You go sit. Breakfast is just about ready," Daniel said as he took a toast out of a rack he used to toast the bread on the stove top. He brought Carol some more coffee and then when the food was ready, he called everyone to the table. As they ate, Liam asked, "Uncle Daniel, you don't have a Christmas tree. We need a tree cause Santa will not know where to put our gifts. Do you have any trees we could have, Uncle?"

"Of course, but it will be hard to get. The snow is very deep. But that's not a problem, I have snowshoes. I'll go get one right after we finish breakfast," Daniel said.

It took a while for Daniel to find a suitable tree. The trees were half-buried under the snow. He finally located one he thought would be okay. Using his axe to clear the snow away, he chopped the tree down, one that was not very tall but was bushy enough. He dragged it home and was shaking the snow off the tree when the boys joined him outside.

"We'll stand it up in the house and when it's all melted off, we can start decorating it," Daniel said. The boys picked up the bottom end, and with Daniel carrying the top, they brought the tree into the house. Once the tree was set up Liam said, "We made some decorations. See!" When Daniel saw them he said, "These are really pretty decorations. They'll look really nice on the tree."

That evening, after supper, Carol asked, "Daniel, do you have a way to play Christmas music? We can't decorate a tree without music."

"Well, let me see. I think I have something on my computer," Daniel replied. He booted up the computer and in a short time said, "Yes, I have one Christmas album—the Neil Diamond Christmas album. Will that do?" As the music played in the background, they took turns placing the decorations on the tree. Carol brought out little LED lights powered by batteries. When they were placed on the tree, both boys agreed that it made the tree just perfect. When they had finished with the decorating, Daniel made everyone hot chocolate. As they drank their hot chocolates, they sat around the tree, singing along with the music.

On Christmas day, the boys were up early and were surprised by the gifts under the tree.

"See I told you Santa knows we're here," Daniel heard one of the boys say as their parents made their way to the stove to get their morning coffee. Daniel wished everyone a Merry Christmas and said, "I don't have any presents for you, but I promised that on my next visit I'll have something special for everyone."

"Don't you worry about that. Your present to us is this place. Who can say they had an old-fashioned Christmas like we're having? It is so special to be able to show the boys how people used to live before TV and Wi-Fi," Carol reassured him. Then, looking at the boys, she said, "Go ahead, open your presents. Make sure Uncle Daniel gets his."

She sat back and watched the boys' reaction when they saw what they got. "It's a gun and there's even a target we can shoot at! Thanks, Mom and Dad!" cried Liam, unable to believe what he had just gotten. He turned to his brother and asked, "What did you get, Dennis?" Dennis was still struggling with the wrapping, and when he finally saw what he got, he exclaimed, "I got a gun too!" The guns were exact replicas of real Winchester rifles, with lever action cocking to shoot a small spongy bullet. Once they had opened their presents, they turned to Daniel and Liam said, "Open your present, Uncle Daniel! Let's see what Santa brought you!"

Daniel saw the present was a long, narrow box and after seeing the boy's present, he kind of knew what his present was going to be. He unwrapped the present to find that it was indeed a gun—a Winchester .33 rifle, like the one the boys got—but for real.

"I got a gun too!" he said, feeling like one of the kids. "Charlie, you shouldn't have. What did you get me a rifle for? I never thought of getting one. Thank you!"

"I know you're thinking you won't ever need a rifle, but I think you should have one living here on your own," Charlie said. "If you look in the box, you'll find a box of bullets too." Daniel examined the rifle. Raising it up, he looked through the sight. The boys followed his example.

"I had one of these when I was on the police force and became a pretty good shot. I won many shooting competitions with it. The chief said I was one of the best shots on the force," Daniel explained.

"Look, Uncle Daniel, my rifle looks just like yours. It even has the same handle to cock it!" Dennis said as he showed the little rifle to Daniel.

"Yes, it does look the same, but this one is for real. Guns can be very dangerous in untrained hands. You know you should never play with real guns, don't you?" Daniel asked.

"Oh yes, my daddy said we have to be responsible with guns and never to point a gun at any people," Dennis replied in his innocent little voice. Then he added, "When you were a policeman, did you ever shoot anyone?"

Daniel was a little taken aback by his question, but he answered the little boy's question. "No, I never had to. But why are we talking about that? It's Christmas! Come here, let's see your rifle!"

"Well, boys, I think it's time for me to start getting the Christmas turkey ready. Maybe Daddy can set up the target so you can practice shooting your guns," Carol said as she got up and headed for the kitchen.

Daniel kept the stove at an even temperature as the turkey roasted in the oven, filling the house with a delicious fragrance. Carol worked all day preparing the food. She would serve her famous turkey dressing, mash potatoes, carrots, turnips and pickled beets all from Daniel's garden. She had brought fresh vegetables to make a green salad. And for dessert, Carol made apple crisps from the apples Daniel had picked. Carol had never cooked on a wood stove before, and she surprised herself by not burning anything. With the boys' help, the table was set. And when everything was ready for their Christmas meal, they sat down to enjoy it. Charlie gave thanks for the bountiful food and they all dug in and ate 'til they were full.

After a week of fun-filled activities, Charlie and his family said their goodbyes with big hugs and kisses.

"I think I'm going to miss having you. It's been wonderful having you all here. Goodbye, Charlie, thanks for coming and for the rifle. Having you here was so great. If you get to town before I do, say hi to Lilly and my dad," Daniel said.

"Will do. You take care. I worry about you, so far away in this bush," Charlie said.

"I'll keep safe, I love being here. It's my home now, so stop your worrying. I know how to take care of myself," Daniel said confidently. They hugged each other. Charlie got in his truck and drove away.

As the winter months passed, he realized he missed having bacon and eggs for breakfast. Porridge was okay but not everyday. Christmas and the meat Charlie had brought had spoiled him. He hadn't been able to go fishing since the snow had drifted in. One morning as he ate his porridge he thought, *Maybe I could raise pigs?* Then he thought again. *No pigs would be a lot of work. Maybe I could get some chickens?* His grandfather kept chickens over the winter. They just had to have the right shelter. When he had finished eating another idea came to mind. *I could get a cow. Then I'd have fresh milk. I could make yoghurt and cottage cheese. Grandma used to do that.* A plan started to form. *If I got animals, then I'd have to build a barn. I could cut down some trees and build the barn with them.* Later that day, he put on his snowshoes and went to see if there were suitable trees he could use.

That evening, he sketched a drawing of what his barn would look like. The sketch he drew was of a log, square structure with a flat roof sloping toward the back. He drew two doors in the front with a row of windows above the doors. He was not sure how big to make it—he would have to see how long the trees were. He leafed through the handicraft book and found a section about how to set in doors and windows, and another section on making cement. *It will be a lot of work to do by myself,* he thought, but he was determined. "I can do this," he said out loud. *I'll need some materials to build this and some better tools; maybe a sharper axe and a chainsaw,* he thought.

Daniel had found Zeb's chainsaw in the odds and ends shed, but it was old and hard to start. It would not last for very much lon-

ger. He made a list: plywood, nails, cement, roofing tiles, windows—
these were the big-ticket items. He kept the list handy and every time
he thought of something he would need, he wrote it down.

Now that he had formulated a plan for his barn, he became
very impatient because it kept on snowing. The snowbanks were now
shoulder height, making it very hard to clear a path. With the way
it snowed, it seemed like it would stay around all year, he thought.
As the weeks passed, he filled his days by chopping wood, shovelling
snow and whittling the chess pieces. He went cross-country skiing
but had to leave Misty home alone, because the snow was to deep for
her to walk in. When he returned, she would take his boots and hide
them. One time, he found one boot in the wood box and at another,
he found a boot under her bed. The third time, both boots were
gone and Daniel was a little upset with her and said, "Where did you
hide my boots, Misty?" Misty just laid on her bed with her head over
her paws and did not move. It took Daniel an hour before he found
them. One he found way at the back under his bed, and the other
one between the wall and his desk. When he came back from skiing
this time, he decided to place his boots in the closet under the stairs
where Misty would not be able to go.

Although Misty gave him trouble, she was his only companion.
She loved playing fetch and rope war. Daniel spent a lot of time with
her, teaching her to sit and stay, roll over, shake a paw, and to go
fetch and return her favorite toy—a ball Daniel had made with an
old sock. She knew Daniel's routine so well, it seemed like she could
read his mind. Daniel found that the best time to study was in the
evening when the house was at it's warmest, and the kettle was simmering on the stove. The simmering made it feel like he wasn't alone
and he found it very soothing. Most evenings were spent studying,
but he took a night off every week to watch a movie from the ones
Lilly had given him. For Misty, it was a time to rest on her daybed
beside the stove.

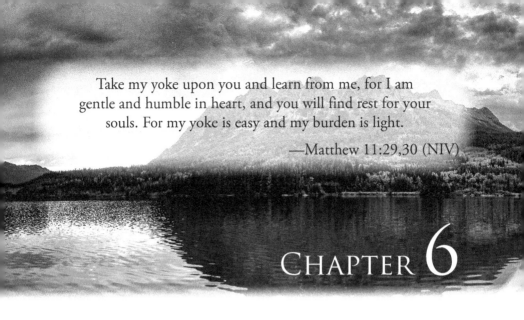

Take my yoke upon you and learn from me, for I am gentle and humble in heart, and you will find rest for your souls. For my yoke is easy and my burden is light.

—Matthew 11:29,30 (NIV)

CHAPTER 6

The spring that Daniel so patiently waited for finally came. As the snow melted away from the trees, Daniel started cutting down trees that he would need to build the barn. Once the trees were down, he trimmed off the branches and pulled the tree out of the woods to the clearing. When the ground dried out, he would use his truck to bring them to the building site. Once the snow had gone from the yard, he knew the road would be opened, so he decided to go to town for the supplies he needed. His list was long as he had also included the gardening supplies he would need.

"We're going to be pretty busy building the barn and putting in the garden," he said to Misty as they drove to town. Misty did not care. All she knew was that she was going for a truck ride. He drove straight to the lumber supply store. He asked a clerk for help to find all the items on the list and asked where the best place would be to buy a chainsaw. The clerk told him that they sold chainsaws and he took him to that department. Daniel was a little taken aback by all the different saws—they came in all types and sizes. Daniel picked them up one by one and chose one that was light but big enough to do the work he needed it for.

Most of the items on the list were loaded on his truck except for the windows. Those had to be ordered. He did not like that. That meant he would have to come back to town for them. *Maybe Charlie could pick them up and bring them to me?* He thought. He decided to go see Charlie and surprise him again.

When Daniel drove in the yard, Charlie was on the porch looking to see who was driving up.

"Daniel! You survived the winter! Am I happy to see you!" Charlie said as he greeted him with a manly hug. Daniel hugged him back and said, "What, you did not think I'd make it? Misty and I did very well, if I may say so myself."

"Come on in." Charlie invited Daniel in the house, and said, "Carol look who has come to see us. The recluse has come back to join the world." Charlie offered Daniel some coffee and they sat at the kitchen table to chat. Daniel told Charlie of his plan to build a barn so he could keep chickens and a cow.

"That's quite the undertaking, Daniel. What type of material are you going to use to build?"

"I'm thinking of using logs. I've been cutting down trees. The ones that are long and straight, I think they'll make good logs. I figure I can place one log over the other, one at a time. Might take me a while but I think I can do it," Daniel answered.

"It sounds like you've been thinking about this for a while. I could come help you later on this summer if you want some help," Charlie offered.

"I'm not going to say no to that, Charlie. It would be great to have help. Thanks. Oh, before I forget, I've ordered some windows for the barn but they're not going to be available for a while. When you come, would you bring them up?" Charlie agreed to do that. They continued to talk for a short while. After he had said good-bye to Charlie he decided to go see Lilly and his dad.

Lilly and his dad were so happy to see him. Lilly shamed him into staying for the rest of the week by telling him Little Beth would be very sad if he wasn't there for her birthday. Beth played shyly with him at first, but after a day with her, she came to him showing him her favorite dolly. The birthday party was very enjoyable, and when he saw how happy Beth was, he was glad he had agreed to stay.

They were having supper after the party when Ken asked, "Daniel are you planning to stay up in the mountains all summer?"

"Yes, I'm going to be very busy this summer. I'm planning to build a barn," Daniel answered.

"Really?" asked Lilly. "Wouldn't that be hard to do by yourself?"

"I've got it figured out. Charlie said he'll come help me later in the summer," Daniel replied.

Lilly and Ted went to put the birthday girl to bed and when they returned, Lilly had a present for him.

"I've got you something to keep you in touch with civilization. I know you want to live like they did in the past, but I think you should have this," Lilly said handing him a box. Daniel took the box and opened it.

"You got me a satellite radio?" Daniel said after he opened the box.

"Yes, and a subscription for a year. You'll use it, won't you?" Lilly asked.

"Of course, I will, thanks! I never thought of buying one. It's an excellent idea! I think you know me better than I know myself. Do you know how to set this thing up?" Daniel asked as he checked the radio.

"I can install it for you. I've got one and it can be done in no time," Ted answered.

The next day, he returned home and as he drove back, he thought about all he had to do that summer. Not only did he have to put in a garden and keep it up, he had this barn project too. It would be a lot of hard work but he liked keeping busy. Before he had left town, he had gone to see the chief to ask to get his leave of absence extended for another year. A year had passed already. *Time sure went by fast*, he thought. So much was different now. His whole outlook on life had changed over the year. He was no longer troubled by the horrific events he had witnessed working for years in the police force. Now he felt free, at peace—there was now a lightness to his life. *Maybe I should quit this police business*, he thought, but now was not the time to make that decision. As he drove, he listened to the music on his new radio. He loved the music, it made the drive seem shorter.

Once back at home and all the supplies he bought were unloaded, he went to try his new saw. He gassed and oiled it. On the first pull, the saw started, startling him so that he almost dropped it. He was not used to a saw starting on the first pull. The old saw never started on the first pull.

"Well, how about that, it started just like that," he said to Misty. "Let's go see if it can cut a tree down." Misty followed him to the tree line. Daniel picked a bigger tree and in no time, the tree was lying on the ground. "It sure makes a difference having a new saw, ah Misty? I think we're in business." The dog looked at him and wagged her tail in agreement.

As the days went by, Daniel kept busy keeping the house clean, making sourdough bread and all the other domestic duties that came up. He turned over the garden and planted it. Daniel had helped his grandmother plant her garden, but this garden was his first try on his own. Before seeding it, he would read the back of the seed packets and would follow the directions very closely. This year, he thought he would try to grow some corn. His grandmother had grown corn and he loved fresh corn on the cob. Zeb had told him that it did not grow very well here. The nights got too cold for the corn to form ears. But he would give it a try. It took longer to plant the garden than he had anticipated but once he had finished, Daniel looked it over and hoped his efforts would pay off.

Daily, Daniel went to cut down more trees and waited for the ground to dry so he could bring them closer to the building site. Finally, the day came when he thought he had cut down enough trees to build his barn. The ground had dried so he got his truck and loaded the trees in it. He took them to where he was going to build. He cleared and leveled an area for the building site with a shovel and a pick. As he worked, he had to stop once in a while to swat away the mosquitoes off his face and arms. He did not remember so many mosquitoes being around the last summer.

He was now ready to build the barn. He measured and staked out the foundation—fifteen feet by ten feet. Once that was done, he framed in the foundation with the largest logs he had and pounded spikes in to keep the logs in place. He was going to make a concrete floor so he divided the floor space into six sections, each five-feet square. He would be mixing the cement by hand so he figured this would make it easier by filling one section at a time. He decided to partially fill each section with gravel from the lakeshore. Before he could do that, however, he had to make the access down to the lake easier to walk.

All this time, the bugs kept getting worse. They would buzz around his head, get in his nose, mouth and ears. Finally, one day after he had swallowed a few bugs, he stopped work. His neck was so itchy. When he looked in the mirror, he could not believe all the bites he had on his neck.

"Misty, I wish I had some calamine lotion," he said to the dog. "I wonder if Zeb had anything for bug bites." Daniel went to the cupboard where Zeb had kept his medication. Daniel had never cleaned that cupboard and was surprised to find all kinds of different items in there. Old medications Zeb had not taken, old pain killers expired five years ago, some laxatives and a bottle of calamine lotion—expired of course. He kept the lotion and threw away all the other items. As he reached for the last of the bottles, he noticed something at the far back of the cupboard. He could not believe it. On the little package was written "Mosquito net." He unwrapped it and found a shirt made with netting.

"Well, look what I found, Misty, a mosquito net shirt. Thanks, Zeb," he said as he looked up. He rubbed in the calamine lotion over all the bites then decided to take the rest of the day off.

The next morning, Daniel went to see what he could do to make walking down the slope a little easier. Suited with the net shirt, he walked down the slope and tried to figure out what he could do. After some time, the best idea he came up with was to build some steps, maybe put in a set of stairs. He could pound in some posts in the bank and anchor the stairs to them. He worked all day building the stairs with two by fours. On the next day, he pounded in the posts. By the third day, he had a set of stairs going over the steepest part of the slope, making it so much easier to go up and down.

Now he could get on with building the barn and the business of hauling the gravel from the lakeshore to the work site. He worked for a week, filling buckets with gravel and hauling them to the site. After partially filling the sections with the gravel, and stockpiling some gravel on the side to use for when he mixed the cement, Daniel took a rest; going for a long sauna to soothe his achy body. Misty was worn-out following him back and forth and could not understand why he would do such a thing.

After a restful day, he was ready to tackle mixing the cement. He shoveled sand and gravel in the wheelbarrow, added in the cement, then added some water. And with the shovel, he mixed it all around until it was a good, pouring consistency. When he was satisfied with the mixture, he dumped it in the first section of the floor. He found that he would need another wheelbarrow full to fill the section. After mixing the wheelbarrow a third time, the first section was filled. He trowelled the cement until it was nice and smooth.

He found working with cement was hard work. His shoulders hurt and a blister was starting to form on his left thumb. Although it was only one in the afternoon, Daniel decided to take the rest of the day off. He was exhausted. He felt so grimy and clammy, then noticed he was covered with cement dust. When he saw Misty coming to him, he said, "Misty, let's go to the lake. I need to cool down and wash this dust off my clothes."

When he got to the lake, he took off his boots, and walked into the lake with his clothes on and swam around for a while. Misty did not like that Daniel was in the water and as he swam, she came to him and took a hold of his arm and pulled him to shore. Daniel let her pull him. When they were on shore he said, "Misty, you are one funny dog. Good girl, you'd be good to have in a sinking boat." He patted her on the head then took off his wet clothes and walked back to the house.

As he walked, he passed his hand through his hair only to find that he still had grime in his hair. He hung his clothes on the line and went straight to the shower. The water felt warm. He hadn't noticed how cold the swim had made him. The swim and the shower had revitalized him and now his energy was restored. He thought of going back to his cement work but decided against it. It was much too hot to do that work, but he then remembered the garden. He hadn't paid much attention to it so he supposed that it would be in much need of some care.

The rest of the afternoon he spent weeding around the small vegetable plants and hilling the potatoes. With all the rain—and now the warm temperature—the garden was growing very well. It pleased him to see it. As he went in to make supper, he heard thunder in the distance and noticed clouds coming up from the west. He looked at Misty and said, "I think we are in for more rain, we better go cover the cement or it will be ruined."

When he got up the next morning, it was pouring rain and it continued for three days. Daniel did not like the delays, but this place was teaching him to be patient, to wait and endure the upsets.

When it finally stopped raining, the ground around the building site was all mud and the mosquitoes were even worse. When he lifted the tarp from the cement, he was surprised to find that it had cured perfectly. Daniel's spirit rose—all his hard work had not been for nothing.

By the end of the week, Daniel had another section filled in. With more delays caused by more rain, it took him almost a month to finish the cement floor. Now that all the cement was good and hard, it was time for the first row of logs. Daniel selected the biggest and straightest log he had, sawed it in half, lengthwise, and set one half on the edge of the cement in the front of the building, and the other half at the back edge, laying them cut side down. For the sides, logs were notched at both ends to fit in the logs that had been put in the front and the back. He nailed the four corners in place. For the second row, he notched the logs to fit on the first row of logs. This took more time than Daniel anticipated. Once he had the second row of logs up for the four walls, he pounded a long nail in each corner where the notches were. By the end of the day he had started on the third row.

Misty had watched him all day from a shady spot she had found. When she saw him put down his tools, she went to him. "Hey there Misty, what do you think? I think we did enough for a day. Let's go cool off with a swim." Misty gave him a bark and ran down the path to the lake. When he got to the lake, he took off his sweaty clothes and ran into the water.

One afternoon, Misty started to bark and would not come to Daniel when he called for her. He finished nailing the log, stepped down the ladder he was on and as he walked by an axe, he picked it up. As he came by the house, he saw Misty was barking at a girl and a guy. The second the girl saw Daniel, she took off running down the trail to the lake, the guy right behind her. Daniel just stood there wondering why the two were running away so fast. "Well, they're sure not very friendly," he said to Misty as he looked down at her. It was then he realized he was holding the axe. He started to laugh and said, "I would run too if I saw a scruffy looking guy holding an axe. They probably thought I was the Mad Hatter." He walked to the edge and watched as the two paddled off in their canoe.

By the end of the month, he had the four walls up to six-feet high. He divided the interior with a log wall, making one side five-feet wide—the side for the chickens—and ten-feet on the other side for the cow. He cut two openings in the front for doors, one for each side. He framed the sides of the door openings with two by six planks. Over the doors, Daniel framed the openings for two windows and filled the space between the windows and the edges with some logs. The front wall was two-feet higher than the back to give the roof a slope. Now he was ready to start building the roof for the barn. He had to lift large logs for the roof supports. He worked all day devising a way to best do this. These were the biggest timbers he had—very heavy. He set up a tripod on the top of the last row of logs and hung a block and tackle to it. He wrapped a rope around the end of the log then pulled it to the top of the wall. Now he had to get the other end up. He would have to build a tripod on the back wall too.

"I think we did enough for today, Misty, let's go for a swim. You look like you could use some water. I wish I could have a cold beer just now." Misty loved it when Daniel talked to her. She responded with a bark or two. They played in the water until Daniel could no longer feel his feet. Although it was the end of summer, the water in the lake was still very cold.

As he sat down for supper, he heard a vehicle drive up his driveway. Charlie and his boys had come.

"You sure have good timing, Charlie," Daniel said as he went to greet his company. "Are you guys hungry? I was just going to have supper." Daniel had made a large batch of spaghetti sauce. All he had to do was to cook up more noodles. The boys went straight to Misty to play with her.

"Yeah, I think the boys are hungry. Come on in, boys, you can play with Misty later." In no time, Daniel had their plates ready to eat. After they had finished eating, they all went to look at what Daniel had built.

"Whoa! Daniel, you sure have been busy. It actually looks like an old homesteader's barn. I've got those windows you ordered. Where are you going to put them?" Charlie asked.

"They'll go in the space above the doors. I hope they will fit in the space I made. Right now, I'm working to get the roof on. I'm glad you're here because I need help pulling those large logs up on the walls. It's very hard to do on your own. We can start with that tomorrow. Let's go sit and talk," Daniel replied. Charlie gave him a smile and agreed. They talked for a while then retired for the night.

The next day, with Charlie's help, the support logs were lifted and nailed into place. Plywood was sheeted over the support logs and roofing tiles nailed over those. The windows were set in. Daniel was happy to see that the windows fit just right in the opening. By the end of the weekend, Daniel's barn was all enclosed except for the doors.

"You know Daniel, I have some old doors at the farm that you could have. They were from Grandpa's old house. They've been laying around. I just about took them to the dump last year," Charlie said.

"That's awesome, Charlie. I was wondering where I could get old doors. New doors would have looked out of place on this barn. I'll pick them up the next time I come to town," Daniel said. As he looked at the barn he added, "Now I'll have to chink up all the cracks between the logs. I think that will take me a while. Charlie, thanks for all your help."

Daniel decided to take a few days off and enjoyed Charlie's company. Charlie taught the boys how to fish. It pleased the boys when they caught enough fish for their supper. The day before they were going to leave, they all went for a long hike up the trail that led to the top of a mountain. They were on their way back when Misty suddenly stopped. The hair on her back went up and she started to growl.

"What is it, Misty?" Daniel asked as he looked in the direction the dog was looking. He spotted a black wolf just to the side of the trail, not very far ahead of them. Daniel grabbed on to Misty's collar and said, "Boys, do you see the wolf? It's okay, I don't think it will hurt us. Just stay close together."

The wolf did not seem to fear them. It skirted the trail and ran passed them. Once the wolf had gone, Liam said, "Did you see the color of it's eyes? They were baby blue. It sure looked spooky."

"Yeah it sure was and it sure was big. Bigger then Misty!" Dennis added.

In the morning, as Charlie and the boys were getting ready to leave, Daniel said, "Thanks for all the help Charlie. I don't think I could have put the roof on by myself. Thank you. Drive safe and I'll come see you soon."

"Daniel you're welcome, you keep safe," Charlie replied. He got in his truck and drove away.

After Charlie left, Daniel went to look at his garden. He had spent most of his time working on the barn and had not spent a lot of time caring for his garden. The plants appeared to be growing well, and it looked like he would have a good harvest. He weeded around some of the rows and hilled the potatoes a little more. For the rest of the summer, he divided his time working in the garden and working at filling the cracks in the barn's walls. As he worked, he played the radio, listening to music and to the news. It made him feel like he was still part of the world.

When fall came, he harvested his garden. Consulting his notes he had made the previous summer, he canned green beans, tomatoes and made pickled beets. He had not planted any cabbages this summer—he never ever wanted to see a cabbage again. His garden had produced well, except for the corn. He had found a few ears but they were small and not well formed, not worth his effort. He noticed that the potatoes and the carrots were bigger this year, probably because there had been a lot more rain. All in all, he was pleased with what the garden had produced. After he had picked the apples, he decided it would be nice to bring some apples down to his family. He hadn't seen anyone except for Charlie in a long time. He missed them and wondered how they were doing.

When he arrived at Lilly's house, she was out so he and Misty sat on the front steps and waited for her. As he waited, he called his father. He too was busy but told him he would be at Lilly's for supper. Daniel realized that his family had busy lives and he was not part of them. That bothered him. He would have to make the best of every visit and let them know he was still part of them.

When Lilly drove in, she was very surprised to see her brother. "Daniel, I'm so happy to see you, I missed you so!" she said, giving him a hug. She went back to the car to get Beth out of her car seat. The little girl gave him a smile but would not let him pick her up.

"Dad will be here for supper. It will be so great having all of us together again. How was your summer? You were gone all summer! What did you do with all that time up there?" As she talked, he sensed that his sister was a little annoyed with him.

"Lilly, why are you upset with me? Is there something wrong?" Daniel asked.

"Something wrong? No, nothing is wrong," she said. She was a little surprised he had picked up that she was upset. "Dad will be here soon. I have to get ready for supper." She picked up Beth and went in the house leaving Daniel standing outside by himself. He went back to sit on the steps and waited for his father.

"Daniel, what a nice surprise, how are you, son?" Ken asked giving Daniel a manly hug.

"I'm good, Dad. What's with Lilly? At first, she was pleased to see me and then she became upset with me. Is she okay? She left me out here and never invited me to come in," Daniel said, a little confused.

"Son, I think this is between the two of you. How long will you be staying?" They both went to sit on the front steps.

"I've got to get some supplies, then I have to go see Charlie to pick up some doors for the barn," Daniel replied.

"You built the barn?" Ken said with surprise.

"Yeah Dad. I got it built. There were times when I just about gave up. The mosquitoes were so bad. Somehow, I don't remember having any mosquitoes last year," Daniel said. With a nod from his dad, Daniel continued saying, "Charlie came and helped me with the roof, but I did everything else by myself. The summer just flew by. I guess I should have come for a visit before now. It upsets Lilly when I'm gone for too long. I thought she was okay with me to be away. I've got to talk with her."

Lilly came outside and with a big smile on her face she greeted her father. She gave him a kiss then invited both men in the house. After they had supper, Daniel helped Lilly clean up the kitchen.

"Does Ted miss supper often? How are you two doing?" Daniel asked.

"Ted and I are in a bit of a slump these days. He has been working long hours, overseeing the renos and hiring new staff. He just thinks he should be there; it's his baby. He promised he'll be home for supper once all is settled. He's doing very well in the business. He's good at what he does and loves it," Lilly said as she washed the sauce pan. Then she looked up at Daniel and said, "It's not that bad. It's just me. You know how I can be, very needy at times. I've got to find something for me."

"Are you upset that I was away for so long? You did not seem very happy when I first saw you," Daniel asked.

"Daniel, if you were here, I would probably rely on you instead of standing on my own two feet. You caught me at a low point. Ted had just told me he would be working late and I just felt sorry for myself. I should not have taken it out on you. I'm sorry for being so rotten to you," Lilly said giving him a smile.

"Lilly, you're forgiven. When will Ted be home?'" Daniel asked.

"He should be home soon. He's always home in time to put Beth to bed," Lilly answered.

When Ted got home he found everyone in the living room enjoying little Beth playing. When she saw her dad, she ran to him to be picked up. "Hey, there's my little munchkin! I see your uncle came to see you. Were you nice to him?" Beth nodded. Lilly joined them, and together they went to put Beth to bed. When Ted and Lilly returned, they went to sit outside.

"What a wonderful night! Look at that moon. I love this. All my favorite guys, all here with me," Lilly said as she sat on the lawn swing with Ted by her side.

"I've brought something for you guys. I'll be right back," Daniel said as he left to go to his truck. He returned with a big basket full of apples. "These are from my place. I picked them just yesterday. Taste them, they're nice and sweet." Everyone tasted an apple and agreed that they were tasty.

"I just hired a baker at the restaurant. I'll get her to make pies with these. Thanks, Daniel," Ted said. After Lilly thanked Daniel for the apples, she started questioning him about what he had done all summer. Daniel told her what he had done with the barn and said, "Would you like to see pictures of what I built?"

"Oh yes, Daniel, I want to see that!" Lilly exclaimed. Daniel retrieved the pictures and explained the building progression from clearing the site to finishing with putting in the doors. As Lilly viewed the pictures, she was amazed and said, "That's the barn you built? I'm impressed. You sure did a lot of hard work."

At the end of the week, after Daniel had all the supplies he would need for winter, he said his goodbyes to his family and drove to Charlie's place. He had to ask Charlie for another favor. It dawned on him that he relied on Charlie a lot. When he got there, the family was having supper, which again made Daniel feel like he was imposing. But Charlie's family was so inviting that he forgot all about that feeling. Daniel caught up with how their summer had gone and showed them pictures of the barn.

After supper, Daniel went outside to help Charlie with the chores. They were feeding the chickens when Daniel remembered the favor he wanted to ask Charlie. So he said, "Charlie, I tried to order some chicks for next spring and was told that they did not take orders 'til the beginning of the year. Would you put in the order for me? You might have to pick them up if we have a late melt."

"Don't you worry, I'll take care of it," Charlie answered.

"Thanks, Charlie, I'm always imposing on you these days. Thanks for all the support you've given me," Daniel said.

"Daniel, I'm glad to be of help. I think I owe it to you. Over the years, you have done some heavy lifting around here. It's my turn to return the favor. Come on, I'll show you those doors. They're in the garage." The doors were wood panel, full of nicks and scratches—a little battered but they were not warped. After looking them over, Daniel decided they would work just right so they loaded the doors on Daniel's truck.

The next morning, Daniel was back on the road. It felt good to be returning home. Was he becoming a loner? Maybe there was something wrong with him, he wondered. Misty was tired after playing with Charlie's boys. She happily laid on the seat and went to sleep.

Once back home, he returned to his routine, doing his chores in the house and going to work on the barn. Putting in the doors proved to be a little harder than he first thought. He had to do some slight adjustment to the openings, but with the help of his chainsaw and axe, he had both doors in by the end of the day. When he backed away to take a look, it pleased him to see that the barn was finally all enclosed.

When most of the chinking was done, he went to work on the interior, putting in hard insulation on the floor and on the walls in the chicken's area. Once the insulation was taped so there were no gaps between the floor and the walls, plywood was nailed over it. Two by fours were nailed in place to make perches so the chickens could roost. He built a stall for the cow and a wall to separate the space to make a store room. By springtime, the barn would be ready for the chickens and the cow.

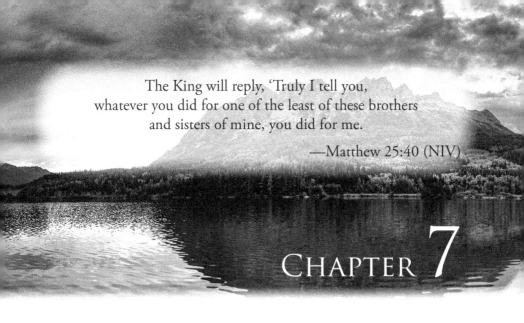

The King will reply, 'Truly I tell you,
whatever you did for one of the least of these brothers
and sisters of mine, you did for me.

—Matthew 25:40 (NIV)

CHAPTER 7

Daniel spent his second winter with Misty as his only company. He kept himself busy with household duties, shoveling snow, making improvements on his barn, and chopping wood for the ever-demanding stove. Having a warm house became his main concern, and he became an expert at doing it. He experimented with new food recipes and tried to make different foods with the same ingredients. This winter, he did not have a tub of meat like the one Charlie had brought him last Christmas. He missed the fresh fish he had all summer.

The snow had drifted in over the ice, making it impossible to go fishing. What meat he had was canned; canned tuna and salmon, some canned ham and some canned chicken. He was getting over-obsessed with his craving for fresh meat so he decided to try his hand at snaring a rabbit. He found some snaring wire in the old shed of odds and ends, and with his snowshoes, he walked to where he found rabbit prints in the snow. There he set the snare. The next afternoon, he went to check the snare but found that it was gone—no snare, no rabbit. As he walked back home, he scolded himself. *How could I be so stupid? Why didn't I secure the snare so the rabbit could not run away with it? Now there's a rabbit with a snare around his neck. I could have had fresh rabbit for supper.* When he got home, he had a different thought. *I don't even know how to skin a rabbit or cook it. What was I thinking?*

That evening after another supper of the same type of food, he decided to watch one of the movies that Lilly had given him: The Beverlee Hill Billie's. It was corny but it made him laugh. It was just what he needed. It was a treat, a break from all the studying he had been doing.

Every morning, he kept in touch with the outside world by listening to the satellite radio. Sometimes when he put on the radio, he wondered what kind of disaster had happened overnight. After a while, he noticed that there was a new tragedy just about every day. It made him wonder why people lived like that and he was happy not to be part of it.

The winter proved to be much milder than the last and with much less snow. This winter, he was not spending all his time shoveling snow, but he had time to enjoy some winter sports. Daniel set a cross country ski trail around his property and down to the lake, and managed to keep it open all winter. The snow pack had become hard enough to walk on without falling through, so he and Misty went for long walks following the lakeshore and around the fenced area, exploring their backyard.

Spring at last made its appearance and to Daniel's surprise, the weather stayed warm and the snow quickly melted away. On the first day, he knew the road would be opened. He went to town to inquire about the baby chicks. Had Charlie ordered them for him? He drove directly to Charlie's place, and when he got there, he was welcomed with open arms. As they had supper that evening, Charlie bombarded him with questions. "So how did you spend your winter? Are you tired of being by yourself? Whatever did you do all alone for that length of time?"

"Well, let's see, I kept busy with everyday chores and working on finishing the barn so it would be ready for the chicks. And in the evenings, I would study the law course I'm taking. I finished the course the professor gave me to study," Daniel replied.

"Are you thinking of going to practice law?" Charlie asked.

"Yes, I'm thinking I'll do some work for my dad, help him with some of his cases," Daniel replied.

"Are you going to quit the force?" Charlie asked, surprised that Daniel would do that.

"Yes, I think I will. I can't see myself doing that type of work anymore. I think I can be more helpful as a lawyer then a cop," Daniel replied with confidence.

The next morning, Charlie and Daniel drove to the little town to get the chicks. When he picked up the chicks, he was told to get them out of their boxes as soon as possible so they would not overheat. He thanked Charlie for his help, said goodbye and set for home. As he stopped at a gas station for gas and a coffee, he saw a much older man pulling a young girl by the arm. Daniel could tell that the girl did not want to be with that man by the way she was trying to get him to release her.

Daniel went up to the man and said, "What are you doing? Let her go."

"You want her? You can have her for an hour for just one hundred dollars." Daniel could not believe what he had just heard.

"Are you selling her?"

"No, I'm not selling her; just letting you have her for an hour. You can have your fun with her then return her to me," the old man said.

Daniel saw red. He was just about to punch the guy out when he saw a look in the girl's eyes calling out for his help. "One hundred dollars? That's a little much. I'll give you fifty," Daniel said, handing him a fifty-dollar bill. The man took the money and handed him the girl.

"Have her back here in an hour."

The man walked away and Daniel was left with the girl. He could not believe what he had just done. Now what would he do? He took a closer look at the girl. She was just about as tall as he was, very thin, like she was anorectic. She was wearing a short, black leather skirt and a very revealing knitted top. Her head was covered by a colorful scarf which Daniel saw she was using to carefully cover up the left side of her face. From what Daniel could see of her face, she was strikingly beautiful with dark blue eyes and black hair. It made Daniel wonder why she was hiding behind the scarf.

"Well we can't stand here all day. I'll take you to a woman's shelter," Daniel told the girl. He took another look at the girl and shook his head. *What in the world did I just do?* he wondered.

"No, I don't want to go to a place like that. Take me with you," the girl said in a soft voice. When they got to the truck, Misty was told to go sit in the back. The girl never saw the dog. When they were both in his truck, the girl again said, "Take me with you." As she said that, she turned. The scarf fell away and Daniel saw her badly disfigured face. He tried not to show how shocked he was and said, "You don't even know me. A woman's shelter would be a better place for you."

"No, please, please take me with you. I know you are a good man. I just know it. Take me with you," she said, hiding behind the scarf. She could tell that Daniel was a good guy by the reaction he had when he saw her face. Daniel looked at the chicks in the back of the cab. He had to get them home. He did not have time to argue with this strange girl. He drove away from the gas station and asked, "How old are you? I bet you're not even eighteen?"

"I'm over eighteen," the girl replied in a quiet voice.

"Really, you're over eighteen? You look like you're ten. If I took you with me, it would be child abduction charges I'd be looking at. I'm taking you to the woman's shelter," Daniel insisted.

"No. You can't take me there. I am over eighteen years old. I was born in 1996. Please take me with you, please, please." She started crying. Big tears rolled down her face. She put her knees to her chest and tried to make herself as small as she could. When Daniel saw how determined she was, he gave in and decided to drive home. They did not say anything for a long time. The girl sat with her knees up to her chest and the scarf around her face, just looking outside. She was the first to speak.

"Where are you taking me? There're no houses out here. You're not going to leave me in the forest, are you?"

Daniel was a little startled by her voice. "I live in the mountains. We should be there in an hour or so. I'm Daniel. What is your name?" he asked.

"My dad calls me Kit. My mom used to call me Kitten. My name is Kitten LaChatte."

"That is an unusual name. Who was that man you were with?" Daniel asked.

"That's my dad. He wanted money to buy himself something to drink. He told me he was out of work and needed money. This morning, he was supposed to take me to the hospital, but instead he dragged me to this gas station and said that man would pay money to play with me. No one paid any attention to us until you came. He will be mad when I don't show up in an hour," Kit said in a frightened voice.

"Yeah, that he will, if he's not to drunk. What did your dad do for work?" Daniel asked.

"I don't know. He worked." Daniel gave her a funny look so she just clammed up. She had the feeling she had said something stupid again. Her dad always said she was so ignorant.

"What's the matter? Did I say something to upset you?" Daniel asked. Kit did not answer. She could not show Daniel how ignorant she was. Daniel put on the radio and drove for awhile, listening to the songs of the sixties.

"We're just about at the house," Daniel said, just as Misty gave a bark from the back seat. Kit was so surprised, she let out a loud scream—surprising Misty who gave another bark. Kit was so scared that she slipped down to sit on the floor in front of the seat.

"Hey there, Misty, quiet! You scared Kit. Kit, don't be afraid of my dog. She is a very gentle dog. She won't hurt you. Come, sit back on the seat." Kit slowly got up and keeping an eye on the dog, sat back in the seat. Everything was quiet until they arrived at the house.

"Okay, you're home now Misty," Daniel said as he let her out of the truck. He turned to Kit and said, "Well, this is my home, do you like it?" Kit did not answer. She was stunned. There were no other houses here. She had never imagined a place like this existed. She got out of the truck and stepped on the newly greened grass with her bare feet. It felt cool and very soft.

As she walked on the grass, she totally forgot about the scarf she hid behind, and with the biggest smile on her face, she said,

"Oh Danny, this is so wonderful! This has to be the prettiest place I have ever been! I can't remember ever walking on grass with my bare feet before!" Daniel was a little surprised by Kit's reaction and was amazed to see the look of pure joy on her face.

Daniel turned back to the truck and got the chicks to carry them to the barn. When he opened the box, he was relieved to see that they were all okay. The little balls of yellow fluff were chirping up at him. He couldn't help but smile. He put the box on the ground and opened the side of the box to let them out. As he picked up one to look at it closely, he heard, "What are those?" Daniel jumped. He had been so fascinated by the chick, he had forgotten about the girl.

Daniel looked up and saw Kit was right beside him. He had not noticed that she had followed him. "These are little chicks. Do you want to hold one?" Kit nodded her head so Daniel placed a chick in her hand. She was surprised by how light and soft it was.

"It sure is cute. Will it stay little like this?" she asked as she gently stroked the chick.

"No, of course not. They'll get big. They're chickens," Daniel said sarcastically. The smile on Kit's face changed to sadness. She put the chick down very gently and walked out of the barn. Daniel knew he had offended her. He caught up with her by the truck.

"I'm sorry. I should not have spoken like that. I guess you have never seen chicks before?" Daniel asked.

Kit opened the truck door, got her scarf and wrapped it around her head. Daniel noticed tears running down her face and said, "Kit why are you crying? I said I was sorry."

"Danny, it's not you. It's me, I'm just ignorant," Kit said as she walked away from Daniel.

"What? I never said you were ignorant," Daniel said as he watched her walk away from him.

Kit went to sit on the edge of the deck so Daniel let her be and went to care for the chicks. When he returned to the barn, he saw that they were all bundled up together. But when Daniel set up the water, they all flocked around the water jug for a drink. *I think they'll be okay*, he thought to himself. He set out a tray of chicken feed for them, then went to the house.

Kit was still in the same place when he returned to the house. He went over to her and said, "Come, let's go in the house. You must be hungry. I'll make us some food."

Daniel was just about finished eating his sandwich when Kit slowly walked in the house with the scarf covering her face.

"Kit, I made you a sandwich. Come sit."

Kit walked over to the table and sat down. Daniel placed the sandwich in front of her but she did not take it.

"Is there something wrong with the food? You don't like sandwiches?" Daniel asked. "You've got to be hungry. Go on, eat." Kit reluctantly picked up the sandwich and took a bite. After she had finished eating it she said, "Thank you for the food. Can I go see the chicks again?"

"Sure, let's go see them. I'll show you how to unlock the door so you can go see them anytime you want." Daniel noticed that she would not walk beside him but stayed a couple of steps behind him. He showed her how to work the door latch and when she went inside, he returned to the house. *What a strange girl. She's so sensitive. I have to bring her to a shelter*, he thought.

After he had cleaned the kitchen, he went to see what Kit was doing. He did not see her outside so he went to the barn. When he came closer, he could hear she was singing a song they had heard on the radio. But when he entered the barn, she stopped.

"You have a nice voice. Go on, keep singing."

But Kit shook her head and kept quiet. "You know songs from the sixties?" Daniel asked.

Kit looked up at him, smiled and said, "I've never heard that song before today. I just remember it and I sang it."

"Really? That is very good. I wish I could remember things that easily. Are you going to stay here all night? There is a bed in the house you can sleep on. Come, it's a lot more comfortable than this wood floor." After Daniel checked to see if the chicks had enough water, they both went to the house. Daniel showed her to the bedroom and where the bathroom was.

"Danny, are you going to lock the door to the room? I don't like to be locked in," Kit asked. Daniel thought that this was a very strange question.

"Kit why would I lock the door to the room? You're free to come and go as you please. Why would you ask me that?" But Kit did not say anything.

"I'm going to take you to a shelter tomorrow. It's getting late, I'm going to bed."

When Kit heard that, she stood up and said, "I'm not going to any shelter. I'm staying here. I like it here. The shelter is full of mean and nosey people. I'm staying here. All I ask is that I get a little bit to eat and that you don't beat me. I'll help you with the chicks or do some housework. But I'm not going to no shelter."

Daniel was a little taken aback. He would have never thought that she would be so determined about staying.

"You don't have any other clothes or shoes to wear. You've got to go to a shelter. Please understand that it's the best place for you," Daniel said softly. This made Kit even more determined. She would not go.

"You could go to town and get me some clothes, Danny. I'll stay here and look after the chicks. I'll pay you back by doing work for you. Please, Danny, I'm not leaving here."

"I'll get you a shirt you can sleep in," Daniel said as he went up to the loft. He was tired and did not want to argue with her any longer. When he returned with one of his t-shirts, he said, "Here, you'll be more comfortable if you changed into this. It's late. I've got to get some sleep. Good night."

Kit took the shirt from him and as he walked to the stairs, Kit said, "Thanks Danny. Good night."

When he came down the next morning, Daniel was surprised to see Misty sleeping beside the couch where Kit was sleeping. The minute he stepped by the couch, she sat up and said, "Good morning, Danny. I already fed and watered the chicks. I could make you breakfast if you show me how."

Daniel couldn't say anything. He went outside and checked the chicks. Their feed tray and the water jug were both full. Kit had followed him outside and was now watching him return to the house.

"You didn't believe I could feed the chicks? I saw how you fed them yesterday. Did I feed them okay?" she asked.

"Yes Kit, you did alright. I'm still taking you to the shelter," Daniel answered.

"Danny, if I go to the shelter, I'm not going to stay there. I would go back to live with my dad. He beats me and he would sell me again, but it's better than to have people stare at me as if I'm a freak. Don't you see this is the best place for me? I like it here. Your dog likes me. It slept by the couch all night and when I had to go to the bathroom, it sat by the door waiting for me. I can be very quiet. Just show me what you want me to do and I'll do it. Daniel, please let me stay." With that, Daniel agreed that Kit could stay.

"I still have to go to town. You have no clothes to wear. I just don't know about this. Will you be alright staying here by yourself?" Daniel felt so uneasy. What had he gotten into?

"I'll be just fine. I'll make sure the chicks are fed and watered. I won't touch any of your things. Thanks, Danny. I'll be good. Thanks, Danny!"

Daniel was still not convinced it was a good idea to let Kit stay. He started a fire in the stove and in a little while, he had two bowls of rolled oats ready to eat. He set canned milk, brown sugar and some apple sauce on the table. Kit looked a little confused when she saw what was set before her.

"I never had this for breakfast before. What I ate always came from a box. What is this?" Kit asked, stirring the porridge. Daniel was careful to keep his usual voice when he answered. He did not want to offend her again.

"This is what I call a good breakfast. What I like to do is put brown sugar and apple sauce over the rolled oats, then cover it all up with milk. Go ahead, I think you'll like it."

Kit followed what Daniel did to his rolled oats. She took a spoonful and tasted it. "Yes, it is very good. Danny, thank you!"

After they ate, Kit helped Daniel clean up the dishes. Before he left for town, he set out bread and some cheese on the cutting board along with a muffin. "Kit, I left you some food on the cutting board. Please help yourself."

"Thank you, Daniel. I'll be good Daniel, don't worry," Kit said with a grateful smile.

"I'll be gone all day and it will be dark when I get back. Help yourself to the food, eat all you want. I'll leave Misty here, she can keep you company. Stay close to the house and don't go wandering off in the trees, it's easy to get lost. I don't want you to touch the stove. Just let it be. The house will keep warm."

After a few more instructions, Daniel left. He questioned what he was doing but what else could he do? He couldn't physically pick her up and put her in the truck, could he?

Daniel could not believe he had let a strange girl talk him into staying at his place. What was he thinking? Why was she his responsibility now? He drove straight to his sister's place.

"Daniel I'm so glad that you are back. I was starting to wonder when we would see you. How was the winter? How are you?" she said as she gave him a welcome hug.

"Lilly, I did a crazy thing. Now I'm stuck with this big problem. Man, I'm such an idiot," Daniel replied.

"What is it Daniel? Were you in an accident?" Lilly replied, very concerned.

"No, nothing like that. I put my nose in something I should have left alone," Daniel said, then continued to tell Lilly about how he had acquired Kit.

"Where is this girl now?"

"At my place. I could not persuade her to go to a shelter. She said she likes it there and will not leave."

"It's just like you Daniel, helping the down and out. You did a good thing. But now you have a house guest. Maybe Dad will have an idea. Why don't you go see him?" Lilly said.

"Yes, Dad would know what to do, I'll go talk to him. Thanks, Lily."

Daniel was a little anxious about seeing his dad. He had no idea what his dad's reaction to this would be. But he needed some advice. When Daniel got to his dad's office, his dad was waiting for him.

"How did you know I was coming? Lilly called you?" Daniel asked as he sat in the chair in front of the desk.

"Yeah and she told me about the problem you have," Ken said with a big smile on his face.

"Why do I put my nose in things that are not mine to solve?" Daniel asked.

"You sure this girl is of age? Is the dad looking for her? You could go to the police to have her removed," Ken counselled him.

"Dad, I think she's been abused, she's as skinny as a rail. I don't want to cause her anymore pain. I can't have the police involved in this. That would only frighten her. Could you see if you can find something on her? Her face is badly scarred. I think she was in a fire. If her dad is looking for her, there might be a missing person's report on her. Could you find out?" Daniel continued and told his dad everything he knew about Kit.

"We don't have much to go on but I'll do my best to find out more. In the meantime, I guess you have a roommate."

"Yeah, I guess. She doesn't have anything to wear except for the clothes on her back so I came to town to get her some. Maybe I'll get Lilly to help me with this. Thanks, Dad, I told Kit I'd be back tonight so I'd better get going."

Daniel went back to Lilly's and she agreed to go shopping with him. When Lilly volunteered to pay for half of the items they had bought for Kit, Daniel said, "You don't have to do that. She's my problem, not yours." He felt bad about taking Lilly's money, but she insisted. Once they had finished shopping, Daniel said goodbye and thanked her for all the help.

"Bye, Daniel, you now have someone to spend the summer with. You never know, this might turn to be for the good," Lilly said as she gave him a kiss goodbye.

It was very late when Daniel arrived home. He saw no lights in the house, but Misty came to greet him when he got out of the truck. "Hey there, girl. Why are you outside?" he said as he went in the house. He expected to see Kit sleeping on the couch but she was not there. Alarmed, he sat on the couch and took a deep breath. As he sat it suddenly occurred to him that she might be with the chicks. He ran to the barn with his flashlight in his hand. When he got inside the barn, he spotted her lying down on the wood floor with all the chicks huddled closely beside her.

"Kit. Kit, wake up. Come, let's get you in the house. Kit, wake up," he said as he gave her a little nudge. Kit woke with a jump. For a moment she did not know where she was but quickly realized that she was with the chicks. She slowly got up being careful not to step on any sleeping chicks and went with Daniel to the house.

Once there, Daniel asked, "Kit, are you alright? You must be frozen. It's not very warm outside." He took the blanket that was on the couch and wrapped her with it. "Come on, lay down, it's very late. I'm going to bed too," Daniel said as Kit laid down, closed her eyes and went back to sleep.

The next morning, Daniel found Kit sitting at the kitchen table examining the chess pieces he had made. When she saw him, she set the pieces back down and carefully covered the injured side of her face with her scarf. He noticed that the table was set in the exact way he had set it the morning before. *Strange*, he thought.

"Good morning, Kit, how long have you been up?' he asked her, but Kit did not answer. He went over to the stove to start a fire so he could make coffee. Once the fire was going he asked, "You must be hungry?" Kit nodded. "As soon as the stove is hot enough, I'll make rolled oats. In the meantime, I'll go see the chicks."

He was just about out the door when he heard her say, "I already fed them. They eat a lot for little things," Somehow it did not surprise Daniel. Kit knew how to make herself helpful. Kit sat quietly at the table looking at what Daniel was doing. She noted what he did to prepare the cereal and how he made coffee. When he placed a bowl of cereal in front of her, Kit asked, "Danny, what is this thing?" holding up a chess piece. Daniel gave her a smile and replied, "That's a chess piece. Do you know how to play chess?"

"No, I don't think so. What is chess?" Kit answered in a soft voice. Daniel was pleased to see that he had not offended her and said, "Chess is a game. I can show you how to play if you want."

"It's called chess… what do you do with these pieces?" She could not figure it out. A grown man playing with small wooden pieces. She put the piece back with the others and started to fix her cereal the way Daniel had done the day before.

As they were eating their breakfast, Daniel asked, "How did you spend your day yesterday?"

Kit did not answer until she had finished her bowl of food.

"I spent it with the chicks, they're so cute. I like to pick them up. They're so soft!"

Daniel gave her a smile and went to get some coffee. As he poured himself a cup, he asked, "Would you like some coffee?" Kit was surprised to be asked. Her dad had never offered her any coffee.

"Yes, please Danny, I would. Thank you for asking me," Kit said. She got up and ran to the cupboard to get a cup.

"I should be getting the coffee for you. Next time, I'll do that," she said, bringing her cup to Daniel. He poured her some coffee. And with his coffee in hand, he walked outside to enjoy the morning sun. Kit followed him. "I got you some things from town. I left them in the truck," Daniel said, drinking his coffee.

"Oh, Danny, thank you, I'll repay you. I'll work hard for you. Thanks for letting me stay. Is it okay if I went to get them, Danny?" Kit said very excited.

"Yeah, go ahead. The bags are in the back seat."

Kit ran to the truck and returned with her arms full of bags. Kit was so amazed by all the things Daniel had gotten her. She could not speak. She opened a bag and could not believe all the clothes in there: pants, t-shirts, socks, underwear, boots and shoes. In another bag, she found a hair brush and comb, and all kinds of hair things and other toiletries. In another bag a coat, robin egg blue in color, one with two layers, an outer shell and a fleece.

Kit thought it was the most beautiful coat she had ever owned. She just broke down and cried. She looked at Daniel and tried to thank him, but the words just stuck in her throat. Daniel had never seen anyone react like this for getting new things. *What had this girl been through?* he wondered.

"You okay? Why are you crying? Do you like the clothes?" Kit nodded, but she could not say the words. She found it was hard to find the words that would convey the gratitude she felt.

"Let's see if it fits," Daniel said as he went over to her and helped her put on the coat.

"It's a little big but I think it will be alright. The sleeves fit just right on you," Daniel said once Kit had the coat on. She pulled the coat snugly around her. It felt so warm.

"Th-thanks, Danny. You are so kind."

"You're welcome Kit. My sister picked it out for you," Daniel said with a big smile on his face.

"You have a sister? I don't have a sister or brother," Kit said, then abruptly stop herself from saying more. She wasn't sure if she should say anything personal to Daniel. What if her dad found out? She quickly turned back to her new clothes and kept quiet. Daniel sensed that Kit was keeping something back. He would not push her. *She'll open up when she's ready*, he thought.

"Kit, I'm glad that you like the things I got you. There's a dresser in the bedroom. You can put your clothes in it. I've got some chores to do," Daniel said.

He went to the garden. As he worked the soil, he thought about this strange girl living with him. There was something about her that was amiss. He had to talk to her but he did not know where to begin.

Kit went in the house and brought her clothes to the bedroom. She took each item, folded it neatly and placed it in the dresser. She placed the hair brush and the comb on the dresser. She had never received such kindness before. She decided that Daniel was a person she could trust.

After she had put away all the items, she went to join Daniel outside. She sat at the garden edge to watch him. "What are you going to plant?"

Daniel was surprised she knew he was going to plant anything. He asked, "Well, this is a vegetable garden. I'm going to plant potatoes, carrots, peas. Have you planted a garden?"

"Yes, when I was a little girl. I remember taking care of it with my mother. Are you going to plant corn? I like corn."

"No, I don't think so. Last year, I did but it did not grow well. Did you plant corn?" Daniel asked.

"Yes, we did. It grew good," Kit answered, remembering the happy days with her mother.

"Do you have a secret on how to grow corn?" Daniel asked.

"My mom never told me how she did it. I was just little then."

"Where is your mom now?" Daniel reluctantly asked. He was afraid of upsetting her.

Kit sat on the edge of the garden and played with a blade of grass. Then she softly said, "My mom died when I was eight." Daniel put the shovel down and went to sit by her.

"That must have been hard on you. My mom died when I was in my teens. I miss her everyday," Daniel told her. That surprised Kit, but now she felt she had something in common with him.

"When she died, my whole life changed," Kit said but would not say anymore. She got up and said, "I'm going to see the chicks." *Strange,* thought Daniel as he went back to his digging. He felt there was something she wanted to tell him and wondered what it could be. He did not see Kit until supper time.

As they ate their supper that evening, Kit asked, "Danny, is playing chess hard to do? What do you do?"

"I'll teach you if you want. It's a game of strategy. Each different piece moves differently. Want to give it a try?" Daniel asked. Kit nodded her head so Daniel went to get the checkerboard he had purchased the last time he had been in town. He explained the game and as he placed each piece on the board, he taught what each piece was called and how they moved on the board.

He had finished whittling all the pieces and was pleased with how the pieces looked. The kings were the tallest, shaped like figures in robes and had a square on top; the queens were a little shorter, shaped like the king but with a round head and a smaller square on the top; the bishops had a slightly different shape and had a round head that came to a point; the knights were flat, square pieces. Daniel had attempted to whittle them in the likeness of a horse. The rooks were shorter then the bishops, with a round body and a flat top. The pawns were the shortest, had a tapered body and a little round top.

Kit became very anxious and said, "Danny, there sure is lots to know about this game, I don't think I'll be able to play it. Maybe some other time." She did not want to show Daniel how ignorant she was.

"Okay, Kit, if that's what you want. We can play another time," Daniel answered. He took the board with the pieces on it and placed it on the side table by his chair in the living room.

A week went by and Kit started to relax. No one had come by looking for her. There was one thing Kit found strange. She noticed that after supper, Daniel would go to his desk and read his books. She had never seen anyone read so much so one night, she asked, "Why do you read those books? You're not at school."

"I'm studying to be a lawyer. It's like school without a teacher," Daniel said, returning to his book.

"Oh, I did not know you could go to school at home." After a little while, she said, "If I asked you something, promise not to laugh?"

"Kit, why would I laugh? Ask. I won't laugh, I promise," Daniel assured her.

"Well, it's kind of stupid," Kit said with her head down. Then in a very soft voice she said, "Would you teach me how to read?"

Daniel looked at her and said in a gentle voice, "You can't read? Why can't you read? Is it because of your injuries?" Daniel hoped this did not offend her.

"No, I stopped going to school before that," she said, hesitated a little then she continued, "After my mom died, I stopped going to school."

Daniel was not sure he understood right. "What? You were eight. Why did you stop going to school?" Daniel inquired.

"Danny, it's very hard to talk about this. My dad said never to tell anyone," Kit replied, very fearful.

"That sounds very ominous, Kit. I'm listening." Daniel went to sit at the table with her. He could tell that she was shaking. He asked, "Kit, what is it? Why are you so stressed? It can't be that bad."

"Believe me, it's bad, Daniel." She stopped talking. She did not know if she should tell. Daniel saw that she was wrestling with something but did not say anything. After a short time, she decided that she could trust Daniel and had to tell someone. So she said, "My mom was the one who took care of me, my dad never was around and if he was, he was drinking. After my mom died, I was dad's responsibility and he did not like it much. The summer my mom died, I spent all the time at my best friend's house, so I did not see dad very often. When summer ended and school started, I needed new clothes and school supplies. When my dad saw that he would have to spend money on me, he said he had no money to send me to school. I argued with him, saying I had to go to school, that all kids went to school. He did not like the way I spoke to him, so he came at me and punched me right on the nose. I fell backwards a bit dazed. My nose was bleeding so I ran to the bathroom to make it stop." Kit stopped speaking, she was shaking even more.

"You don't have to say anymore, Kit. It's upsetting you too much," Daniel said, trying to comfort her.

"No, Danny, I want to tell you. Now that I feel safe, I can tell what happened to me. Like I said, I went to the bathroom to clean up. It took a very long time to stop the bleeding. When I came back to the kitchen, I saw my dad by my mom's bedroom door. He told me to get my things, that I was going to have my mom's room from now on. I thought he was doing me a favor because he felt sorry he had punched me, so I did not question him. I moved my things in the room and when I was done, he closed the door and locked me in. He had even covered the window with a board. I banged and banged on the door, pleading for him to let me out but he was gone. That night was the first of many nights I went to sleep without anything to eat." Kit stopped and looked at Daniel for his reaction. There was a look of disbelief on his face. Kit continued. "You don't believe me, do you?" she asked.

"But surely, someone must have come looking for you?" Daniel asked.

"Oh, he said that he had told my friends and the teachers that he had sent me to live with my aunt in the States. Because he was a nasty drunk, they never came back to question him."

Daniel was dumbstruck and asked, "How long did he lock you up for?"

"When he was home and not drinking, he let me out. I would clean the house and wash the dishes he had left in the sink. If there were any leftovers, I would eat them instead of throwing them out.

Or I would sneak them in my room so I would have food for the times he forgot to feed me. He showed me how to do the laundry. I learned very fast not to argue with him. If I behaved, did what he said, he would feed me and even let me watch TV. But he made sure he locked me in every night."

"What did you do by yourself?" Daniel asked.

"I played with my Barbie's, pretending that my friend was with me. I played with my mother's things. I found some writing paper in my mother's desk and I would practice writing my letters and draw pictures. I read my kid's books with the words under the pictures; A is for apple, b is for bat. I still know what all the letters are for." Kit smiled to herself when she remembered that. "When I ran out of paper, I asked my dad if I could have some more. He blew up and yelled, 'What would I do with paper?' I thought he would hit me again, but he did not. The next day, he brought me a box full of scrap paper. I think it was from an office because it was typed on one side. I thanked him and was happy I had something to write on again. I tried to read what was on the paper but I did not know how to read those long words. I only could read small words," Kit said with relief.

"That sure was generous of him," Daniel commented, almost sarcastically. "How long were you locked up for?"

"I was locked up 'til the fire." Kit stopped talking and big tears started rolling down her cheeks.

"Kit, it's too hard on you. You can tell me more later," Daniel said.

"No, I want to tell you now," she said wiping her eyes. "I woke up in the hospital. I did not know where I was or why. All I knew was that I hurt a lot. They told me that I was one lucky girl. A fireman had found me just in time, just before the roof caved in they said. I did not think I was lucky," Kit stopped and went to get some water. When she returned to the table she continued, "At first my dad came to see me everyday. Everybody thought he was a very concerned father, but he only came to see me to make sure I did not tell anyone about what he had done to me."

"Did you tell?" Daniel asked.

"No, he threatened to kill me. He said, 'It will be very easy to put a pillow over your face, and no one will know.'"

"Surely he would not have done it. You're his daughter!" Daniel said in disbelief.

"He never cared for me. He locked me up for three years so he would not have to spend money on me. He would have killed me!" Kit replied, and continued to say, "Once he knew I was going to survive and not say anything, he stopped coming to see me. My burns healed very slowly. I was in the burn unit for three years. After I went in the foster care system cause my dad told them he could not care for me. A very nice woman took me in. She enrolled me in school but I did not do well. I stayed with her 'til I was eighteen. Did you know once you're eighteen, you're an adult and cannot be in foster care?"

"Yes, is that when you went back to your dads?" Daniel asked.

"No, they put me in this group home. I hated it there. There was a guy there that kept saying to cover my face, that it disgusted him. He was so mean. The others living there were all scared of him. We complained to the director but he did nothing about it," Kit answered.

"How long did you stay there?" Daniel asked.

"I lived there for two years. I was on my own. No one looked after me. They expected me to go get a job. I don't know what a job is." Kit stopped and shook her head, and said, "There's so much I need to learn. I'm so ignorant!"

"Kit, you're not ignorant. I think you're very smart. Now let's go on with your story. Only if you want to," Daniel said as he touched her hand. "Can I ask how you ended up with your dad again?"

"Yes, okay, I'm sorry. As I said, I went to a home and I stayed there because it was close to the hospital. I had to go for skin grafts. I was in and out of the hospital getting my face fixed up. I was just out of the hospital after having my nose fixed when my dad visited me at the home. He told me that he had rebuilt the house and that he wanted me to come live with him. I said no. So, over the months, he would come just about every day. He would bring me clothes and other nice things. He was really nice to me. After a while, I thought that he must be sorry for what he had done to me so I agreed to go live with him. I was there a few days when he told me I had to start making money for him. I asked him how would I do that. That's when he told me if I let men play with me, they would pay money. I did not understand but I somehow knew it would not be good. The next day, I had a doctor's appointment, he was supposed to drive me to the hospital but instead he took me to the gas station where you found me." Kit stopped and looked at Daniel then said, "You know, it feels good to have that off my chest. Danny, thank you for rescuing me. You are the best."

Daniel sat there, incensed by what Kit had just told him. He could not understand the brutality. "That monster should be in jail. How could he do that to his own daughter?" Daniel said.

"Danny don't let this take your goodness away from you. I survived," Kit said, giving him a soft kiss on the cheek. Daniel was taken aback. Now it was Kit who was consoling him.

"Kit, I'm so sorry that happened to you. You should get your father arrested. We'll go to town tomorrow and press charges on him. What a monster!" Daniel was furious.

"Danny, I don't want to go to town. I want to stay here. My dad is not important anymore. What he did is in the past. Danny, please calm down. I told you because I wanted someone to know what I lived through. I'm really tired now. Good night, Danny," Kit said trying to calm Daniel down.

Daniel gave her a hug. "Good night, Kit. Have a good sleep."

"I will, Danny, I feel much better now. I don't have to keep that ugly secret anymore. Sleep tight."

The next morning, Daniel was up early. He had thought about what Kit had told him the previous night. He felt he should do something—but what could he do? Kit did not think it was important and that troubled him. Throughout breakfast, Kit made small talk and Daniel tried to keep up with what she was saying, but he was preoccupied with what Kit had shared with him. Maybe if he went fishing he could clear his head. He helped Kit clean the kitchen and said, "I'm going fishing to catch our supper. I'll be back in an hour or so." Kit did not know what "going fishing" was but kept quiet because she did not want to look ignorant. She noticed Daniel walking toward the trail that led to the lake, so she went to get dressed. With her new boots and coat, she went outside and followed him. Daniel was surprised when he saw her following, and when she came closer, he asked, "Have you ever tried fishing?"

"No, is that what you're doing?" Kit said.

Daniel stopped himself from saying what he thought. It suddenly occurred to him that Kit might not know what fishing was so he said, "Yeah, that's it." He reeled in the line and cast it out again. "There's a hook at the end of the line. When the fish bites it, I'll reel it in."

Kit gave him a smile. "How do you know there's fish in the water? I can't see any."

"Oh, they're in there. You'll see when I catch one," Daniel replied, certain that he would. The ice had receded away from the beach but still covered the rest of the lake.

"Maybe it's to cold for them to bite. They must be cold in that water."

Daniel laugh and said, "You don't think I'll catch one, do you?" Kit was getting a little cold but stayed. She wanted to see Daniel catch this fish. Cast after cast and no fish—she was about to go back to the house when Daniel started to reel in the line very fast.

As he finally brought his catch to the shore, he said, "Just look at that! It's the biggest one I have ever caught. A nice lake trout! He'll make a very nice supper." Kit was surprised. This was the first time she had seen a live fish. She backed away from it when she saw it flopping around on the beach. That evening, Kit had her first taste of fresh trout. She had fish before but it certainly never tasted like this. There was no mention of the conversation they had the night before, but it still bothered Daniel.

He heals the broken hearted and
binds up their wounds.

—Psalm 147:3 (NIV)

CHAPTER 8

A fter their breakfast the next morning, Kit helped Daniel cut up potatoes to prepare them for planting. Kit seemed more cheerful. She kept singing a song to herself as she cut the potatoes.

"Make sure there is an eye in every portion," Daniel said to Kit.

"Yes, Danny, I know. It's sure funny potatoes having eyes," she said as she carefully looked over the potato. Once all the potatoes were ready, they went to the garden to put them in the ground.

"Sounds like were going to have a visitor," Daniel said when he heard a vehicle coming up the drive.

"Oh no! I don't want anyone to see me, Danny!" Kit ran into the house. Daniel watched as Charlie's truck came to a stop by the house. Charlie's boys were the first to be out. They were very excited to see their uncle.

"Uncle Daniel, we brought you a cow. Where is Misty?" they said. Daniel called Misty and she came running out from the barn. The boys went to play with the dog. Daniel greeted Charlie and said, "I was wondering when you'd be coming. Let's see that cow. Is she a wild one that does not like to be milked?"

"No, I brought you a nice gentle one."

They both walked to the trailer. Charlie let the cow out of the trailer and walked her to the corral. "A little Jersey cow. Thanks, Charlie. I think we will get along well."

Meanwhile, Kit watched as the two men walked the cow to the corral. *What would Daniel do with a cow?* she wondered. She had never seen a real cow and was surprised to see just how big it was. As they were coming back to the house, Daniel noticed Kit outside. He stopped and called to her. "Kit, come meet my cousin Charlie and his boys. Come, Kit, it's okay."

Charlie was a little surprised to see that there was a girl living with Daniel but did not say anything. Kit slowly came to them, hiding her face behind her scarf.

"Kit, I'd like you to meet my cousin Charlie. Charlie this is Kit."

"Kit, I'm pleased to meet you, but a little surprised," Charlie said with a big smile on his face. By then, the boys had seen Kit and they came running up to them.

"Kit, these two boys are Charlie's sons, Liam and Dennis." Kit noticed that both boys were looking at her covered face but did not ask any questions. Kit greeted them pleasantly but felt very uncomfortable.

"I'm going to see the chicks Danny. Okay?"

"Sure, Kit, it's okay with me." When the boys heard that Kit was going to see the chicks, they asked if they could join her. Kit wished she could go by herself but did not object.

"Oh, look at them. I like them when they are little like this. Once their feathers start growing in, they're not so cute. They're just dumb chickens then," Liam said. His brother agreed with him. Kit was a little dismayed by what Liam had said. As far as she was concerned, these little chicks were her little buddies.

"Don't call them dumb, they're so cute. I spend lots of time with them. They're my friends," Kit said.

"I wouldn't get too friendly with them. They're not pets. When they get big, we eat them." Now Kit was saddened and felt very stupid. Of course Danny would eat them; why else would he raise chickens? She got up and left the barn. The boys were left wondering what they had said wrong.

Charlie and Daniel saw Kit leaving the barn followed by the boys. They heard Dennis say, "What did you go and say that for? You upset her!"

"What did you boys say to Kit to upset her?"

Before they could answer, Kit turned and said, "They did not say anything wrong. It's just me. Liam and Dennis just made me realize something." She left them and went in the house.

Charlie told the boys to go play with Misty, as he and Daniel went to sit on the deck.

"How did Kit get to be here?" Charlie asked.

"She's been here since the day I picked up the chicks. I was going to take her to a shelter but she wanted none of it. Charlie, she's been abused. She needs a place to feel safe now. I can't ask her to go somewhere else." Daniel continued to tell Charlie how he had found Kit, and what she had told him the other night.

"That sure is an awful story. That guy should be hung! Are you going to report him?" Charlie asked.

"I don't know, Kit wants to live here and does not want to think about her dad. She says he's not important. I think she wants to forget what happened to her," Daniel said as the boys came to join them. They said that they were hungry. "Well, we better get some food in you two," Daniel said.

Supper was a very stressful time for Kit. She would have preferred to stay in her room but did not want to be rude to Daniel's family. They had just about finished eating when Liam asked, "Kit, can I ask you a question? If you don't want to answer, it's okay."

Kit looked at him and said, "Liam, what do you want to know?" She knew the question was going to be about her face.

"Kit, what happened to your face?" he asked.

Charlie started to say something but Kit stopped him and said, "I was in a very bad fire. They told me I was lucky that I got out alive. I was in a hospital for a long time to make my face look better. I could get more work done on it, but for now there's nothing that can be done. I know it is hard to look at," Kit covered her face with her scarf.

"Oh, I don't mind your face, Kit. I know you must have suffered a lot. I burnt my arm when a was little," Liam said as he pulled his sleeve up to show the burnt scar. "It really hurt and mine was smaller than yours."

Kit gave him a smile and asked, "How did you burn your arm?"

"I fell against a hot stove. It was an accident. My mom freaked out. Remember, Dad?" Liam said.

"Yes, I remember. It was very nerve-wracking what with you crying, and your mom running around not knowing what to do. It's a good thing I was home when it happened," Charlie said, messing up Liam's hair.

Kit noticed how loving Charlie was to his boys and how confident the boys were with their dad. She said, "You are such a loving family. You two are very lucky boys to have a father that loves you." After she said that, she relaxed and everyone else felt more at ease.

Once supper was done and the kitchen tidied up, Charlie asked, "Who is going to milk that cow? She must be tired of waiting. Daniel, let's see if you can still milk a cow." They all headed to the barn, Daniel carrying a pail.

"It has been years since I milked a cow. I hope she's as gentle as you told me, Charlie," Daniel said.

"Uncle Daniel, Dad said you did not like cows when you were young. Do you like cows now?" Dennis asked.

"Well, cows are okay," Daniel said as he sat on the little stool. Everyone looked on as Daniel milked the cow. In a short time, Daniel had a pail just about full.

"She's a very good cow. I think you will get along just fine," Charlie said.

Once Daniel had finished milking the cow, Kit and the boys went to feed the chickens. As she filled the tray with chickenfeed, Kit asked, "Where do you boys live?" The boys told her that they lived on a farm, and they also had chickens, cows and pigs. They also told her about their mother and why she had not come with them. Kit liked the boys. They reminded her of her life before her mother had died. As they went back to the house, the two boys were chatting with Kit like they had been long time friends.

The next morning, Kit was sorry to see them go. Kit hugged each of the boys and said goodbye to them. After Charlie shook Daniel's hand he promised to visit when seeding was done.

"I'm sad to see them go. They are such nice boys. They must play outside a lot," Kit said once they had left.

"Why would you say that?" Daniel asked.

"Well, they have very nice tans," Kit answered.

"Oh, Kit, their skin is that colour because their mother has dark skin," Daniel said, trying his best not to offend her.

Kit was so frustrated and said, "I'm so stupid. I should know things like that."

"Kit, don't be so hard on yourself. You were brutally treated when you were young. It's not your fault. You're smart, you'll learn—give yourself some time," Daniel said as he cleaned away their breakfast dishes.

Kit went to her room. She felt so ignorant like her dad always called her. She stayed in her room until she heard the screen door bang shut. *Daniel must be outside working in the garden*, she thought. She went outside and found him there.

"Hey, Kit! Are you okay?" Daniel asked when he saw Kit by the garden. "Danny, I'm okay. Want some help?" she asked.

"Would you hand me the carrot seeds? They should be on the table on the deck."

Kit returned to the garden with a package of seeds and handed him a packet. He opened the packet and put some seeds in his hand. As he bent down to sow the seeds, Kit said, "Can I do some?"

Daniel showed her how to sow the seeds, and said, "You can finish sowing the carrots. I'll start another row for onions."

Kit took meticulous care seeding the carrots. As she did, she started singing a song she had heard on the radio the night before. It amazed Daniel that Kit could sing the song. She remembered all the words and the tune. They spent the entire day planting seeds in the garden.

"Thank you for helping me with the garden, Kit, you were a great help. Took me a couple of days to plant last year."

"You're welcome, Danny, I like helping," Kit replied. She pointed to a patch at the far end of the garden and said, "What's growing over there?"

"That's the strawberry patch. It's all overgrown. I never had time to keep it up last summer."

"I'll clean it up, Danny, just show me what plants are strawberries."

After Daniel had showed Kit the strawberry plants, he said, "Thanks again, Kit. It'll be real nice having strawberries."

Kit felt good to be able to help and to feel appreciated. "Danny, thank you for letting me help. I'll get started on this right away."

The next morning, Kit was the first to get up. When she went out to feed the chicks, she heard a strange sound, like glass breaking. She followed the sound and when she came around the house, she was shocked to see ice rolling up the bank. In disbelief, she ran back in the house.

"Danny! Danny, come see! There's ice!"

Daniel had been in deep sleep, and when he heard Kit, he woke up with a jolt and jumped out of bed. He could hear Misty barking. As he was putting on his pants, he heard Kit say something about ice.

He met Kit on the stairs and asked, "Kit, what in the world is going on? What ice?"

Before Kit could answer, he was out of the front door and came to a sudden stop when he saw the ice. The lake was clear of ice, but now all the ice was on the shore and rolling up the bank. As it rolled in, it made a tinkling sound, like that of fine glass breaking.

"What is happening, Danny? Is the ice going to bury us?" Kit was so frightened.

"No, it'll stop before it gets to the house," Daniel assured her. "It must have been windy last night and it pushed all the ice on shore. It will be okay. We'll just have to wait 'til it melts." He walked off the deck and called Misty over. "It's okay girl, a little ice won't hurt us." He patted her on the head. He continued to the edge of the ice and looked over the bank. It was still very windy, making big waves on the lake. When the waves hit the shore, it pushed more ice in and up the bank. Daniel had heard of this happening but had never seen it. It amazed him how powerful nature was.

That morning at breakfast, Kit asked, "What are you going to do with all the milk we have?"

"Good question, you're going to have to drink more of it," he said with a big smile on his face. "We can make butter, and yoghurt. My grandma used to make cottage cheese too. I'll have to go to the health-food store and ask for some help. Maybe we'll go to town tomorrow."

"Danny, I'll stay here. I don't want to see anyone. Okay, Danny?" Kit said. Then she remembered the ice. She believed Daniel when he said the ice would stop rolling in, but it made her very uneasy.

"You don't have to go. I'll leave early and try to be back before it gets dark."

"Danny, if that ice hasn't stopped moving, you can't go. Please, Danny," Kit said in a weak voice.

"Okay, Kit. I'll go when the ice stops moving."

By afternoon, the wind died down and the lake became calm. The ice now covered up the edge of the bank by about four-feet in and was three-feet deep. To Daniel's dismay, it also covered one corner of the garden so he went to shovel it off.

Kit became a little braver and went to pick up one of the bigger pieces of ice. As she picked it up, it crumbled up in pencil-size pieces.

When Daniel left early the next morning, the sun was shining and the ice was slowly melting away. He promised Kit he would try to be back before dark. Once in town, Daniel met with his dad in his office.

"Daniel, I did not expect to see you back so soon. Is there something wrong? Did you bring the girl with you?"

"Oh, no Dad, I just came to town for the day. Charlie brought me a cow and now I have to figure out what to do with the milk. I need some advice on how to make yoghurt and cheese. I'll go to the health-food store and see Helene. I'm sure she can help me. Dad, did you get any new information on Kit?"

"Yes, I did. I went to speak to the chief. He knew her mother. She worked at the police station more than ten years ago. She died in some freaky accident. He said her dad was a big drunk but did not know his whereabouts. There is no missing report on her. How is she doing?".

"I think she's going to be alright. She has been through some very bad abuse. She told me her story the other night," Daniel continued to tell his father what Kit had told him.

"That guy should be charged. You should go speak to the chief about what she told you," Ken replied.

"She does not want to think about it. She just wants to have a safe place to live."

After visiting with his father, Daniel said goodbye and drove to the health-food store. The store was on the edge of town. Daniel had been there many times over the years and knew the owner. She had been friends with his mother. "Daniel is that you? You haven't been here for ages. Where have you been keeping yourself?" Helene said when she saw Daniel walk in her store.

"Helene! Oh, it's so nice to see you," he said as Helene came to give him a hug. "A lot has changed since we last met. I'm here to ask you for some advice." He went on to tell her all that he was doing. In no time, Daniel had all kinds of equipment and instructions on what he could do with the milk he had. "Thanks again, Helene, it was very nice seeing you again. I promise to keep in touch," Daniel said and he left the store.

Keeping with his promise to Kit, Daniel drove home and arrived just as it was getting dark. Kit was asleep on the couch but woke up when she heard the screen door bang shut.

"Danny, you are home, I'm so happy to have you back. I was so worried," she said crying.

"Why, did something go wrong? Are you alright?" Daniel asked.

"I'm okay, Danny. But I think something bad happened to Misty," she replied.

"What happened? Where is she?" Daniel was very alarmed. "What happened Kit?"

"I don't know. Just before supper time, Misty started to bark. So, I went outside to see what she was barking about. I saw these two grey dogs just on the edge of the woods not far from the barn.

The cow looked very nervous so I decided to put her in the barn. When I did, that's when Misty took off after those dogs. I called and called her but she did not come back. Oh, Danny, I think those dogs did something bad to her." Kit was crying so hard she could barely speak.

"Kit, I hope not. Wolves are very unpredictable. It's late, there isn't much we can do tonight. She might come back in the morning. I'll go look in on the cow. Maybe I should milk her," Daniel said heading for the back door.

"I milked her. I don't think she likes me. She did not stay still like she did for you."

Daniel was astounded. "You milked the cow? How did you know how? Have you milked a cow before?"

"No, I never did. It was the first time I have been near a cow. Danny, I watched you this morning. But I must be doing something wrong because she kept moving away from me all the time. I only got half a pail," Kit replied.

"Kit, you amaze me. It's late, you go to bed. I'll just go take a look around to see if everything is okay," Daniel said. Kit sat on the couch and waited for him. When he returned, he told Kit that he saw no signs of Misty. They said goodnight to each other and went to bed.

Early in the morning, Daniel heard whimpering at the front door. He jumped out of bed and flew downstairs. There by the front door laid Misty. It looked like she had been caught up in a whirl-wind. Other then having her hair all matted and a big chunk of hair missing on her left shoulder, she looked all right. "Misty, come," Daniel said as he let Misty in the house. The dog slowly walked to her bed and laid down.

Kit was by her side. She knelt and gave Misty a hug. As she stroked the dog she said, "Misty you're back. I'm so happy to see you." Tears were rolling down her face. Then Kit's attitude changed. She got back up on her feet and scolded Misty. "Don't you ever run off like that again. You could have been badly hurt. You worried us so. You hear me? Don't ever run off again," she kept saying as she hugged the dog again. Misty was a different dog after that day. She never ventured alone, but kept close to Daniel or Kit. Mostly, all she did was lay on the deck and watched.

The ice had finally melted from the bank and when Daniel went to go down to the lake, he found the stairs he had made were destroyed. The force of the ice had pushed the support posts up and they were laying on the ground. The steps had come off the runners. Now he knew why the path to the lake had been so bad. This must have happened before. A few days later, Daniel had the stairs back in place and he took Misty to the lake to play fetch. He tossed her a stick but the dog ignored it.

"Misty, go fetch," Daniel said as he threw her another stick. But Misty turned and returned to the house. Daniel scratched his head. He remembered when she loved to play fetch. He followed her and watched her as she went off to sit on the deck to resume her guard duty. Daniel tried to play with her but she moved away not willing to submit and show her tummy.

Kit saw this and said, "Misty is not the same. She used to like playing with you. Now she just lays there and waits. It's like only half of her returned to us."

"We'll give her a few days, she might come around," Daniel said.

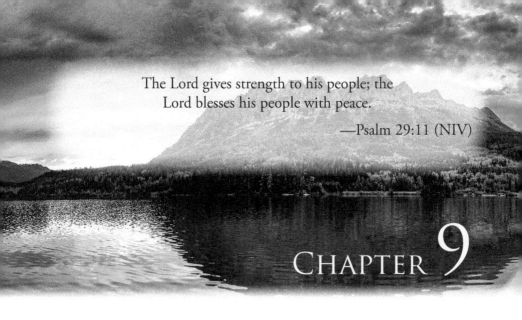

The Lord gives strength to his people; the
Lord blesses his people with peace.

—Psalm 29:11 (NIV)

CHAPTER 9

A s Daniel and Kit were enjoying the beautiful afternoon, they heard a vehicle coming up the drive way. Daniel did not recognize the truck, but when it came to a stop by the house, he recognized his father and the Chief.

"What a surprise!" Daniel said as he greeted the two men. Kit had gone in the house and looked through the window to see who got out of the truck. She knew one of the men. He looked older but she was certain she knew him. She walked outside and went to join the men. Daniel introduced her to his father and the chief. Kit gave Barry a closer look. She remembered him being taller and with more hair, but she was certain it was him by the way he smiled at her.

"Uncle Barry, is it you? Do you remember me?" she said covering up the burnt side of her face.

"Kitten! What a surprise to see you here. How are you? When Daniel's dad informed me you were here, I had to come to see you. He told me what happened to you," Barry said giving her a hug.

"I'm alright. Uncle Barry, Danny has let me stay here. He is the kindest man. But I wish he had not told about me." Daniel noticed that Kit was a little nervous so he invited them to the house for some coffee. After coffee, Daniel took them for a tour of his place and they ended up sitting on the front deck.

Barry went to sit close to Kit and said, "Kit, I know you don't want to speak about what happened to you. Can I talk to you about your mom?" Kit nodded so he continued, "Your mom worked at the police station when I first started on the force. She was very helpful to a green rookie. Everyone at the station liked her. No one was more surprised than me when she announced that she was getting married. We were all happy for her. One day, just after she married, she came to work with a bruise on her face and more on her arms. She did not say anything but we knew who had given them. My partner and I went to pay a visit to your dad and we warned him. We told him that if his wife ever came to work with bruises, we would come for him and make him disappear. She never came to work with bruises after that. Once she had you, she would bring you to the office. We would make such a fuss over you. Do you remember when she would bring you to the office?" Kit nodded.

"I'm so sorry I let you down. I believed your dad when he told me that he had sent you to your aunt in the States." As he talked, Kit's eyes were filling with tears. She realized that there had been people who had been concerned about her. *If only they had asked more questions*, she thought.

"It's very upsetting to hear what your dad did to you. We can't let him get away with what he did." Kit shook her head. "Kit, listen to me. You will not have to see your dad. He will never know where you are. We can interview you and videotape it. Ken is a lawyer and he can represent you. Please trust us. We can get your dad locked up for the rest of his life." Kit sat beside Barry for a while without saying anything. He could tell that she was shaking.

"Kit, you can trust us, please let us do this for you. I promised your dad I would come after him if he ever hurt your mom. By hurting you, he hurt your mom. I have to keep my promise," Barry told her.

"Are you going to make him disappear?" Kit asked.

"Yes, in a way. He will go to jail and we will never see him again," the chief said. "Kit, I know it's hard reliving the bad memories. If you don't want to do it for yourself, do it for your mom."

Kit sat still. When she heard Barry say, do it for your mom, she remembered how her mom had taken such good care of her. If she

107

would have lived, her life would have been like being in heaven. But she had lived through hell. No, she would not let her awful dad get away with trying to destroy all the good her mother had done.

"I'll do it," Kit said in a very soft voice. "I'll tell everyone how bad my father was to me. He should be locked up. But once he is, I don't ever want anyone to talk of him ever again. Okay, I'll do it."

"That's my girl. Now just a minute. We'll set up for the interview. Ken will ask you questions," Barry said as he went outside to get the equipment he would need. Ken and Kit sat at the table waiting for the interview to begin.

Once the camera was set up, Barry said, "Okay, all is ready. Kit, if it becomes too much to talk about, just say so and we will stop." He went to sit on the couch by Daniel.

Ken started by asking her name and how old she was. Then he asked, "Tell me about your life with your mother."

"My mother was the best. She took very good care of me. We did everything together. I loved her so much."

"Where was your dad?" Ken asked.

"He was around. We would see him for supper, then he would go out. He never took care of me, he never said anything to me. He would talk to my mom but never to me. It was like I was not there."

"What happened to you after your mother died?"

With that question, Kit took a deep breath and told Ken the story she had told Daniel. She ended by saying, "My dad locked me up in my mother's room. During the day, I would play with her things. I loved the smell of her clothes. Sometimes I would pretend my friend was with me. We would play with my Barbie's. My mom had a lot of pillows on her bed. I made a cocoon with them. When I went to sleep, I would crawl under them and tell myself not to cry. I would pray to Jesus to take me to be with my mother. Sometimes in my dreams, I would be with her. I felt someone picking me up. I could feel my mother holding me and telling me how much she loved me. But in the morning, I was alone. I spent a lot of time sleeping."

"Kit, I think we have enough. We will give this to the prosecutor and get your dad arrested. Don't worry, Kit. You are doing the right thing," Ken promised her.

Ken and Barry put the equipment away, and Kit went to help Daniel start supper. As they ate, everyone noticed that Barry was quiet. Daniel tried to make small talk, but after a while they ate in silence. After supper, Kit told Daniel that she would clean up, so Daniel went to milk the cow. Ken and Barry tagged along.

"Something bothering you, Barry?" Ken asked as they walked to the barn.

"Yeah, something is. I don't think I can ever forgive myself. I was at that fire. I remember when they took Kit out of there. The fireman said that he just about missed her. He found her under a pile of pillows with just her face showing. He said that if it had not been for those pillows, Kit would not be alive. I went to see her in the hospital but she was sedated so I was not able to speak to her. Her father was there every time I visited. He was so concerned. It seemed to me that the father was there for her so I stopped going to see her. I can just kick myself!"

"Did you talk to her father?" Daniel asked.

"Oh yes. He was very subdued. Didn't want to talk much," Barry answered.

"Did you ask him how Kit got to be in that room?" Ken asked. Barry was very remorseful and said, "He told me that she had come for a visit, for a school break. I should have never trusted that bastard! Why didn't I just keep going to see her?"

"Barry, you are not to blame. You can't read another person's mind. You're only human. Kit is in good hands now. She's going to heal and get better," Ken said, trying to console Barry.

"If I see the bastard, I just might brake his neck myself! Why do things like this happen to innocent little girls? I should have known!" Barry just could not let it go.

"Dad, you better make sure Barry is not there when they arrest him. I'd hate to see the chief go down because of scum like that," Daniel said to his dad.

"Don't worry, Daniel, I'll take care of the chief. And I'll make sure Mr. LaChatte is caged up," Ken replied.

When the men returned to the house, Kit had prepared some dessert for them, and as they walked in, she said, "Would anyone be interested in dessert? These are the first of the strawberries and Danny's first batch of yoghurt. I tasted it, it's pretty good with strawberries!"

Daniel was very surprised that Kit had even thought of making dessert, so he said, "You made dessert, how lovely! Good thinking, Kit. Any takers?" All three eagerly agreed to have some so Kit dished the strawberries in dessert bowls and drizzled a generous amount of yoghurt on top. As they ate, Daniel said, "We have to thank Kit for these strawberries. She has a knack of making things grow. These are so good. Thanks, Kit." He gave her a big smile.

After they finished dessert, they all went to sit in the living room. Ken said, "I see you made yourself a chess set. I was looking it over before supper. I never knew that you were so handy with a knife. The pieces are very well made. I'll play you if you're up for the challenge, Daniel."

"Okay, Dad, I'll play but you'll have to go easy on me. I haven't played for a while," Daniel replied with the biggest smile on his face. Ken shook his head and said, "As I remember it, you'll have to take it easy on me. The last game we played, you wiped me out."

Daniel set up the chess set on the table and the game started. Kit sat by Daniel and studied every move that they made. She noticed that Ken was very quiet when it was his turn to move. But he would try to distract Daniel as he considered his next move. She loved to see the interaction between the two of them. She could tell they both loved each other very much.

After some time, Ken won the first game. "How about we play in teams. Kit, who do you want as a partner?" Daniel asked. Kit was a little taken aback, but with some coaxing from Daniel, she picked him to be her partner. The game was reset, and Ken and Barry had the first move. When it was time for Daniel and Kit to make a move, Daniel told her where to move. When Daniel took out the opponent's queen, Kit cheered but was not so happy when they had their queen taken out. The game ended very close with Ken and Barry the winners. That evening, Kit went to bed feeling at peace with herself.

The next morning after they had breakfast, Ken and Daniel went for a walk down to the lake. As they went down the steps,

Daniel said, "I had to rebuild these steps." When Ken asked why, Daniel said, "The ice took them out. You should have seen it, Dad. The wind blew all the ice up on shore and it kept rolling in over the bank. See how it has eroded the bank? I hope it doesn't happen every spring. It sure can be destructive. It's good that the house is some ways away from the bank."

"Nature sure can be powerful," Ken agreed.

As they walked back to the house, they met Barry and Kit by the car. When Barry saw them, he said, "Well, Daniel it has been very nice to be here but we'd better get going. It's a long drive back." He shook hands with Daniel and turned to Kit. He gave her a hug and promised to return to see her soon after he had taken care of her father. After Ken said goodbye to Daniel and Kit, they were off.

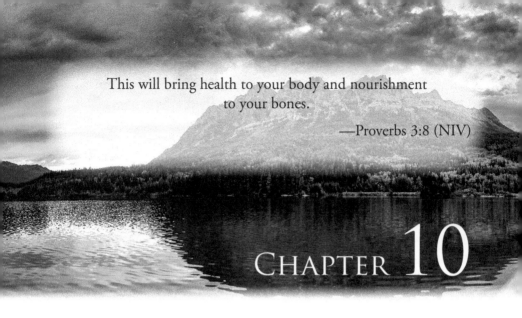

This will bring health to your body and nourishment
to your bones.

—Proverbs 3:8 (NIV)

CHAPTER 10

As the summer progressed, Kit learned more and more about her new home. She loved the outdoors, to listen to the birds sing, smell the flowers and work in the garden, singing as she weeded. Some hot afternoons, she would join Daniel for a swim. She was not a swimmer, but she loved to splash about, although for only a short time for the water was so cold. She loved going for long walks with Daniel. On the walks she would pick up wild flowers and make bouquets. She learned what the flowers were by looking them up in the wild flower book Daniel had kept. She now could identify most of them, the Oxeye Daisy, the little Canada Violet. The wild Roses were her favourites. Best of all, she befriended a chipmunk and named him Chips. She enticed him to get a piece of bread from her hand and in no time, she had Chips coming right to her hand to take it.

By late summer, Kit had grown more confident in herself. With the proper food, she was no longer a skeleton. Her face had filled in. Even the burned half of her face looked better. She grew more confident in asking Daniel questions, and she knew he would not make her feel like she was ignorant.

Daniel had brought equipment to make butter, and both he and Kit had read the instructions on how to use it. It was Kit who oversaw the churning of the butter and the making of yoghurt. Although it took some time to churn the butter, she did not mind for as she churned, she would sing along with the radio. Daniel sometimes stopped his work to listen to her sing. He told her that he loved the sound of her voice, and when he did, she would tell him he was just silly. They had a steady supply of butter and yoghurt, and with Daniel's first batch of cottage cheese turning out so well, they had plenty of that too.

The heavy, manual chores were Daniel's responsibility. One day, he was cleaning out the chicken coop when Kit asked, "This chicken poop is sure stinky. You should take that stuff away."

"What do you mean? This is going to decompose and turn to manure. It's good for the garden," Daniel informed her.

When Kit heard that, it horrified her and she said, "No, you can't do that. You can't put poop on the garden and then eat the food."

Daniel started to laugh and said, "It's not poop anymore when we put it on the garden, it's fertilizer. It gives the plants nutrition."

"Well, I don't care what you say, I'm not eating anymore of those vegetables," Kit said in defiance.

"So, what will you eat then, Kit?" Daniel asked.

"I'll drink milk and eat the cheese and the fish you catch," Kit replied. She touched her stomach, she said, "I think I feel sick."

When Daniel heard that, he laughed and said, "Kit, you are just starting to regain your strength. If you don't eat properly, you'll get sick. If you get sick, you will not be able to live here anymore."

Kit turned to walk away and thought, *Danny does have a point. I can't be getting sick and besides, the vegetables were very tasty.* So she resolved to forget about this manure business and continue eating what she had been.

As Daniel cleaned the coop, the chickens were in their outside enclosure so Kit went to join them. She sat on a stump left from a tree Daniel had chopped down when he made the enclosure. Kit had made friends with the black rooster and a little brown hen. As Kit sat down, the rooster came to her and flew up on her lap. He loved sitting there while Kit rubbed his neck and back.

She asked, "How are you today, Cornelius? Are you being good to the hens?"

Daniel heard what she said and could not help but to laugh. "Kit, you called the rooster Cornelius? Where did you get that name?" Daniel asked, teasing her.

"I remembered my mom told me the name of the rooster on the Corn Flakes box," Kit said, looking down at the rooster on her lap.

Daniel noticed Kit sounded very sad so he asked, "Kit are you okay? I've noticed you have been very quiet lately. Why is that?"

"Danny, when I remembered the name, I remembered something else. Something I never wanted to remember. Maybe if I told you, I'd feel better," Kit said, trying to remove herself from her thoughts.

"Yes, Kit, what is it?" Daniel was now very concerned, "What did you remember?"

"Well, Danny, it is very bad. I wish I had never remembered it. I don't know if I should tell you, it's too bad," Kit said with tears starting to roll down her face.

"Kit, I've heard bad things before. I think you want to tell me. Go ahead," Daniel urged her.

She turned to the rooster and said, "You are a very nice rooster. Go down and be good." She put the rooster down and said, "I remembered the first time my dad let me out of the room. I was so happy and when he told me to go clean the kitchen. I obeyed him. I was out, that's all that mattered to me. I did what he wanted me to do, and when I finished cleaning, I asked him if I could go see my friend. That was such a big mistake. He got so mad and yelled, 'No you can't, you're going back in the room!' I pleaded with him not to lock me up and I asked to go to see my friend again. He grabbed my arm so hard it made me cry. I yelled, 'Let me go, let me go!' That's when I saw his hand go up, and the next thing I remember was waking up in my mom's bed."

Kit looked at Daniel and saw the anger in his face. "He hit you?" Daniel asked softly.

"Yes. I remember getting up and going to the bathroom. There was dried blood on the side of my face and my right eye was swollen shut. I could not move my arm without it hurting very bad. I hurt so much that I went to the locked door and begged my dad to help me. But he didn't. I don't think he was home." She waited for Daniel to react and when he didn't, she continued, "The next time dad came in the room and saw the blood on the bed, he told me to go wash the sheets. When I told him I couldn't move my arm and when he saw it was all swollen, he did it himself. Once he had finished with the bed, he told me he would be gone for a few days. He left the room and returned with a big box of Corn Flakes. So now you see why I remember this. Sure is weird, don't you think?" Kit finished wiping off her tears.

"Kit, it's criminal. How could he have done that to you? I'm so sorry, Kit." The story Kit had just told him upset him to the core. He turned away and went to chop wood. He placed a big stump on the chopping block and raised the axe over his head and brought it down with all his might. He was so angry. With every hit, he wished it was that bastard he was hitting. How could someone abuse his Kit? As he continued chopping wood, other injustices came to mind.

After a while, Kit went to see Daniel and said, "Danny, are you going to chop wood all day? You're all sweaty. Maybe you should take a break. I brought you some water."

He put down the axe and took the glass from Kit. "Thanks Kit. I'm just so angry and hitting something helps." As they walked back to the house, Kit asked Daniel not to talk about it again.

At harvest time, Daniel found it much easier with Kit's help. They picked and canned raspberries and tomatoes, pickled beets, dried peas and beans. They dug up the potatoes and carrots and put them away in the bins downstairs.

Most of the garden was in when Barry came for a visit. This time, Kit did not run to hide when she heard the vehicle come up the drive. She was the one who went to greet Barry.

"Uncle Barry, it's so nice to see you. How are you?" she said cheerfully.

"I'm well, and how are you? You look like you have spent a lot of time outside. You look great," Barry said with a big smile on his face. Kit was pleased with his greeting. They walked to the deck to join Daniel.

"I just made some coffee, would you like a cup?" Daniel said.

"That would be just what I need. Thank you. It sure is a long drive to get here." Daniel went in the house to get Barry a cup. As he returned to the deck, he heard Kit ask if he had put her father away.

"Yes, he's in jail and will be there for a long time. When we arrested him, he denied that he had locked you up. He said that you were in the States. So we asked to talk to your aunt but he wouldn't give us her name. The more he talked, the more we knew he was guilty."

"Good. Now I don't have to talk or think about him," Kit said in a detached voice.

"Kit, I got your dad to sign over the house to you. It's all yours. I brought you the deed." Barry brought out a paper and gave it to her.

Kit looked at it and said, "I don't know if I want it. Maybe I should sell it." She sat looking at the paper and said, "The house is mine? But I want to stay here. Danny let me stay here," Kit said.

"Kit, you can stay here. You don't have to worry. You have a home here," Daniel replied. Kit calmed down and after a short silence she said, "Uncle Barry, would you take care of the house? Maybe I could rent it out. Then I could pay for my own things and not use Danny's money."

"If that's what you want. I know of a new officer looking for a place. I'll take care of it," Barry said.

"Barry, can you stay for the weekend? We would like to have you over as a guest," Daniel asked.

"I'd like that. This place has such a peaceful feeling." Barry sat back on his chair and let out his breath. He realized that he needed a place to rest and Daniel's place was perfect. Barry thought he would rest, but Daniel had another idea. They spent two days cutting down dead trees for fire wood. By the time Barry left, the woodshed was full of chopped wood.

"Thanks for all your help Barry. You sure can split wood. I probably have enough wood to last me the winter," Daniel said walking Barry to his car.

Barry laughed. "Chopping wood helped me get all my frustrations out. I should be the one to thank you. Bye, Daniel, and take care." Barry said as he shook Daniel's hand.

Kit was already standing by his car. "Bye, Uncle Barry. Thanks for helping me with the house. Come back to see us very soon," she said, giving him a hug.

Now that he had his winter supply of wood, Daniel decided to winterize the barn a little more. He wrapped the inside wall that divided the barn with a tarp. This way, there would be less drafts going into where the chickens were kept. He went over all the logs and chinked all the cracks he had missed in the spring. His grandmother used to keep chickens all year round so he knew chickens could be wintered over. He just hoped that all his efforts would help the chickens survive.

Each day, Daniel and Kit enjoyed the fresh eggs. However, they had not enjoyed a supper of roasted chicken. So on his birthday, September 30th, Daniel decided to treat himself. He did not want Kit to know he was going to butcher a chicken, so he got up early and went to the chicken coop. Killing the chicken proved to be very difficult. Daniel had to talk himself into doing it. He had seen his grandma do it many times but had wondered how she could. Now he knew. If he wanted to eat, the chicken would have to die.

After the deed was done, he plucked the chicken and cleaned it. He placed the chicken in a pan and as he returned to the house, he met Kit as she was going out.

"Good morning, Kit," Daniel said. But before he could say more, she asked, "What is in the pan?"

Daniel was a little hesitant. He did not want to upset Kit. "Kit, do you know what today is?" She shook her head.

"Today is my birthday and we're going to have a special supper," Daniel said with a smile on his face.

"What will make it so special, Danny?" Kit asked with a smile. The smile on her face faded when she saw what Daniel had in the pan.

"No, you didn't. Which hen did you take?" Kit whispered. If she said it louder, she would cry. Daniel did not answer and continued inside the house. Kit ran to the chicken coop. These were her chickens but at that thought, she realized that the chickens were not hers. They were food for them to eat. She stopped at the door and sat by it. She did not want to know which hen was missing. She had to adjust her thinking. Chickens were food not pets. She proceeded into the coop and fed the chickens and picked up the eggs. She did not look for the missing one.

When Kit came back in the house, Daniel had coffee ready and the stove hot enough to make their breakfast. "You alright, Kit?" Daniel asked as he saw Kit come into the house.

"I'm okay, Danny. Happy birthday! It's very nice outside today," Kit said in a joyful voice.

Daniel noticed that she was avoiding looking at him, and he knew she did not want to talk about what he had done. "Thanks Kit. Do you want any coffee?"

Kit went to get a cup, went to the stove and poured herself some coffee. She still did not look at Daniel. "Kit, I know you're upset. Please let's talk about this. Believe me, it was hard for me to butcher that chicken, but it must be done if we are to eat. It happens every day. It's just that I had to do it instead of somebody we never see."

"I know, Danny. It's just that we raised those chickens. They became close to me. Charlie's boys told me not to get close. I just did not listen. I thought it would never happen. Can I ask you one thing, Danny?"

Daniel nodded so she asked, "Danny, there are four chickens that are my favorites, the black rooster, the little brown hen and the two speckled hens. Please don't take those, okay?"

Daniel gave her a smile and said "Kit, they're just chickens but if you want, I will not take those. Okay?"

"Yes, thank you. Now let's not talk about it anymore. Okay, Danny?" They sat at the table and ate their breakfast in complete silence.

Later that day, Kit went to the garden to pick the small ears of corn. Kit had planted the corn although Daniel had told her it would never produce any corn. She came in the house carrying a basket half-full of small corn ears.

"What do you have there, Kit?" Daniel asked when he saw her come in the kitchen.

"See, corn. We can have it for supper. It's my birthday gift to you. There's still some Swiss chard in the garden and we can have some new potatoes. We're going to have a wonderful meal," Kit said.

Daniel gave her a big smile and said, "That sounds great Kit, thanks!"

Once the vegetables were cooked, Daniel took the roasted chicken out of the oven. The chicken was golden brown, and it smelled so delightful. The table was set with the special plates settings Daniel had found when he cleared out the top of the cupboards. Daniel set the food on the table and everything was ready for Daniel's birthday supper. Kit sat looking at the roasted chicken set before her. It looked so tempting, she completely forgot that it once was a live chicken. Daniel opened one of the wine bottles he had bought for special occasions. They both enjoyed the meal enormously.

"Happy birthday, Danny," Kit said, raising her wine glass to wish him all the best.

When they had finished eating and had cleaned up the kitchen, Kit went to sit on the deck chair. After a short time, Daniel came to join her and asked, "What are you looking at?"

"Nothing in particular, just admiring the view. See how beautiful it is. The leaves are so colorful, with their yellows and oranges. It's such a contrast to the deep green of the evergreens. Makes for a perfect picture. Don't you think?" Impressed by her choice of words, she smiled up at Daniel.

He returned the smile and agreed. The view was spectacular; the snow-capped mountains stood out against the deep blue sky. There were sprinkles of yellows and oranges from the poplar and birch trees amongst the evergreen trees, making for a post card picture.

"Yes, it is lovely, but it won't last for long, the leaves all fall off and then we're left with the black and white of winter."

They sat for a while longer watching the sun set. "That was a very good meal. Perfect. How about we watch a movie for tonight's entertainment?" Daniel said.

They both went into the house and Daniel went to put in a DVD in his computer. They sat together on the couch and watched Dirty Dancing. When the movie was over, Daniel asked, "Did you enjoy the movie, Kit?" He had seen that Kit had not taken her eyes off the screen.

"Oh, yes, it was just so great. I wish I could dance like that!" At that thought, she became quiet. She knew that no one would ever want to dance with her. "Danny I'm tired, I hope you enjoyed your birthday. Good night." Daniel said goodnight and Kit went to her room. When Kit went to bed that night, she knew it had been the best day in her adult life.

A few days later, Charlie came with a load of feed for the cow and chickens. "This should last you the winter, Daniel." He reached in the front of the truck and brought out a bag. "Carol insisted I bring you this fruit," Charlie said as he handed Daniel a large bag of bananas and oranges.

"Thanks, Charlie. I have not had these in ages. We'll enjoy these immensely. Thank Carol for me." Charlie stayed with them a full day, helping Daniel with odd jobs around the place. As Charlie was getting ready to return home, he said, "Daniel are you sure you want to live through another winter up here?"

"Yes, this is my home now. Where else would I live?" Daniel replied.

"Is Kit alright with spending all winter here? Isolated from the rest of the world." Charlie was a little concern for the two of them.

"I've told her about being snowed in and not being able to leave. She's okay with it and is looking forward to it," Daniel replied.

Winter descended upon them. Kit got so excited to see the first snow. She got her winter coat and boots and went outside. Daniel stopped what he was doing and watched her dancing and singing around in the snow. She was so light on her feet. She looked liked a snow fairy. It brought a smile to his face.

"Danny the snow is so beautiful, why don't you come out?" Kit shouted when she saw Daniel watching her. Daniel had been studying so it did not take much coaxing to make him join her. Once outside, Kit took his hands and they danced around in the snow. She was like a little girl enjoying herself. Daniel realized he had not taken a break from studying in a long time. It was time he loosened up and had some fun.

"Kit, let's make a snowman. The snow is just right for it," Daniel said, a bit out of breath.

"I've never made a snowman before. Show me how," Kit said as she watched Daniel form a snowball and roll it in the snow. As he rolled the ball, it became bigger and bigger.

"Kit you make another ball and we'll put it on top of this one. I'll make a smaller ball for his head." Once the balls were put on top of each other, the snowman was as tall as Daniel. Rocks were used to make his eyes and a carrot for his nose. Kit put one of her scarves around his neck then said, "Look at him, he looks just like a snowman I saw in a picture a long time ago. This has been so much fun, Danny, but now my fingers are frozen. I think I better go inside." Kit had the biggest smile on her face.

Daniel nodded and said, "Yes, my hands are cold too. We have been outside all afternoon. Let's go inside and warm up."

The evenings were getting longer. Kit often asked Daniel if she could watch a movie so he would set it up for her. The movie she asked to watch was almost always Dirty Dancing. After a few times of her watching the movie, Daniel noticed that she was starting to imitate the lead female character in the movie. Kit would try to dress like the girls in the movie, but with the clothes she had, it did not always turn out like she wanted. Alone in her room, she would try new ways to style her hair but never let Daniel see her in her new do. One evening as she sat on the couch watching Daniel studying, she said, "Danny there's a lot of things I need to know. I was cleaning upstairs and I saw the bowl of money on your dresser. I don't even know how to count money. Would you teach me?"

"Of course, Kit. I never realized you would not know that. When you were in that group home, didn't you have money?" Daniel asked.

"Yes, but I never needed to buy much. The director of the home would buy the food for the house. She took care of my money and would buy what I needed. I did not like going where there were lots of people so I never went shopping. If I needed money, she would give me a twenty-dollar bill. When I bought food at the hospital cafeteria, I would give them the twenty, and they would give me some money back, but I never knew why they did. I never knew how to count the money."

Daniel smiled at her. He went upstairs to get the bowl of coins he had. He described each coin and what each was worth. Once Kit had the concept on how money worked, Daniel asked, "Kit, you told me you stopped going to school when you were eight. Did you go to school when you were in foster care?"

"Yes, I went to school but I never learned anything. I was fifteen when I got out of the burn unit so they put me in a class with other fifteen-year-olds. The teacher talked about things I never heard about. There was math class and science class and Phys-Ed. I just hated that class. The teachers thought that my injuries had affected my brain so they did not even try to help me," Kit explained in a sad voice. "The school never said anything to my foster mother."

"Oh, Kit, I'm so sorry that happened to you. There is nothing wrong with your brain, that I know. Like I told you before, I'm willing to teach you," Daniel said.

"Thank you. I will try very hard. I want to learn." Kit paused for a moment and said, "Danny, you study at home. You have your books. Maybe I could get my own books and go to school at home. Is that possible?"

Daniel saw how excited she was to learn so he said, "Kit that is very possible. You can take courses by correspondence but we'll have to wait 'til spring. We're snowbound remember?"

"Really, I can do that? I would like that very much. Maybe for now, I can try reading those books that are in my room. I was looking at them and they have some big words that I don't know," Kit said.

"Kit, when you read and don't know the word, why not write it down? Then we can go over the words and I'll show you how to pronounce them," Daniel volunteered.

"That is a good idea. Thanks, Danny, you're the best," Kit said as she ran to her room to get a book.

As the winter progressed, Daniel and Kit established a routine. They did their everyday chores—cared for the cow and the chickens, shoveled snow, chopped wood, and all the other things that needed to be taken care of. This winter, Daniel found time to do fun things as well. He taught Kit how to walk with the old snowshoes, and in a short time, she could walk a fair distance with them. Daniel joined her on his cross-country skis and they both went for long walks around the property. Other days, they would take the toboggan and slide down the snow drift going down to the lake. Kit loved the ride down but was not to enthused by the walk up.

Kit had walked by the chess set everyday and remembered the night when Daniel had played chess with his dad and Barry. She wanted to ask Daniel to play but she could not bring herself to ask. One evening, she took hold of her fears and surprised Daniel by asking, "Would you like a game of chess Danny? I think I remember what you showed me before."

Daniel was a little surprised and he asked, "You want to play? Why now, Kit?"

"Well, when we played when Barry and your father were here, I saw what the game is about. I know how much you like to play and you can't play by yourself, so if you want to teach me, I'll play with you," Kit answered with a big smile, and added, "I've been thinking of asking you to play ever since your dad left, but I was afraid you would think I was stupid."

Daniel returned the smile and said "Kit, I would never think you were stupid. If you want to play, let's give it a try. What color do you want, white or dark?"

Kit did not know what Daniel was asking and said, "What do you mean?"

"Kit, see on these pieces, I left the red bark on so I call them the dark pieces. And those are the white," Daniel said as he showed Kit a piece with red bark on the edge of the base.

"I like the red ones, so I'll take the dark pieces," Kit replied.

"Good, I'll be white so I have the first move," Daniel said and moved a pawn up one square. Kit made the same move with her red piece. As they played, Daniel would correct Kit if she made a wrong move and reminded her that the object of the game was to protect the king. After a while, Kit saw what Daniel was doing and tried to stop him, but she was too late and her king was caught in checkmate. Daniel found Kit to be a fast learner and said, "That was a good game, Kit, you learn fast. Did you like it?"

"Yes, that was more fun then I thought! Next time, you won't win so easily," Kit said with a laugh.

It was Christmas Eve, a bitterly cold evening, Daniel came in from milking the cow and he said, "The northern lights are especially bright tonight. You should go see them." Kit put on her coat and went outside. The northern sky was lit up by all kinds of beautiful greens and purples. It was like the colors were dancing, changing shapes as they did. They watched until they could not endure the cold any longer. As Kit took off her coat she said, "That was wonderful. Do you know what makes the lights?"

"I think it has something to do with the sun and the earth's atmosphere but I'm not sure just how it's done," Daniel replied. "Why don't we watch a Christmas movie, that will make it feel like Christmas. I have just the right movie, 'It's a Wonderful Life.'"

The next day they celebrated Christmas. Although Kit was with him this year Daniel felt that there was something missing. He missed being with his family, this would be the third Christmas he had been away.

By the end of the winter, after Kit had viewed Dirty Dancing for the twelfth time, she asked, "Danny, would you teach me how to dance? I wish I knew how."

"Well, how do you know I can dance?" Daniel asked as he closed the book he had been reading.

Kit would not be put off and said, "Danny you know. Please teach me."

"Well, Kit, I can't dance like they do in that movie. When my sister and I were teenagers, she got in her head she wanted to be a ballroom dancer. She talked me into being her partner so I learned some steps. I'll show you what I know." Kit was so pleased she got up and ran to give him a quick kiss on the cheek.

"When can we start?" she said enthusiastically. "Can you show me now?"

Daniel shook his head and gave her a big smile. He remembered how his sister had been. There had been no way to say no to her, and he knew that Kit would not take no for an answer either. "Okay, we'll start with something slow." He went to the radio and found some slow music, something they could waltz to.

Kit was a natural. She learned the steps very quickly. In no time, they were waltzing around the room. Once Kit thought she knew the steps, she said, "Danny this is pretty easy. Can you show me another dance?" She had the biggest smile and could not wait to learn more steps.

"It's getting late, Kit. I'm a little tired. We'll dance again tomorrow," Daniel said.

Kit was a little sad. She did not want this evening to come to an end. She liked being close to Daniel. Nevertheless, she said, "Okay, Danny. You are a very good teacher. Thanks!"

The next morning, Kit was the first up. Daniel found her wrapped up in her warm comforter, reading her book on the couch. "I'll get the stove going right away. It's cold in here," Daniel said, crumpling some paper to start the fire. "It must be colder outside. The house is not usually this cold. I had hoped that the colder weather would be over by now. Once the fire is going, I'll go check on the animals."

"I'll come with you. I hope the chickens did not freeze up. I wish we could bring them in the house."

Daniel did not answer her but thought to himself. *There is no way I would live with chickens.* She got up and went to dress, and followed Daniel outside. Once at the chicken coop, they found the chickens all huddled close together. "I think they're alright, Kit. See, the water is not frozen. It's above zero in here. I'll check for some eggs." Daniel did not find any. It was just too cold for the hens to lay eggs.

This year, the snow was slow in melting. It would be nice one day, but the next it would snow another inch or so. On one warm afternoon, Daniel decided to clean out the odds and ends shed, something he had in mind to do for a long time. Most of the stuff in there was junk so he piled it up to take to the dump.

He found some nice planed boards, nails, a gas can in good condition, and some tools. These things he organized in the shed. Once that was done, he turned his attention to the gas generator. It was a small unit so he wheeled it out and brought it to the back of the house. He had it half-apart when Kit came out and asked him, "What are you doing? Why are you taking that apart?" She came closer to have a look.

"I'm trying to fix this generator. If I can get it going, we can run it when the power gets low," Daniel said.

Kit had no clue of what he was talking about and said, "I don't understand. Are you saying that thing will make the lights work?" As Daniel worked, he explained how the generator worked and how it would be helpful if he got it to. Parts were all over the table at the back of the house. He cleaned out the gas tank and made sure the gasoline was clean, cleaned the air filter, and replaced the spark plug with a new one he had bought. After many afternoons, he had it all back together and it was ready to be started.

The generator started by a pull cord. He braced his foot against the machine and pulled and pulled. He adjusted the choke, then pulled again. After what felt like a million pulls, the machine finally sputtered to life but only for a short time. He made a small adjustment to the choke and pulled again. This time the machine sputtered up and kept on running. Kit had observed what Daniel had done and when the machine started, she jumped up and down saying, "You did it, Danny, you fixed it! I knew you'd do it."

"Yes, finally, I thought my arm was going to fall off my shoulder. Now we have back up for our power," Daniel said, rubbing his shoulder. He wheeled the generator back to the odds and end shed and connected it to the power supply.

Give careful thought to the paths for your feet
and be steadfast in all your ways.

—Proverb 4:26 (NIV)

CHAPTER 11

I t took some doing but Daniel finally persuaded Kit to come to
town with him. As soon as the snow finally melted, he had gone
to town to see about getting Kit her lessons. When he returned,
Kit was there to meet him and she asked, "Did you get my books,
Danny?"

"Kit, no, I'm sorry. I met with the principal of the school and he
told me that you would have to come in to get tested."

Before he could explain, Kit jumped in and said, "Get tested?
What is that? I don't want to get tested, he will see how ignorant I
am. Oh, Danny, why can't I just get the lessons?"

"Kit, slow down. He wants to test you to see what you know.
The principal needs to know at what level to start you at and what
kind of lessons you need to learn. The test will tell him that. Stop
saying you're ignorant Kit. You are very smart. You learned to read
very quickly. Stop being so hard on yourself," Daniel assured her.
He added, "I got you this book. It's by the same author of the books
you've been reading." When she saw the book, she thanked Daniel
but still was not happy about having to go to town.

"We'll go stay at Lilly's house. I already talked to Charlie. He
and the boys will be coming here for spring break and care for the
animals, so we can take our time in town. You can get used to having

people around you and then we'll go see the principal," Daniel told her, as he prepared their evening meal.

"So you have everything planned?" It made her mad that he had made these plans for her life without first talking to her. "What if I don't want to take these lessons?" She stopped talking for a minute and thought about what she had just said. She continued, "Oh, Danny, you know I do! I want to learn things everyone else knows. I want to be smart. Why is it so hard?" She dropped to the couch and started crying.

Daniel went to her and put an arm over her shoulder. "Kit, dear, you have to take it one step at a time. We'll go to town and stay at my sisters. Once you are used to being with her and the family, we'll go see the principal. You don't have to see anyone else. I know it's hard for you but I think you will be happy you did it."

"Danny, I'm sorry, I'll go but you have to promise you'll be with me when I take the test."

"Kit, I promise but I'm not going to give you any answers," Daniel said, now teasing her. "I think supper is ready. Let's go eat." He wiped her teary face and helped her to the table.

Charlie arrived a week later. They were all very pleased to be at Daniel's place again. "It's so wonderful to be here again, this place has such a beautiful feel to it," Carol exclaimed. When she saw Kit she said, "You must be Kit. My boys told me all about you. It's like I already know you." She went to Kit and gave her a hug.

It did not take long for Kit to become comfortable with Carol. Kit saw how Carol cared for her boys, and it reminded her of the way her mother had loved her. The boys went to play with Misty but she just lay still and would not play with them, so they asked, "Uncle Daniel, is something wrong with Misty? She doesn't want to play."

"Oh, she's not well. She went to chase off some wolves and came back different. I don't really know what happened to her. She likes it when you pet her, but she does not play anymore," Daniel replied. They sat by Misty and petted her for awhile. Then with sad faces, they went to sit by their father until supper was ready. They spent a quiet evening together.

The next morning, Daniel and Kit left for town. Kit was very nervous and could not sit still. She asked, "Do you think your sister will like me? Oh, what if I scare her little girl? Are you sure we can stay there?"

"You'll love my sister. She has a very big heart. You'll see," Daniel said about his sister.

Kit was still worrying about taking the test, and said, "Danny, what if I can't answer the questions? I don't know if I should do this. They'll think I'm so stupid."

Daniel looked at her and said, "Kit, you'll do alright. It's not a test that you can fail. Stop fretting. Take one step at a time." Kit got what he was saying to her and then she realized that he was talking to her like she was a little kid. That was something she did not want. She wanted Daniel to see her as a grown woman. She became very quiet and sat still. Daniel noticed the change and asked, "Something wrong, Kit? Did I say something to upset you?"

She looked at Daniel and gave him a big smile. "No, Danny, you're right, I'll take it one step at a time." She decided that she had to grow up and become a woman that Daniel could love.

When they arrived at Lilly's house, Kit became very nervous. Before she got out of the truck, she covered her face with her scarf. She mustered up her strength and followed Daniel to the door. Lilly greeted them warmly. She gave her brother a big hug, and turned to Kit and said, "Kit, welcome to my home. It's so nice to finally meet you. Come in."

Lilly led them to the kitchen and said, "I just made some lemonade. Would you like a glass?"

"Yes, that is just the thing I need. How about you, Kit?" Daniel said.

"Yes, please, I'd loved one," Kit said graciously. She wanted to make a good impression so Lilly would not think her to be ignorant. As Lilly brought the glasses to the table she said, "Beth is having her nap, she should be up soon."

"So, Lilly, tell me what is new with you and Ted?" Daniel asked.

"What's new? You haven't been here for so long. Daniel you must come back to see us more often. I started my own business.

Remember last year I said I had to find something to do? Well, I took a cosmetology course. After I got my certification, I could not get any work so Ted suggested I start my own business. I learned that the burn center wanted someone to help their patients with their rehabilitation. I put in an application and got the contract. I did not like leaving Beth with a babysitter so Ted suggested I work from home. He remodeled the room by the back door and I now have my own shop to work in. Want to see it?"

"Yes," Daniel said very surprised, "I would. Come, Kit, let's go see Lilly's shop." They followed Lilly to the back of the house.

When Lilly opened the door, Daniel was surprised to find a room that looked like a barber shop. On the wall, at the back of the room, was a shelf full of wigs of all colors and styles. Other shelves held shampoos, nail polish, makeup and all kinds of cosmetic products. In the middle of the room, there was a barber chair in front of a large mirror, and off to the side, a sink used to wash hair.

"Whoa, this is wonderful. Can you cut hair?" Daniel asked as he looked himself in the mirror.

"Yes, I cut hair. I just finished a haircutting course. Do you want a hair cut? You look like one of those bush guys you see on TV."

As Lilly cut Daniel's hair, Kit stood at the door. She saw the close rapport they had and she liked the way they teased each other. Once Lilly was done cutting Daniel's hair she asked, "Kit, would you like me to style your hair?"

Kit was suddenly alarmed. She had been in deep thought and did not expect Lilly to ask her a question. With fear in her eyes, she answered in a meek voice, "No, no, thank you, Lilly." She turned and headed for the front door. Daniel hurried to catch up with her.

"Kit, hey, what's the matter?" he said, grasping one of her arms. "Stop, Kit, it's okay. You don't have to get your hair cut. Now, please calm down." Kit stopped walking and looked at him.

"Daniel I'm sorry. It's just things are…" She could not finish her sentence but collapsed in his arms and started to cry.

Daniel held her and rubbed her back saying, "Kit, it's okay, remember we said we would take it one step at a time. Getting your hair done is probably a step you can take when you get to know Lilly better. Now let's go and finish our lemonade. Okay? You alright?" He looked at her and saw her nodding. He brushed off the tears from her cheeks and led her to the kitchen.

Once in the kitchen, they saw little Beth sitting on her mother's lap. "Hey, there's my little girl." He went to Beth and gave her a kiss on the cheek. "Want to come see your Uncle?" he asked, extending his arm to pick her up.

"Uncle Daniel, it's so nice to see you! I missed you!" She said in her little girl voice and she raised her arms to be picked up. Daniel picked her up and went to sit beside Kit.

"Beth, I want you to meet my friend, Kit. Kit, this is my niece I told you about."

"Hello, Kit, you have pretty eyes. Do you love my Uncle Daniel?" she asked.

Kit looked at Daniel and gave him a smile. Then looking at Beth, she said, "Beth, yes I love your Uncle. He is the kindest man I know. He takes very good care of me." She looked at Daniel and gave him another smile.

"Kit, would you like to see my new tea set my daddy got me? We could have tea," Beth asked Kit. She turned to her mom and said, "Mom, can Kit come and play tea with me in my room?"

"Yes, dear, if Kit wants to," replied Lilly.

When Beth and Kit had gone, Lilly said, "So that's your Kit. I'm sorry I upset her. I should have been more considerate to her needs. They taught me at school that people who were traumatized are very sensitive and need special care. I should have waited for her to ask me."

Daniel gave her a smile and said, "Kit will get over it. She is trying very hard to learn how to respond in a normal way. It's hard for her to trust adults but children, on the other hand, she'll take to them just like that."

As she played tea with little Beth, Kit realized that she had over-reacted to Lilly's offer to cut her hair. *I must have hurt Lilly's feelings by my response*, she thought. *Why can't I just do things right? I have to grow up and stop being afraid of everything*, she admonished herself.

131

While she was in thought, little Beth asked her if she wanted to see her Shopkins. "What are Shopkins?" Kit asked, a little confused. Beth took her to a shelf filled with little figurines, not more than two centimeters in height. They looked like things you would buy. One was of a shoe, one of a cake, one of a chocolate sundae, one of a carrot, one of a milk carton—Kit was amazed to see all the different kinds of figurines Beth had, and Beth had names for all of them.

"Okay, but what do you do with these?" Kit asked.

"Well, you can put the Shopkins in the little baskets and pretend you are shopping. Or you can pretend you have a store and you put them on the shelf so people can shop. Which one is your favorite, Kit?" Beth said.

"Well, let's see. I think I like the ice cream cone one. Which one do you like?" Kit replied.

"My favorite is the strawberry shortcake one. See, you can see the little strawberries on top." Beth picked it up and placed it in Kit's hand. Just then, Lilly and Daniel walked in the room and they joined Beth and Kit in playing with the Shopkins.

When Kit had been alone with Beth, she had let her scarf fall away from her face. But when she saw Lilly, she brought it up and covered her face. Beth noticed and said, "Kit, it's alright to show mommy your face. She helps people with hurt faces. She makes their faces look like they were not even hurt. She could do that for you."

Kit was surprised a little girl would say that to her. Beth had not taken any notice of her face until now. She had not asked about what had happened. She just accepted Kit as she was. Kit looked at Lilly and asked, "You can really do that?"

"Yes, I'm a qualified cosmetologist. I can show you how to put on makeup to minimize your scars. But we'll have to do that tomorrow. It's just about supper time and I don't want us to be rushed," Lilly replied.

"Yes, Lilly, I'd like that and maybe you could show me what I can do with my hair. I'm sorry about how I reacted before," Kit said. As she finished saying that, Ted walked into the room. For a second, Kit felt trapped. She quickly covered her face and looked away.

"Oh, Daddy, you're home!" Beth ran to him to be picked up.

Daniel knew that Kit was uncomfortable with Ted who she had never met, so he said, "Kit, remember I told you about Ted? This is Ted, Lilly's husband. Ted meet Kit." Ted gave her a big smile and said, "Kit, it is so nice to finally meet you! Lilly told me about you." He turned to Beth and said, "I see you're playing with your Shopkins again. Did you tell Kit all of their names?" Beth nodded her head.

"Well, we'd better go see what Ted brought for supper, come, let's go eat," Lilly said.

Kit was a little disappointed that she would have to wait until the next day. Being anxious and wanted to see what Lilly could do for her, she spent a long sleepless night wondering how it would turn out.

She was the first one up the next morning, and when Daniel got up, he saw her sitting and waiting at the kitchen table. "Good morning, Kit, why are you up this early? Did you sleep okay?"

"No, Daniel, I could not sleep. I could not stop thinking about what Lilly will do about my face. Do you think she will be able to help me?" Kit asked as she started to pace up and down the kitchen floor.

"Kit, you'll have to wait to see. I'm sure Lilly will do the best she can," Daniel answered.

"Yes, I think so too. Oh, I wish she would get up so we can start," Kit said just as Lilly joined them in the kitchen. She gave them a big smile and said, "Good morning, you two, you're up early. Let's have breakfast, then we can go to my shop and get started."

Kit was so anxious, she could not eat. She just nibbled on a piece of toast and wished breakfast to be over. Finally, it was time for the girls to head for Lilly's shop, and Daniel was free to go do what he wanted.

Kit was so nervous but very pleased that she was finally sitting in Lilly's barber chair. Lilly showed her the different products she would be using and explained what she was going to do.

"Kit, first we'll wash your face with this cleanser. After we'll put on this moisturizer." Kit washed her face and applied the moisturizer. "Okay, now we're ready to start. I'll show you how I apply the concealer."

Lilly applied some concealer on Kit's face. With a facial brush, she patted the concealer evenly over her injuries. She applied some makeup and blended it with the brush. She finished off with a thin layer of face powder. With each step, Kit saw the scars slowly disappearing.

"Oh, Lilly, I was never told the scars could be covered up. Look, you can hardly see any of them. Why was I not told about this before?" Kit asked.

"I don't know but I usually only see people when they have finished their treatments," Lilly replied.

"Oh, I never finished mine. I was going to but that's when Daniel rescued me. Do you think I should go back to have it finished?" Kit said as she examined her new face in the mirror.

"That's up to you Kit. I'm not the one to ask that question. You'll have to ask a doctor," Lilly answered. "Now let's see what we can do with your hair?"

"Yes, it's getting pretty long. The last time I got my hair cut was when I was at the group home," Kit said.

While Lilly was giving Kit a makeover, Daniel went to the police station to catch up with his old partner and to talk to the chief. When he got there, the chief invited Daniel to come into his office. "Hey, Daniel, it's nice to see you. How are you? It's been some time since I last saw you."

"I'm doing well. It's good to see friends and family again," Daniel answered.

"So, Daniel, are you coming back to take up your old position?"

"Yeah, well, the thing is, Chief, I've thought about it for a while now. I have decided that I'm giving up police work. I've been studying law and I'm going to take the bar exam this fall. Then I'm planning to go to work with my dad," Daniel replied.

"I'm sorry to see you go, Daniel, you did good work in the police force. The force needs men like you but if it's not what you want, no one can push you into it. I'm glad to hear that you'll be working with your dad," the chief said. He paused for a minute and asked, "How is Kit?"

"She's good, she came to town with me," Daniel said. He continued to tell him about where Kit was and what she was planning to do. He ended by saying, "She said she wanted to see you before we returned home."

"Tell her to give me a call. It will be good to see her again."

After Daniel said he would tell Kit, they said goodbye. As he was leaving the station, his former partner was just coming off shift. He saw Daniel walking out of the station and ran to catch up to him, "Daniel, wait up."

When Daniel turned, he saw Jay walking toward him.

"How have you been? I was starting to think that you had gotten eaten by a bear. Do you have time to go have a beer?"

"Hey, partner, sure good to see you too," Daniel said, giving Jay a bear hug. They headed to their favorite haunt. As Daniel sat down he realized how hungry he was so he ordered a hamburger. When his order came he took a bite out of his hamburger and said, "Man, does this ever taste good. It's one of the things I miss, living in the mountains. I have fresh fish and chicken but no beef."

"Well that settles it, you'll just have to move back," Jay teased. As they ate their meals they caught up with what they were doing then said goodbye.

When Daniel returned to Lilly's, he heard music coming from downstairs. He followed the music and found his sister with little Beth and Kit line dancing. He stood by the entrance of the room and watched. Their backs were turned away from him so they did not see him. As he watched, he noticed that little Beth kept up with her mom and Kit. When the dance step made them turn to face him, he observed Kit's face—she looked beautiful. It was little Beth who saw him first.

"Uncle Daniel, come see how mommy fixed Aunty Kit's face. She is so beautiful. Don't you think so?" Kit was looking at him with the biggest smile he had ever seen her give.

"Kit you look lovely," he said returning her smile.

Kit took him by the hand and said, "Danny come dance with us. It's lots of fun. Come, please."

But Daniel would have none of it. "No Kit, I draw the line at line dancing, it's not for me. That dance is for people who can think with their feet. Go ahead, you three were doing really well. Go, keep on with your dance."

In the meantime, Lilly had turned the music off and looking at her watch, she said to Beth, "It's that time already, your daddy and grandpa will be here any minute. Come, Beth, we have to setup for supper."

Daniel saw the reaction in Kit's face when she heard what Lilly said. He said to Kit, "You worried about meeting my father?"

"Oh, grandpa is your father, of course. I've decided that I'm not going to shy away from people anymore. It's the way I reacted for so long, I have to make a conscious effort not to now. It's hard to change how you react to things but I'll do it."

"That's good to hear, Kit," Daniel replied.

"Lilly did a really good job in covering my scars, don't you think?" Kit asked. Daniel agreed. Lilly had done a great job. "Lilly said she'll take me shopping but I don't want her to spend her money on me. Do you think Uncle Barry would give me some money from the rent of my house? I should call him. Would you have his phone number?"

"I saw Barry today. I can call him if you want," Daniel said.

"No, I want to call him. I have to start doing things for myself." After Daniel had given Kit the number, they both went upstairs just as Ted and Ken were coming through the door carrying insulated bags.

"What do you have in those bags, Ted?" Daniel asked.

"Just my special ribs. Lilly wanted to make tonight a special event," Ted said. "It's not every day we have all the family together. Kit, you look like Lilly worked her magic on you. You look lovely." Kit thanked him and gave him a smile although she felt a little embarrassed by the attention.

With new confidence, Kit called Barry and he agreed to meet with her the next afternoon. When Daniel and Kit walked in his office, Barry did a second take when he saw Kit. She even walked differently, he thought. He went to meet her, greeting her with a hug and a kiss on her cheek.

"Kit you look lovely. How are you?" he said as he led them in his office and indicated for them to sit in the chairs in front of his desk. After making small talk, Barry said, "Would you like to go see the house? I took out all the old furniture and bought new stuff. I hope you like it."

"Yes, I would like to see it. Thank you for doing that," Kit replied.

"We have to let the renters know you want to see the house. I'll call them and set a time for us to go." He reached in his desk and took out some papers. "I opened a bank account in your name. This is the latest statement." He handed the papers to Kit.

She looked a little confused and said, "Uncle Barry, I don't know what to say." She took the papers, looked at them and said, "I don't know what all these numbers mean. Can you help me?"

Barry went over the numbers and how to read the statement. Once Kit understood he said, "We could go to the bank so you can apply for a bank card. Then you can use the card to buy the things you want."

"Really, I can have my own card? And I can pay for my own things? Yes, I would like that. Can we go now?" Kit asked impatiently.

After they were finished with banking, they returned to Lilly's house. When Kit saw Lilly, she said, "I'm all set to go shopping, Lilly. See?" She held up the card then continued, "Uncle Barry and Danny helped me get the card. The woman at the bank wanted to see ID, and when I told her I did not have ID, Uncle Barry talked to her and that's when I got my card."

"How nice Kit, I'm glad for you. We can go shopping once Beth is up from her nap," Lilly said with a big smile. She liked to see Kit so energized. Although Kit had known Lilly for only a short time, she felt she could trust her.

She asked, "Oh, Lilly, what is ID? I did not ask that woman what ID was because I did not want her to think I was stupid."

That made Lilly a little sad. *No one should be made to feel stupid*, she thought. She replied in the kindest way she knew. "ID, it's something you show to tell people who you are. Here, I'll get my purse and show you mine."

After Lilly had shown Kit her ID, Kit said, "How did you get all those cards? Should I have them too?"

"You should have a Medicare card and a social insurance card. Don't you have a Medicare card already?" Lilly asked.

"If I did, I don't know where it would be. How do you get those cards?" Kit replied, a little concerned.

"Don't worry, you can get a replacement card," Lilly answered trying to ease her worry. "I have a phone number we could call to see what you can do to get a new card. Do you want to call them?" Lilly asked. Kit was not sure what she would ask, so she let Lilly make the call. She was directed to apply online. Lilly found the site on her computer and brought up the form. She helped Kit fill in the information on the online application. Once they had successfully applied for the Medicare card, Lilly found the site to apply for the Social Insurance Card and had Kit fill in that form.

"Thanks, Lilly, for all your help. When these cards come, I'll have ID like everybody else," Kit said, and went to give her a hug.

"You're very welcome Kit. I'm glad I was able to help you."

The shopping excursion was a learning experience for Kit. This was the very first time she had ever gone to a mall. She was over-whelmed by all the stores and all the people. Lilly saw that Kit was uneasy, so she quickly made their way to her favorite clothing store.

Once they were in the store, Lilly asked, "Kit are you feeling alright?"

"Yes, Lilly, I am." She would not let her fears stop her from buying the things she wanted.

"Okay, I'm glad you are. Now what kind of clothes are you looking for?" Lilly asked.

"Well, I need some summer clothes. Some shorts like the ones they wore in Dirty Dancing? Maybe a summer dress and some san-dals. Can you help me find clothes like that?" Lilly was surprised by Kit's request, but with the help of the sales clerk, Kit came home with quite a few new outfits, new shoes, and a new purse. She could not wait to show Daniel.

Once they returned to Lilly's, Kit showed Daniel all her new things. "Did you like going shopping?" Daniel asked.

"Yes, I did. At first it was a little scary being in that big mall, but Lilly knew where to go. Do you like the things I bought?" Kit replied. Daniel gave her a smile and said, "Yes, they're very nice. When do you want to go see the principal? We should call to make an appointment. What do you think?"

"Oh, Danny, I called the principal this morning when you were out seeing your father. He said I could come tomorrow morning at ten. He said that he was all ready for me to take the test," Kit answered.

Surprised, Daniel replied, "Really, you called the principal on your own? I'm very proud of you Kit."

The next morning, Daniel took Kit to school and was going to meet the principal with her, but she told Daniel that she could do this on her own. As she walked in the school, she felt overwhelmed but fought off her fears. The principal met her in the hall and showed her to a room full of computers. He asked her to sit at one of the computers and said, "This test is to find out what you know and what you don't know. I want you to go through all the questions and answer all of them."

"But what if I don't know the answer?" Kit asked.

"Well, let's look at a question. See, it's multiple choice. One of the option is 'I don't know.' So, if you don't know the answer, select that option. Just relax, this test is not one you can fail," he replied.

At the start of the test, Kit had no problem answering the questions but toward the end, she found she could not answer many of them. When she was done, the principal advised that he would review her answers and call her when he had her study material ready. "Do you have internet access?" he asked.

This made Kit uneasy, but she said, "No, I don't. Does that matter?"

"Yes, a little. Would you have a computer?" he asked.

"I don't have one but I can buy one," Kit answered.

"Okay, I'll download as much material I can on thumb drives and give you text books for the material I can't download. That way, you don't have to have all these big text books. Would that be alright?"

"Yes, I don't know much about computers, but Danny can help me," Kit agreed.

To celebrate Kit's effort, Daniel took her to a restaurant for lunch. As they sat waiting for their food, she told Daniel about the conversation she had with the principal. Daniel said, "Well, we'd better go buy a computer. We'll go after our lunch."

They were still at the restaurant when Daniel got a call from Barry saying, "The renters agreed we can go see the house. They're at work now so it would be a good time to go."

"We're just finishing up. We'll meet you there. Kit knows the address," Daniel said.

They came to a stop in front of a new stylish house. Daniel was under the impression the house would be a run-down shack, but when he saw the house, he was amazed and asked Kit, "This is your house?"

"Yes, it's bigger than what I remember," Kit said as she got out of the truck. They went in the house and toured the place. Barry told Kit that he had taken all the old furniture away and had the entire interior repainted. He also informed her that the renters were planning to move out at the end of the summer, so he was going to have to start to look for someone else to rent. Once they had been all over the house, they said good bye to Barry and headed for Lilly's house.

"Did it bother you to be in the house again?" Daniel asked Kit.

"No, it's alright. I did not stay here very long and it now looks completely different. I can't believe it's really mine. Do you like it Danny?" Kit asked.

"Yes, it's very nice. You would be very comfortable living here," Daniel said. Kit's face changed, and Daniel knew he had said the wrong thing.

"You think I want to live in that house? Danny, please let me go back home with you. You can't leave me here, please, Danny," Kit cried out.

"No, no, Kit calm down, of course you can come home with me. It's your home. I'm just saying that if you ever got tired of living in the bush, you have a beautiful house to come to," Daniel said.

The week came to an end, and it was time for Daniel and Kit to return to their home on the mountain. After she gave big hugs to Lilly and Beth, she thanked Lilly for all the help she had given her. Kit went to the truck to wait for Daniel to say his goodbyes. She had never felt so loved. She now sensed she was part of a caring family. When Daniel got in the truck, he noticed that Kit had big tears in her eyes. "Kit, you okay? Is something troubling you?" Daniel asked.

"I'm okay, Danny, just sad to be leaving," Kit said as she wiped the tears off her face.

As they backed out of the driveway, they heard Lilly say, "Don't stay away for too long. Bye!" Daniel waved goodbye and with a honk of the horn, drove away.

It seemed that the drive home went on forever. Kit was very anxious to look at the study material the principal had given her and to learn how to work on her new computer. She had no time to look at it after picking it up the night before.

It was late afternoon when they finally got home and were greeted by Charlie's family. When the boys met Kit, they could not believe she was the same Kit they had known before. She looked like a grown woman with a new hairstyle and new clothes. She even talked differently but that did not stop them from asking her to come to see the new chicks.

After Daniel unloaded the items they had bought, he went to sit down with Charlie and asked, "How did your week go?"

"It was great but I think the boys are ready to return home. Carol had them doing all kinds of chores which they never do at home. She had them help with making the bread, churning the butter and doing the dishes. She involved them in everything she did, telling them that this was how young boys used to live before the invention of electricity," Charlie continued. "This has shown us that we pamper them to much, letting them watch too much TV and play computer games. I think when we get back home, I'm going to teach them the everyday running of the farm."

"Well, I'm glad you came to stay the week, thank you. I had a good visit with my family. Got to know little Beth a little more. Kit had a great week too. I think she's finally coming out of her shell."

"Yes, I noticed. She does seem to have more confidence in herself," Charlie said.

Meanwhile at the chicken coop, Kit was surprised to see all the little chicks. She knew that two of the hens were sitting on clutches of eggs but had no idea how many chicks would hatch.

"Oh my, do you know how many there are?" she asked the boys.

"We counted twenty. The two hens have ten chicks each. Dad put us in charge of them. We feed them and make sure they have water," Dennis said. He turned, looked up at Kit and said, "Watch out for the rooster, he's nasty. He attacked me the first time I tried to touch the chicks."

Kit laughed and asked, "Did he hurt you?"

"No, not really. He scratched my leg. Dad said to shoo him outside before we play with the chicks."

"I'm glad you told me that, Dennis. He's usually friendly to me but he must think he has to protect his chicks. I'll watch for him," Kit said as they were leaving the coop.

Kit went back to the house. Carol was packing the boys' things and when she saw her, she said, "Did the boys show you the chicks? They are pretty proud of themselves."

"Yes, they did. They're good boys. Thank you for coming to help us out. We spent a very good week in town. I'm glad I went," Kit said.

"Your very welcome, Kit. I like to see you happy," Carol said as she went on packing.

Do everything in love.

—1 Corinthians 16:14 (NIV)

CHAPTER 12

Finally, Daniel and Kit were alone again. As soon as their company left, Kit opened the box the principal had given her. On the top of the books was a letter from the principal addressed to Daniel. *Why would the principal write to Daniel?* Kit thought. She put it aside and took out a box full of thumb drives and wondered what they were. When she unpacked the books, she noticed that there were several math textbooks of different grade levels. *Odd*, she thought. There were also books on history and a few science books. She decided to go find Daniel to give him the letter and to ask him to set up her new computer. "Danny, the principal wrote you a letter," she said when she found him.

"Well, what does it say?" Daniel asked.

"I don't know. I did not open it. It's addressed to you," Kit said giving him the envelope. Daniel opened it and read it out loud. "'Dear Daniel: Since I will not be able to check Kit's work or help her with her learning progress I'm asking you to take my place. Kit tested very low in math so I included math books from lower grades. I suggest that she try the easy level first and work up so she will have a good working knowledge in math. The thumb drives are all labelled by subjects and in what order to take them. Kit informed me that you would be willing to help her and I commend you for doing that

143

for her. I hope all works out well for the both of you.' Looks like he made me your teacher. Let's go see these books."

As they walked to her room she asked, "What is math? Is it important to know?"

Before Daniel answered, he picked up the math books and saw they were from grade school. He said, "Math is learning to work with numbers; learning to add and subtract, multiply and divide. Do you remember learning that?"

"I know how to add and subtract a bit, but that's all. I guess I have a lot to learn, huh, Danny?" Kit said.

"Don't you worry, you'll learn really quick, you'll see. Let's set up the computer, then we'll have a look at a thumb drive," Daniel said as he unpacked the computer from it's box.

And that started Kit on her learning path. She found it easier to learn when her mind was rested, so she would get up early every morning to do her studies. During the day, she would do all her daily chores and help Daniel with any help he needed. In the evening, Kit would review what she had studied in the morning and if she needed any help, she would ask Daniel.

After spending a week in town, Daniel found it hard to get back to his normal routine. He had gotten used to sitting around and visiting. Now that he was back home, there were a lot of things he needed to do and one of them was to get the garden ready for planting. As he went to the garden, he noticed the apple trees were in full bloom. He could not remember seeing the trees with so many blooms. *We'll have a good crop this year*, he thought.

Daniel got some manure and spread it on the garden, without Kit knowing about it. When he had dug it all under and was finished preparing the soil, Kit came to help with the planting. Daniel could not believe that they had seeded the entire garden in a day. He was getting to be an old hand at this, he thought. Before they went in for supper, Kit went to care for the chicks and Daniel went to milk the cow. As they were coming back to the house, Daniel asked Kit, "Have you seen Misty? She's not in the barn. I did not see her all afternoon."

"No, I saw her by the shed when you were fueling the generator. I thought she was looking for a shady spot," Kit replied.

After calling for Misty and she did not come, Daniel became alarmed. He set out to look for her and did not return to the house until it was dark. He called and called but Misty never came back. She was gone.

"She'll be back. She never ran away before. She'll be back," Daniel said trying more to convince himself. The next morning, Misty had not returned, so Daniel went to look for her some more. But no Misty.

One afternoon, after Misty had been gone for a week, Kit decided to cheer up Daniel. He was so sad about losing Misty. She put on some makeup and did her hair the way Lilly had showed her to do. Daniel was surprised to see her all dressed up and asked, "What's the special occasion, Kit?"

"I just thought we needed a little fun. Let's do something different, maybe we could have a nice supper, afterwards, we could dance. We haven't danced all summer," Kit replied.

"That's a good idea. We do need some cheering up but I'm not so sure about the dance part. But okay, let's do it," Daniel said.

Daniel made his special dish with noodles and canned tuna. Kit loved that dish especially because of the added homemade cheese. Coupled with the garden salad, their meal was delicious. To many, this dish would not be special, but to them it was. After they ate and cleaned up, Kit put the radio on and found some music to dance to. The first song had an upbeat tempo. They did the jive. Kit enjoyed the fast dance and loved it when Daniel would whirl her around. After a few faster dances, Daniel said he needed a rest, but Kit talked him into one more slow dance. "Sure, one more then we will stop, okay?" Daniel insisted.

Kit found a slow song and they waltzed around the room. As they danced, Kit smiled at him, and unexpectedly kissed him on the lips. At first, Daniel returned the kiss but quickly broke it off. Kit knew she had done something wrong, but before Daniel could stop her, Kit said she was sorry. She ran to her room and closed the door.

Daniel noticed the closed door. She never closed her door. He went to the door and said, "Kit please, I'm sorry."

He could hear her crying but he did not know how to comfort her, so he went outside to think about what just happened. Kit was still in her room when he returned to the house. He did not see her again that evening.

The next morning, Daniel made breakfast and still Kit did not come out of her room.

"Kit, breakfast is ready, please come join me. Please, Kit, you can't stay in your room forever," Daniel pleaded. Daniel had finished his cereal when Kit walked in the kitchen, got a cup of coffee and sat down at the table. She did not look at Daniel.

"Kit we have to talk about what happened last night," Daniel said.

Kit took a sip of her coffee, looked at Daniel and said, "You mean about the kiss?"

"Yeah," Daniel replied.

But before he could say anything else, Kit said, "I'm sorry, I should have known that a handsome man like you would not fall for someone who looks like this." She pointed to her scarred face. In a soft voice she continued, "I just wanted to show you that I love you, Daniel."

"Kit, let me try to explain. I did not stop kissing you because of the way you look. I think you look lovely. It's just that I don't want to put you in a situation that you are not ready for. Last year when you came to live here, you were like a little girl. Now you're like a teenager, what you're feeling might be just a crush. You have a little more growing to do before you'd be ready for an adult relationship. You don't have to rush things," Daniel said.

Kit interrupted and said, "Oh! Is that what you think? You think it's a crush?" Kit had to smile. What Daniel had just said gave her hope. She said, "I may not know much but I do know my heart, and it tells me that I love you, Daniel."

"That's just the thing, Kit, you're just starting to learn about these feelings. All you know is living here with me. What if, when

146

you leave here, you outgrow me? What if you meet someone else you love more?" Daniel said.

"Never! I will never want anyone but you, Daniel. I know what's in my heart. I love you. You may know more then I do, Danny, but I know my heart," Kit said again, giving him the biggest smile. After saying this, she went outside to care for the chickens.

Daniel sat on the couch for a while and thought about what Kit had said. He knew in his heart that Kit was right. He saw the love she had for him every time she looked at him. What stopped him was he did not want to take advantage of her. He would never want to hurt her. But who was he kidding? It was him. He did not want to make a commitment. He did love her but could not bring himself to accept the situation.

So Daniel determined to spend less time doing things with Kit, but he knew that would be almost impossible to do, especially in the evenings. Kit was always there with him. She helped prepare the meals, they would eat together, clean up together, study in the same room—and if he went for a walk, Kit would join him. Although he wanted to spend less time with Kit, he found he spent more. Since he had taught her how to play chess, they would play just about every day.

As summer came to an end, Kit noticed that Daniel tried to do things without her but she was determined to show Daniel that she was ready for a serious relationship. It was Daniel's birthday so she decided she would make him a cake. There was only one thing holding her back, and that was starting a fire in the stove. She was deathly afraid of the flames and the heat. After Daniel had gone, she went to the stove, and with unsteady hands lifted one of the stove lids and put it on the top of the stove. She crumbled up some paper, put it in the stove, then put wood on top. Her hands were shaking uncontrollably when she reached for the matches. Standing close to the stove, she struck the match and it lit. When Kit saw the flame, she dropped the match. It fell in the stove lighting the paper. There, she had done it. Now all she had to do was put more wood in to get the oven hot.

When the oven was just about at the right temperature, she mixed the cake, following the recipe closely, poured the batter in a cake pan and placed it in the oven to bake. Once the cake was in the oven, she sat down and took a deep breath. She tried to stop herself from shaking. She had done it: she had faced her biggest fear. When the cake was baked, Kit put on the oven mitts and slowly opened the oven door. As she reached in the oven, the heat hit her face, making her jump. She just about dropped the cake on the floor.

Daniel had been gone all afternoon gathering fire wood. As he stepped through the door, he smelled the wonderful aroma of something baking. He walked to the table and saw a card and a bouquet of blue Showy Daisies beside a cake. When he looked up, he saw Kit by the stove stirring something in a pot. Daniel was so surprised for Kit had never gone close to the stove. He knew she was afraid of it.

"Kit, you alright? You started a fire?" Daniel said with alarm in his voice.

"Happy birthday, Daniel. I did it! I took control of my feelings and started the fire to make you a birthday cake. I'm making your favorite no meat chili. It may be a little different but I tried to follow your recipe."

"Oh, Kit, it will be just fine, but why didn't you ask me to start the fire before I left? It must have been hard for you to do. You sure you're okay?" Daniel said.

"I'm very well, thanks, Danny. I wanted to surprise you. Supper is just about ready. I hope you like it," Kit said with a big smile.

"I'll wash up and be right with you Kit. Thank you. That chili sure smells good," Daniel said.

After a while, Daniel returned for supper. "This is very nice, Kit! I like the way you make chili, it's better than when I make it," Daniel said as they ate. Kit's chili was made with their garden vegetables. She had added beans and lentils, then spiced it up the way Daniel liked. After they finished their chili, Daniel lit the candles on the cake and Kit sang him a happy birthday. As she was cutting him a piece, she asked, "How big of a piece do you want?"

"Oh, give me a big piece. It's been a long time since we've had cake," he replied. When he finished eating that piece, Daniel said, "I'll have another piece. Thank you Kit, for making my birthday so special. It was a wonderful surprise."

Once the kitchen had been cleaned, Kit went to sit on the couch to read her book. Daniel did not want to study, so he asked, "Kit, tonight is special; would you like to dance?" They had not danced since the "kiss" incident.

"Really, Danny? You want to dance?" Kit said and ran to put the music on. Kit had wanted to dance all summer but was careful not to ask because of what had happened. She now felt so happy to be in Daniel's arms again. When Daniel suggested a slow dance, she became a little nervous. As they danced, Daniel became very serious which made her even more nervous. So she asked, "Danny is something the matter?"

Daniel gave her a smile, and said, "Kit, thank you for the lovely birthday surprise. It was very lovely." He stopped dancing, brought her close, lifted her face up to his and kissed her. Kit was so surprised but returned the kiss enthusiastically. When they broke from the kiss, she said, "Do you think I'm ready now Daniel?"

Suddenly, Daniel stepped back from Kit and said, "Kit I'm sorry. You misunderstood, I was just thanking you for what you did."

"Oh! I misunderstood? You still think of me as a little girl and will never think I will ever be ready. Will you, Danny?" Kit said trying to hold back the tears.

Daniel walked to the back door and before walking out of the door, said in a loud voice, "I don't know, Kit."

Kit was so hurt. She went to her room, and as she looked around the room, she knew what she had to do. She would show Daniel she was a grown woman and make it on her own. She went to the dresser and took all her clothes and packed them in a bag. When she had all her things packed, she took the bag to the living room and placed it on the couch.

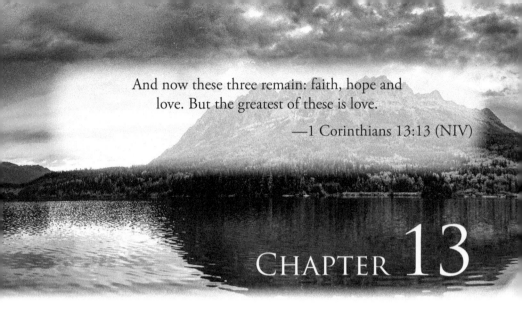

And now these three remain: faith, hope and
love. But the greatest of these is love.

—1 Corinthians 13:13 (NIV)

CHAPTER 13

The next morning, Kit was up early. She hadn't slept all night, but she was still determined to do what she had decided the night before. She sat on the couch and waited for Daniel to get up. A short while later, he came down the stairs and stopped abruptly when he saw Kit.

"What's all this, Kit? What's going on? Why do you have your pack with you?" Daniel questioned.

"I've decided to move back to town. I'll go live in my house," Kit said, holding back her tears.

"You want to move to town? That's rather sudden. Are you sure?" Daniel could not believe what he heard.

"Yes I am. Can we leave this morning?" Kit asked.

"Why do you want to move to town so suddenly? I thought you liked it here," Daniel said, shocked.

"I love it here, Danny. It's just time I start doing my own thing," she answered.

"Okay Kit, if that's what you want. We can leave as soon as the chores are done," Daniel said, going outside to tend to the animals. Once the chores were done and they had a quiet breakfast, they were off.

On the drive to town, Kit looked so sad. She did not say anything nor did she sing along with the radio. When Daniel asked her a question, she would answer in a one syllable word. They were about in town when he asked, "Are you doing this because of the kiss?"

Kit looked at him and said, "You think? You kissed me Danny and I know it meant more than just 'thank you.' I did not misunderstand. I'm not a little girl. Maybe I've just outgrown you."

Her answer surprised Daniel. He knew what she said was right. He had kissed her because he was attracted to her, but the passion he had felt for her alarmed him. He was not sure where it would lead them so he backed off.

The first stop was at the police station to get the key for the house from Barry. They both went in and asked to see him. When Barry came out of his office, he was surprised to see them.

"Hey, you two, nice to see you! How was your summer?" he asked, showing them to his office.

"Summer was great, Uncle Barry. Is the house rented?" Kit asked.

"No, the renters left at the end of last month. I just finished cleaning it up. I was just going to put an ad in the paper to rent it. Why are you asking?" Barry asked.

"Oh, that's good, because I'm moving back to town. I want to continue my schooling. I came to get the keys." Barry nodded and retrieved the keys from his desk drawer. As he gave her the keys, he said, "Here's the key." Looking at Daniel he asked, "Will you be staying in town too?"

"No, I will be returning to my place. I just came to bring Kit to town," Daniel replied. With that said, they left Barry's office and drove to the house. Barry had an odd feeling that all was not right.

After helping to bring her things into the house, Daniel looked around. The house looked clean but did not have very much furniture—a table and four chairs in the kitchen, an overstuffed couch in the living room, and a bed in one of the bedrooms. Kit seemed to be happy with it.

"Thank you for bringing me here, Danny. It's a long drive home and I don't want to keep you," Kit said without looking at him. She did not want him to see how sad she was. If he stayed any longer she would start to cry.

"Kit, I can stay and help you." He went to the kitchen and said, "You don't even have any food here. I can take you shopping."

"No, Danny, I can do that, please go. I can take care of myself," Kit said trying her hardest not to let the tears run down her face.

"Okay, Kit, if that's what you want," Daniel said and went to give her a goodbye hug. "You take care, if you need help, get in touch with Barry." The hug just about broke Kit's resolve but she returned his hug.

She turned away from him, and she said, "Goodbye, Daniel. Have a safe drive back home."

He turned and just like that, he was gone. As she saw the door closing, Kit dropped to the floor and let the tears run free. She felt all alone. How could Daniel be so blind and not see how much she loved him. If only she had a normal face, he would love her. And with that thought, more tears ran down her face.

From Kit's house, Daniel drove to his sister's. "It so nice to see you, Daniel. Where is Kit?"

"I just left her at her house. She decided that she wanted to live in town. I'm going back home. Will you look in on her occasionally?" Daniel replied awkwardly.

"What happened, Daniel? What is the real reason Kit moved to town?" Lilly inquired.

"Lilly, I don't want to get into it. I've got a long drive back, please look in on Kit," Daniel said and got back in his truck and drove away. Lilly could not believe what just happened. Why was her brother behaving like this? *He must have had a fight with Kit*, she thought. Why would Kit want to move to town so suddenly? She loved living with Daniel.

As Daniel drove, he tried to justify what he had done and why he felt so bad. It was Kit who asked to move to town. He hadn't pushed her out. So why did his heart feel so heavy? He had done the right thing, listened to Kit's wishes. Like she said, she had to go on with her life. When he had found her, she was a broken little girl. Now she was a grown woman, free to live the way she wanted. But with all his reasoning, he still felt like he had done something wrong.

It seemed like he would never get home, and when he did, the full realization that Kit was not with him hit him. The house seemed so empty. And for the first time living in his house, he felt alone.

"I lived here before Kit came. I can do it again," Daniel told himself. "Kit was the one…" But he could not finish voicing the thought. He sat on the couch and wondered what had just happened to him.

The first week without Kit just dragged by. Every time he did something, he remembered her. When he made bread, cared for the chickens, cleaned the house—even when he studied—Kit was on his mind. After a few weeks of this, he realized that he would not be able to last the winter thinking of her all the time. It would drive him mad before spring came. He had to get out before the snow came and isolated him.

On the fourth week with no Kit, Daniel decided to visit Charlie. When he arrived at the farm, Charlie came to greet him as Daniel got out of his truck.

"Hey Daniel, what's up. You've never been here this late in the year before."

"Charlie, nice to see you too," Daniel said as he gave Charlie a bear hug. "I've got to ask you something." Charlie led Daniel to the shed he had come from when Daniel had driven in.

"Daniel, you sound very serious, what's the matter?" Charlie asked. Daniel went on to tell him what had happened between him and Kit over the summer, and how he felt now without her. After Charlie had heard the story he said, "Sounds like she loves you and she left because she felt you had rejected her. Do you love her Daniel?"

It was not the first time the question had been asked. Daniel had always found it hard to sort out his feelings, but now he knew he couldn't live without Kit. "Charlie, I don't know. It's like Kit is a part of me. I can't get her out of my mind. If that's what love is then yes, I do love her. She has her own life. I don't want her to make a wrong decision because of me. She had such a raw deal when she was young. I don't want to cause her any more pain."

Charlie smiled at his cousin and said, "Daniel, I think you know what you have to do. There is no guarantee in this life, but lives are meant to be lived. Go to Kit and tell her that you love her. I'll go take care of your place. By the looks of it, you'd better make it quick, because I don't want to be stuck up there all winter."

In the meantime, Kit had started her new life. After the initial shock of seeing Daniel leave and her tearful breakdown, she finally dried her eyes and convinced herself that she could go on with her life on her own. Kit went through the house to see what she had, then decided to go to the mall that was close to her house. Putting on her coat and scarf, she set off. She assured herself that she needed the scarf because it was cold outside, not because she needed to hide behind it.

Once at the mall, Kit felt that everyone was watching her. Panic set in and the confidence she had felt before leaving the house evaporated. She had to find a quiet place to collect herself. She spotted a restroom sign. Once there, she took long deep breaths and convince herself that all was okay. *I can do this. After all, I'm a grown woman. I have to get over this anxiety.*

It's okay, just breathe. Okay, I'm alright. What should I do first? she thought. "Okay, Kit, you can do this. Just go to the food area," Kit said aloud. "I can do this; I'll just do it." She positioned her scarf over her injured face and walked to the food department. She purchased the food items she would need, then went in search for the other items. Once the items were paid for and they were bagged, she set off for home. As she was leaving the mall, she past by a phone kiosk and thought of getting a phone.

After looking over the choices of phones, Kit decided to get a pay-as-you-go phone. The clerk showed her how to work the phone and told her what the number was. When she left the kiosk, she was so pleased to have her own phone now.

Carrying all the bags was a challenge. The bags were heavy and as she walked, she had to stop and put the bags down to give her arms a rest. When Kit finally got home, her arms felt like jelly, but she had accomplished something huge. She had taken control of her fears and that felt very good.

After unpacking the items she had bought, she made herself something to eat. As she ate, loneliness came upon her. She wondered if Daniel had made it home yet and if he was missing her as much as she was missing him. *Probably not*, she thought. *Probably was happy to see me go.*

She wiped a tear off her face and went to the bedroom to make the bed with the new sheets. She found a comforter and a pillow in the closet, and put those on top. Sadness overtook her so she curled up on the bed and started crying.

She must have fallen asleep for when Kit woke up it was dark. For a moment, she did not know where she was. Fear ran through her— then she remembered and thought, *Oh, what have I done? I left the only home I have ever had. Oh, why couldn't Daniel love me? Why couldn't anyone love me?* With that the tears started again. She felt all alone in this world. She laid in bed sobbing 'til she fell asleep.

When she woke up, it was light in her room. Her head and her eyes hurt from all the crying. Kit got up and went to wash her face. She felt so numb. She automatically went to the kitchen, got a bowl and poured some cereal in it.

As she took her first spoonful, the doorbell rang. It was so unexpected that it made her jump, making the spoonful of cereal she was holding go flying. *Who could that be? Nobody knows I'm here*, she thought. She heard, "Kit it's Lilly. Daniel told me you were here."

She went to the door and opened it just enough to see who it was. "Hi, Lilly," she said.

"Hey, Kit, how are you doing? Can I come in?" Lilly asked.

"Yes Lilly, of course," Kit said but made no move to open the door any wider.

When Lilly saw that Kit was not opening the door to let her in, she said, "Kit, are you okay? Is there something I can do for you?"

Kit suddenly realized what she was doing and said, "Lilly, I'm so sorry, I was just remembering the happy time I had last spring at your house, with you and Beth." With that, she could not hold back the tears. Lilly saw Kit's breakdown and hurried to help Kit to a chair in the kitchen.

"Lilly, it's just so terrible," Kit cried.

"What's so terrible, Kit? Has something bad happened to you? Are you hurt?" Lilly asked.

"Lilly, it's Danny. I love him so much but he thinks I'm just a little girl," Kit cried. "He doesn't want someone broken like me."

"Kit, can you tell me what happened between Daniel and you?" Lily asked. "Something must have happened to make you move to town."

Kit nodded her head and told Lilly the story. She ended by saying, "You know what, Lilly? He did not even argue with me when I asked to go to town. All he said was, 'If that's what you want, Kit.'" She tried to imitate his voice.

After Lilly had heard Kit's story, she said, "My brother has always had trouble with feelings. Judging by the way he reacted when I asked him where you were, I think he cares for you a lot. I think he's scared to make a commitment. He'll come around, you'll see," Lilly said trying to comfort her.

"Oh, you think so, Lilly? Oh, I do hope you're right," Kit said in relief.

"In the meantime, what are your plans?" Lilly asked.

"I don't really know. Well, I do somewhat, but I don't know how to start," Kit said. "Does that make sense?"

"Yes, I think so. Do you know what you want to accomplish?" Lilly asked.

"Well, I want to continue my education. I finished all the materials the principal gave me in spring. I have to go see him and see what I should do next," Kit replied, with a hopeful hint in her voice.

"Okay, I could drive you to the school if you want," Lilly replied.

"Lilly, what I need is someone to show me how to take the bus. I don't want to burden anyone. I've got to learn how to do things on my own, like a grown person does. Would you show me?"

"Kit you're absolutely right. I can't do that today, but Beth and I will be happy to go ride the bus with you tomorrow. If that's alright with you?" Lilly said with a big smile on her face.

"Yes, I'm looking forward to that. Thank you, Lilly. Oh, before I forget, I've got a phone. Here's the number."

That started Kit on her way to her new life. Once she learned the bus system, she found she could go places on her own. A week after moving to town, she went to see the principal, returning the books and handing in the reports Daniel had done to show Kit had learned her lessons.

"Kit, you did a lot of work. Looks like you're ready to write the test for your High School diploma. I'll set up a time and give you a call when it's all set," the principal said.

"Really? You think I'm ready? How long will it take to set the test up?" Kit asked, a little nervous about taking a test again. Within the week, Kit returned to school and wrote the test. Now she was waiting for the results.

Wi-Fi was connected to her house and with Lilly's help, Kit learned the ins and out of surfing the net. All the while she worried about Daniel, what he was doing, and if the road was snowed in. Oh, if only he would come for her, she thought.

One day, while visiting Lilly at Ted's restaurant, she asked Ted if he had any work for her.

"Well, Kit, I'll have to see your resume," Ted said in a very professional manner. Kit became very uneasy. What made her think she could work in a place like that?

"I'm sorry, Ted, I shouldn't have bothered you," Kit said, turning to walk away.

But Ted caught her arm to stop her, "No, no, Kit, I'm sorry, I shouldn't have said that. I can be such a jerk sometimes. Please come, we'll go to my office and I'll interview you."

Kit was concerned and asked, "What is an interview?"

Ted gave her a big smile and replied, "It's okay, Kit. We'll just talk. Come in and sit down."

Once they were seated, Ted asked, "Kit, tell me what you can do. It doesn't have to be work related."

"Well, let's see. I have a good memory. I can make sour dough bread. Danny says when I made it, it looked and tasted better. I know how to take care of chickens," Kit said, hoping that Ted would not make fun of her. Ted had to smile as he envisioned a chicken coop on the side of his restaurant.

"Interesting, Kit, I was thinking of serving sour dough bread. Do you have the recipe?" he asked.

"I have it in my head. I know the recipe by heart," Kit replied.

157

"Would you be willing to share the recipe with me? I'll pay you for it," Ted asked.

Kit could not believe what she heard and said, "Really, Ted, you would do that?"

"Yes, I'm always looking for new food recipes. Would you be interested in working in the kitchen?"

"What would I do? I don't know much about cooking. I don't like being where it's hot. I don't know, Ted, this might not be a good idea," Kit said, realizing that she had taken on more than she could do.

"Kit, don't you worry, I'm sure we can find a place that would work out just right for you. Trust me." Kit sat for a while not saying anything, so Ted said, "What do you say, Kit?"

"Are you sure you want me, Ted? I don't want to be a burden to you," Kit replied.

"No, no you would not be a burden. We will train you and show you what we want you to do. How about it, do you want to give it a try?" Ted asked. With some reluctance, Kit agreed.

Kit started work at Ted's restaurant the next day. Ted introduced Kit to Anna, his top chef, and said, "Anna, would you show Kit around the kitchen? She can make sour dough bread. Would you help her make it? Then we can adapt the recipe for what we need." He turned to Kit and said, "I'm going to leave you in Anna's capable hands."

As Ted left, Anna asked, "Have you worked in a restaurant kitchen before?" Kit was so nervous. What was she doing working in a kitchen of all places?

"Oh, no, Anna, I never have. I don't know much about cooking," Kit said in a quiet voice. Anna saw that Kit was uncomfortable, so she said, "Kit, don't you worry. You show me how to make sour dough bread, and I'll show you the workings of this kitchen." She gave Kit a smile and continued saying, "See that apron over there? Go put it on and we can get started on the bread."

As Kit instructed Anna how to prepare the dough, Anna wrote down the recipe. This was the first time in Kit's life that she felt knowledgeable. She liked that feeling and immediately made Anna her friend. Kit's first batch of bread turned out superbly, so Anna added it to the restaurant's menu. As the weeks went by, Kit learned to do more in the kitchen and was assigned more duties. Their friendship grew, and Kit became more confident in herself.

The work gave Kit some relief from missing Daniel, but on days off, she missed him terribly. One afternoon, on her day off, she heard a truck in her driveway. She looked out the front window and saw Daniel's truck. Without one moment of hesitation, she ran out of the house and met him coming up her front walk. She jumped in his arms, placing her arms around his neck and kissed him. Daniel held her tightly and returned the kiss. As they kissed, Daniel carried Kit in the house. Once in the house he put her down and said, "Oh Kit, I've missed you." They held each other for a while without talking. Then Daniel said, "I've been so wrong Kit, please forgive me. I said that you were not ready but it was me who was not ready. I do love you so much." Kit put her hands up to his face and said, "There's nothing to forgive Danny, I love you. I'm so glad you came back to me."

Daniel led her to the couch and asked her to sit. He went down on one knee and asked, "Kit please come back to live with me and be my wife." Kit was speechless but nodded. When she finally managed to get her voice back, she said, "Daniel, yes, I'll marry you, oh yes, yes, yes." She kissed him with every yes. Daniel brought out a ring from his pocket.

Kit was very surprised to see a ring and said, "You even got a ring?" And when Daniel slipped it on her finger, she said, "It's so beautiful, Daniel!" And she kissed him again. He joined her on the couch and said, "It was my mother's ring." Holding her close, they caught up with what they had done since Kit came to town. When Daniel heard Kit had a job, he said, "I imagine you will want to continue to work for Ted?"

"No, Danny, I just took the work because I could not stand staying in this house all day long. I want to be where you are. That's where my home is," Kit answered.

"Well, if we want to go live at my place, we should get married right away. The road is going to be closed soon. What do you think, Kit? Would that be acceptable for you?"

"Yes, Danny, I was thinking the same. I think we waited long enough. But is it possible to get married in a day?" Kit replied. She was so excited, she gave Daniel a kiss, and said, "Let's call Lilly. She will know what to do." Daniel agreed so Kit called Lilly and asked her to come over, but she did not tell her that Daniel was with her.

When Lilly got to the house, she was surprised to see Daniel's truck. She had been right about Daniel. It was Daniel who greeted her at the door saying, "Oh, Lilly, it's so great to see you. You look wonderful. How are you and Beth?" Lily was surprised by the greeting and at how enthusiastic Daniel was.

"I'm very well and so is Beth," she said, following him to the living room. "What are you up to, Daniel?"

"Well, Lilly," Daniel said as he went to stand by Kit, "we need your help. Kit has agreed to marry me and we want to be married today." Daniel gave her a huge smile.

"Can you help us, Lilly? You know how things like that get done," Kit asked. Lilly was a little perplexed, but she knew her impulsive brother—it was just like him to do something like this.

"Kit, are you sure you want to get married right away? You don't have to rush into…"

Lilly was saying this when Kit interrupted her and said, "Lilly, I love Daniel and I want to marry him. Why would I want to wait?"

"Okay, Kit, I know my brother can be impulsive at times. I just wanted to make sure you were certain," Lilly replied.

"Lilly, I'm not being impulsive. I've been thinking about doing this for a whole year now. When Kit moved to town, it made me realize how much I need her," Daniel said.

"Well then, we have a wedding to plan! And to do it in a day! It's a little rushed but I think it can be done. I'll take Kit with me. We'll have the wedding at Ted's restaurant. Daniel meet us there by five," Lilly said.

Daniel called his father and was informed that he was in a meeting. After leaving a message with his secretary to meet him at Ted's restaurant, Daniel drove to the restaurant. Once there, he doubly surprised Ted by his arrival and by informing him that he and Kit were getting married that day.

"Where is this wedding going to take place?" Ted asked. He followed up with, "Why don't you have it here?"

"I was just going to ask that very question! Thanks, Ted, yes, thank you. I could not think of any other place to get married. Lilly said she and Kit will be meeting us here at five. Is that enough time for you to get things ready?" Daniel asked, a little anxious.

"Daniel, no worries, I'll have everything ready. Now relax. You hungry? I'm about to have lunch. Want to join me?" Ted asked as he walked to a table at the back of the restaurant. Daniel accepted the offer and was just finishing eating when his father joined them. Daniel got up and greeted his dad with a hug.

"It's good to see you, Dad. I have something very important to ask you," Daniel said as they sat down.

Ken gave his son a big smile and said, "I know what you want. Let's see. You asked Kit to marry you and now you want me to perform the ceremony. Right?"

Daniel was a little surprised and asked, "Lilly called you?"

"No, son, I never spoke to Lilly. I think I know you well enough. Kit moves to town then you show up a month later. It's not very hard to figure out. When are we to do this?" Ken replied.

"This afternoon, right here. Lilly is helping Kit get ready and will join us here by five," Daniel replied.

"And you, when are you going to get ready?" Ken asked. Daniel looked at what he was wearing and said, "I'm ready. These are the best clothes I own. Is there something wrong with them?"

Ken shook his head and said, "Daniel, this is your wedding day. I think you should look your very best. Now, let's go, I have something that would be just right."

After a while, Daniel and Ken returned to the restaurant and met Ted in a private dining room just as he was finishing with the wedding preparations. As Daniel came in the room, he noticed a fire in the stone fire place in the corner. It made the dining room feel cozy and warm. In the center of the room was a round table, set with beautiful fine china and crystal wine glasses. Everything looked perfect. *Kit will be pleased when she sees this*, he thought.

"Ted, this looks superb. Is there something I can help with?" Daniel said.

"No, Daniel, I think we have everything ready. My chef is handling the food and this room looks like it is all set. You just have to choose the wine you want." When Daniel shrugged, Ted suggested, "How about champagne? But it's up to you."

"Champagne it is. I'm not a wine guy, but I hear ladies love champagne," Daniel said as he saw the chief and his wife walk in.

The two men greeted each other with a firm handshake, and the chief said, "Daniel, I cannot tell you how surprised I was when Kit phoned to tell me you two were getting married. Congratulations! She asked me to give her away. It's a bit rushed, but I'm very happy for the two of you."

"Thank you, Chief, I'm very pleased that you could do that for Kit." Just as he finished saying this, he saw Lilly walk in the room.

She came to him. "Look at you," she said, "You clean up very nicely Daniel. My guess is dad helped you with the clothes? And you had a haircut and trimmed that bushy beard. You look very handsome." She reached up and gave him a quick kiss on the cheek. She continued saying, "Kit is ready." She looked at Barry and said, "I'll take you to her then we can start the celebrations."

Little Beth walked in carrying a basket of petals which she threw as she walked. When Barry and Kit stepped into the doorway, Daniel was so surprised seeing Kit walk in wearing a beautiful, full-length white gown. She looked like an angel. Her hair was styled in loose curls with tiny white flowers dispersed through them. When she saw Daniel, her face lit up and she gave him the biggest smile.

He was so handsome standing there dressed in a light purple shirt and matching striped tie. He had had his hair cut and had his beard nicely trimmed. She walked toward him and stopped right in front of him. Barry took Kit's hand and placed it in Daniel's hand. All this time, Daniel did not take his eyes off her. He brought her hand up and kissed it saying, "Kit, you are so beautiful."

Ken broke the moment by saying, "Daniel, Kit, are you two ready to begin? I think that everyone is here."

Both looked at Ken and replied, simultaneously, "Yes we are."

Ken led them in their vows, then Daniel slipped a wedding band on Kit's finger. "Daniel, Kit I now pronounce you husband and wife. You may now kiss your bride," Ken said with affection.

Once Daniel and Kit finished their bridely kiss, everyone cheered. The couple was congratulated and best wishes were bestowed upon them. Champagne was brought in and Lilly toasted to the newlyweds saying, "To my loving brother and his lovely wife, you make such an adorable couple. May you be happy and loving to each other for the rest of your lives."

Everyone was invited to be seated then the food was brought in. A delicious salad was served first, followed by prime rib, garlic potatoes and a side serving of asparagus topped with cheese sauce. As they were finishing eating, Ken asked, "Daniel, will you be moving to town now?"

It was Kit who answered. "No, I'll be moving back with Daniel. It's our home." She reached up to Daniel and gave him a kiss.

"If that's what you want," Daniel said as he returned the kiss.

"Yes, Danny, it's all I ever wanted. To be with you," Kit replied, wiping a tear rolling down her cheek.

"You all heard the lady! What the lady wishes is what the lady gets," Daniel said with the biggest smile on his face. He could not have imagined that he could be so happy and contented. Why had he been so reluctant about marrying Kit?

The table was cleared and everyone was chatting when music started to play. Daniel knew this was his sister's doing, and as he looked over to her, she said, "Daniel, Kit told me she loves to dance, so the first dance is for you and your bride."

Daniel knew how much Kit loved to dance so he stood up and asked, "Kit, dear, would you like to dance?" She gave him a big smile and took his hand. They danced together a short time, and then the others joined them on the dancefloor. After dancing a waltz and the two-step, Kit requested they have a line dance. Though Daniel disliked that dance, he joined in. Try as he may, he could not keep in step with the others so he went to sit down and watched as the others danced. He watched as Kit and his sister danced. Their steps perfectly matched. It gave him joy to see that Lilly had accepted Kit in the family so easily.

The music and dancing stopped when a wedding cake was brought in. When Kit saw the cake and who was bringing it in, she said, "You made a wedding cake for us? Thank you, Anna!"

"When Ted told me you were getting married, well I just had to make you one. A lovely cake for a beautiful bride," Anna said, giving Kit a hug. She turned to Daniel and said, "So, you're Kit's Daniel. She talked of you all the time. I hope you know how much she loves you. Tradition has it that the newlyweds cut the cake," Anna said handing a knife to Daniel.

After Daniel and Kit had cut a piece, Daniel took a small piece and brought it up to Kit's mouth. When Kit saw what Daniel was doing, she automatically opened her mouth and ate the cake.

"Daniel, what are you doing? Why did you do that?" Kit asked surprised by his action.

Daniel gave her a kiss and said, "Kit love, it's a custom. Now do the same for me." After they had finished with the custom, they served everyone a piece.

"Daniel, Kit, it has been such a lovely wedding but it's getting late. I think it's time I got Beth home," Lilly said.

"Lilly, thank you for all your help," Daniel said, giving his sister a hug and a kiss.

"You and Ted have made it all happen. Thank you," Kit added and gave Lilly a hug. Once Lilly and Beth had gone, Daniel and Kit thanked everyone for making their wedding day so special. And with well-wishes, they were off.

Kit was surprised when Daniel did not drive to her house. She asked, "Daniel, where are we going?"

"Kit, my love, I have a reservation at this fancy hotel in the honeymoon suite."

Kit was surprised. She had thought of spending their first night at her place, not in a honeymoon suite. "A honeymoon suite, ah, what is that like?" She did not want to let on that she had no clue what that was.

Daniel gave her a smile and said, "Kit, let me surprise you, I think you will like it. Just wait and see."

When they got to their room, Daniel said, "It's tradition for a husband to carry his bride over the threshold."

"There sure are a lot of traditions in getting married," Kit said as Daniel picked her up and walked in the room. She could not believe she was in the most beautiful room she had ever seen, with red satin curtains covering the large windows, and a white plush carpet on the floor. As Daniel stood her up, she said, "Oh my, this is so beautiful! Are you sure this is for us? I'm scared of even walking on this carpet."

"Yes, Kit, this is our honeymoon night. I want it to be special," Daniel said, giving her a kiss. Kit took off her shoes and walked to the large canopy bed in the center of the room. The bed had a thick white comforter on which lay rose petals forming a heart. She touched the petals and brought one up to smell it. She looked at Daniel and said, "These are real rose petals."

Daniel came to stand by her and said, "Look, Kit, there's some champagne, would you like a glass?" He walked over to the table where the bottle of champagne was and opened it.

"Yes, Danny, that would be lovely," Kit said as she went to sit in one of two luxurious red chairs overlooking the large window.

He handed her a glass and said, raising his glass, "To you, Kit, you make me so happy. I love you."

They took a sip and then Kit said, "You have given me so much, Daniel. I love you too and always will."

After spending their first night as husband and wife in a honeymoon suite, the newlyweds went to Kit's house to pack up her belongings. They stopped by Barry's office to give him the house key and asked him to care for the house. After saying goodbye to the family, they drove to their mountain home.

It surprised Charlie to see Daniel's truck come up the drive and to see Kit with him. He stopped chopping wood and went to meet them.

"Hey, you two. I did not expect to see you for another few days," he said, shaking Daniel's hand and giving Kit a hug. "Daniel, how did you talk Kit in coming back?"

"Well, Charlie, all I had to do was marry her," Daniel replied with the biggest smile on his face.

"No, you didn't! Really? Now that is the best news I've heard in a long time. Congratulations, you two!" Charlie said as he gave them both another hug.

"I'm sorry that you and your family were not there. It all happened so fast. I hope you will forgive us?" Kit said as she returned the hug.

"I wish I could have been there. But in a way, I think I helped it happen," Charlie replied. "By the look of that sky, I best pack my things and get going. I think we are in for a dump of snow," he continued saying as they all walked in the house.

Within an hour of Daniel and Kit's arrival home, Charlie had packed and was ready to go back home. He said, "Well, I think that's it. Daniel, take care. We'll see you for spring break." He gave him a big bear hug. Then to Kit he said, "I'm very pleased to have you part of this family. I can see you make Daniel very happy. Take care of each other." He gave her a hug. Daniel and Kit went outside to see Charlie off and as Charlie drove away, Daniel said, "Drive carefully. Thanks for all your help!"

The newlyweds were now on their own at their mountain home. They held each other close as they watched the big flakes of snow come down, isolating them from the rest of the world. Daniel realized he felt contented and things had never been so right with his life.

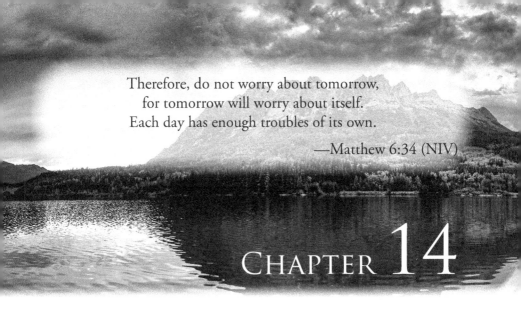

Therefore, do not worry about tomorrow,
for tomorrow will worry about itself.
Each day has enough troubles of its own.

—Matthew 6:34 (NIV)

CHAPTER 14

The days turned into weeks, and the weeks into months. Each day, they got to know each other better. Daniel loved that Kit could show her love for him so easily. Before their marriage, he had been careful to keep Kit at a distance, never sharing any feelings he felt about her living with him or how his previous life had been. Now he was much more open with her, telling her about his life as a little boy, and how he had left the police force to move to their mountain home.

Kit grew more confident in herself and loved to tease Daniel and enticed him to be more playful. With Kit in his life, he learned to relax, and be less serious, less on edge. He loved the freedom and the joy of life she had. This surprised him considering what she had suffered in her youth. One evening as they danced, he asked her, "How do you do it, Kit?"

"Do what, my love?" she asked rubbing herself against him, the way they did in Dirty Dancing.

"You know, you're always happy. Considering what happened to you when you were young, you could have a very negative attitude about life. But you have such a loving way about you," he answered.

Kit stopped dancing and said, "Danny, I don't think about it. It's something that happened to someone else. I'm not that person anymore. I'm yours now. You have made me so happy. That's all I care about."

"Yes, you are my sweet wife. Let's go to bed, it's getting late," Daniel said, picking her up and carried her to bed.

They celebrated Christmas and the New Year all on their own. On Christmas day, they exchanged gifts, not bought ones but ones they made for each other. Kit had made a Christmas cake with apples and cranberries and presented it to Daniel as her gift to him. Daniel had made a wooden centerpiece decorated with cedar boughs and pine cones. Kit loved it and placed it in the middle of the table. With Christmas music playing on the radio, they feasted on a chicken supper with stuffing, and vegetables from their garden. Everything was perfect except that they missed their family.

After the new year, Kit woke up feeling sick. Daniel was up, starting a fire in the stove when Kit ran downstairs and to the out-house to throw up. When she returned, Daniel saw that she had no color in her face and asked, "Kit, you okay? You're a little pale."

"I don't know, Danny, my stomach hurts. Do you think I could have the flu?" Kit said.

"I hope not, Kit. Would you like a glass of water?" Daniel asked. He brought her a glass and touched her forehead to see if she felt warm. "You don't feel like you have a fever. Why don't you go lay on the couch? The stove will be nice and warm soon." Kit took a drink of water and walked to the couch.

"Okay, but first I think…"

Kit could not finish the sentence because another wave of nausea hit her. She ran from the kitchen. When she returned, she looked even paler. *What in the world is wrong with her?* Daniel thought.

Kit went to lie down. She felt better lying down so she stayed on the couch while Daniel made and ate his breakfast. Daniel went outside to care for the animals and to do other chores. When he came back in, Kit was sitting up. He joined her on the couch and asked, "How are you doing, sweetheart? Feeling better?"

"Yes, I actually feel hungry. Maybe I could try some crackers?" Kit replied. After she had eaten, Kit got up, washed her face, and went to get dressed. By supper time, she felt good again so she ate ravenously.

The next morning when Kit got up, the nausea returned. After the second time Kit had run to the outhouse, Daniel became very concerned. Kit looked so sick. He got a blanket, wrapped her in it and carried her to the couch.

"Danny, I feel like I'm going to die. My stomach hurts so much. What is wrong with me?" she cried.

"You must have the flu, my love. Lie down and keep warm. These things don't usually last for long."

Again by supper time, Kit felt good, but this time she ate lightly.

On the fourth morning of Kit getting sick, it occurred to Daniel that Kit could be pregnant. He remembered Lilly being sick in the morning, then feeling better by suppertime. That evening, he said to Kit, "I think I know why you're getting sick in the morning. It's called morning sickness."

Kit gave him a smile and said, "Of course, it's morning sickness. I'm sick in the morning. You silly."

Daniel returned the smile and said, "Do you know what it means when a woman has morning sickness?"

Kit suddenly understood what Daniel was saying and said in a stunned voice, "Oh no, you think that I might be pregnant?"

"It's possible Kit. We never did anything to prevent it," Daniel said.

"Yeah, I know, it's just... I never thought it would happen this quickly," she said. "I'm going to be a mom, Danny!" Then she panicked and said, "But I don't know the first thing about being a mom."

"Kit, don't worry, it's going to be alright. I'll be with you. We're in this together," Daniel reassured her, then continued saying, "We'll have to go see a doctor to make sure all is okay. We'll go as soon as the road opens up." Daniel held her for a long time, making sure that Kit felt loved.

"Yes, and we can tell Lilly and your dad. Oh, Daniel this is just too much but in a good way," Kit said.

Kit's morning sickness continued for another month, but Kit was feeling well again when Charlie arrived with his family for spring

break. Daniel was so relieved to see him. From the first day he realized that Kit was pregnant, he had been worried but had never voiced
any of his concerns to Kit.

"Welcome to our mountain home," Kit said as she greeted them
with hugs and kisses. "How are you all? It's so good to have you here."
Carol took one look at Kit and she knew that Kit was in the family
way. She said, "Kit, how is the mother to be? Look at you, you look
great! Married life suits you well."

Kit was a little surprised by her comment and said, "How did
you know? Did Danny say anything to you?"

"No, I just know the look women have when they are pregnant.
How are you feeling?" Carol asked.

"I'm well now," Kit said.

"It's wonderful news," Charlie said as he hugged Kit. He turned
to Daniel and said as he gave him a hug, "Congratulations man. You
a dad? I just can't picture that."

Daniel returned the hug and said, "Thanks Charlie, I can't
believe it myself."

While the adults were talking, the boys played chess. Liam suddenly said, "Uncle Daniel, we miss Misty. Did you ever find what
happened to her?"

"No, I kept looking for her but I never found a trace of her. I
just don't know what happened to her," Daniel replied.

"She was such a nice dog. I loved playing with her," Liam said.
"I wish she was still here."

"Yeah, me too. She sure was a character," Daniel said in agreement.

That evening, Carol made a special supper to celebrate Daniel
and Kit's union and for the soon to be baby. Candles were set up all
over the house to set a romantic feel to the celebrations. After they
had enjoyed their supper, Carol had another surprise. She presented
them with a wedding gift. To Daniel and Kit's surprise, it was a quilt
that Carol had made for them. When the quilt was spread out, it
depicted Daniel's mountain home. There were four panels that made
up the quilt: one panel was a picture of the house, one of the barn,
one of the pasture behind the house and one of the driveway coming
to the house.

"This is so special, Carol. Thank you. How ever did you do this? It's beautiful! It portrays this place so well. Thanks again," Daniel said, giving her a kiss and a hug. Then Kit joined in saying, "We'll forever cherish this. Thanks, Carol."

Once the kitchen had been cleaned, Carol saw how sad the boys were, so she said, "Boys let's go for a walk. It's nice outside. We can go walk along the lake."

"That's a good idea, Carol. Why don't we all go?" Charlie said.

When they got to the shore, the boys challenged each other to see who could throw a rock the farthest. Once the boys got tired of throwing rocks, they continued their walk and ended up by the barn.

"Let's go see the cow you brought," Daniel said as he opened the barn door. Carol found the wind off the lake a little cold, so she, the boys and Kit decided to go back in the house, leaving Daniel and Charlie at the barn.

As they went in the barn, Charlie said, "She's just young so she might give you some trouble. I milked her a few times. She's a bit jumpy but she'll settle down."

Daniel gave him a smile and said, "We'll get to be friends, she'll learn."

"Is there anything special you want me to do when you're away?" Charlie asked.

"No, nothing special. There's two hens sitting on eggs. They might be hatching little ones before we come back, that's about all. We shouldn't be gone longer than a week," Daniel replied.

The next morning, Daniel and Kit set off for town. They drove a while without talking. Then Daniel said with some relief in his voice, "It feels good to be going to town. It will be nice to see the family again."

Kit agreed with him then asked, "Danny have you been worried?"

Daniel gave her a quick look then said, "Yes. I worry about you, Kit. You were sick for a long time. I want to make sure you're okay. Once the doctor says you're alright then I'll stop worrying."

Kit reached over and gave his arm a squeeze. "Oh, my love, I told you I feel fine. Stop being a worrywart."

Once in town, they drove straight to Lilly's house. Lilly and Beth were sitting on the porch swing when they drove up.

"Hey, how nice to see you two," Daniel said as he got out of his truck. He gave his sister a big hug and went to pick up Beth. Kit was right behind him greeting Lilly with another hug.

"Yes, it's been a long time. How are you two?" Lilly asked. "I'm so pleased to see you both. How was the winter?"

"We are just the best, Lilly. This winter went on for too long. But we kept nice and warm." Kit looked to Daniel to see if he would tell her about the baby, and when he did not, she decided to follow suit. Lilly invited them into the house and offered them something to drink. Then she said, "I have to call Ted to tell him we have company." As she made the call, Daniel picked up Beth, and giving her a hug, he said, "How's my best little niece doing?"

"I'm good, Uncle Daniel, I wish I could see you more often. I miss you," Beth said.

"I miss you too, peanut," Daniel said, then asked, "Do you have any new interesting toys to show me?"

"Oh, yes! Come and see. You too, Aunty Kit! It's in my room," Beth said as she jumped off Daniel's lap and ran to her room. When they got to her room, they were surprised to see a big doll house. It took up a corner of the room and was as high as Beth was tall. "My dad made it for me. See, it opens up in the middle," Beth said as she opened the house up.

On one side of the house, there were miniature shelves and on them were all the Shopkins. Beth pointed to them and said, "This side is the store and on the other side is where my dolls live. I sleep my baby doll here in the day, but at night she sleeps with me. And, see the lights work." She switched the lights on and off. She continued showing them the life-like kitchen, the staircase, and the two bedrooms with plush white carpets.

"This is sure a wonderful dollhouse, Beth. You are one lucky little girl," Kit told her as they sat on the floor playing with the house. Beth was still showing them things on the house when Ted and Ken came home.

172

"Oh, daddy's home," Beth said and ran from the room. Daniel and Kit followed her to the kitchen, and they were greeted by Ted and Ken. It took only minutes to have supper ready to eat. As they ate, they made small talk about life in general. It was when Lilly was dishing out some cake that Daniel made a slip by saying, "Give Kit a double portion. After all, she's eating for two now."

Lilly just about dropped the plate she was handing to Kit. "What did you just say? Are you saying Kit is pregnant?"

"Yes, I am Lilly. I was wondering how long Daniel could keep it a secret," Kit answered with a big smile on her face.

Daniel saw the look of surprise on his sister's face and said with laughter in his voice, "I told you we kept nice and warm."

"Oh, Daniel. Why didn't you tell me when you first arrived? That is wonderful news, isn't it?" Lilly asked.

"We wanted everyone here before saying anything. We think it's good news but a little overwhelming. Would you know of a baby doctor we would be able to see on short notice, Lilly?" Daniel asked.

Lilly went to give Kit a hug, then said, "Yes, I could call my obstetrician and set up an appointment. I'm pretty sure she would be able to take you right away."

"Thanks, Lilly. Kit had morning sickness very bad. I want to be sure all is okay with her and the baby," Daniel replied, squeezing Kit's hand. Everyone looked at Kit making her very uncomfortable. She looked at Daniel and said, "Danny is such a worrywart. I feel fine now but I do think it is a good idea to see the doctor." Everyone congratulated them.

"Do you know when this baby is due?" Ken asked.

"Well, I think it will be sometime in October. When we see the doctor, we'll know more," Daniel replied.

"With the baby coming will you be moving to town?" Lilly asked.

"I don't know. Kit doesn't want to move to town. We will see what the doctor says," Daniel replied. Daniel could tell this was upsetting Kit, so he changed the subject by asking Lilly how her business was doing.

The conversation continued until Ken said, "This has been a very nice evening with everyone together. But it's time for me to get home." Ted usually drove Ken back home, but tonight Ken said, "Ted, it's alright, I'll walk home. I need some exercise after all the food I ate."

"Dad, I'll walk you home. After that long drive, I need to stretch my legs," Daniel said. Turning to Kit, he said, "Kit, you okay with me going with Dad?"

"Yes, of course, Danny. I can visit with Lilly and Ted, and catch up on what has happened over winter," Kit replied. After Daniel gave Kit a kiss, he and Ken said goodnight to the others and left.

As they walked, they chatted about small things. Ken asked about Charlie and how the winter had been. When they were just about at his place, Ken asked, "How are you doing with your studies?"

"Well, I've finished all of the curriculum the professor gave me to study. I've read all the law books you lent me. I'm sure I could pass the bar exam. I'll call my professor and see what he thinks I should do next," Daniel replied.

"Glad to hear that Daniel. I'm sure you could ace it," his father said as they came to the front door.

"There's a semi-final game of hockey on TV, would you like to come in and watch it with me?" Ken asked.

"Okay, I haven't watched a game in a long time. I don't even know the teams anymore," Daniel said. As he walked in the house he remembered with fond memories the many times he and his dad had watched games together. After he called Kit to tell her that he was watching the game, he joined Ken in the living room.

The next week proved to be a very busy one. Kit and Daniel had an appointment to meet with Lilly's obstetrician. After meeting with the doctor, Kit had an ultrasound and blood works done. Once the results of the tests were in, the doctor told Kit and Daniel that both mother and baby were in excellent health, and she confirmed the due date to be at the end of October. The doctor very patiently answered all the questions they had, making Kit feel more confident about becoming a mother.

Daniel met with his law professor, and after some discussions, arrangements were made for Daniel to take the law exam. As he drove back to Lilly's, he started to worry. What if there was something on the exam he had not studied? He remembered what the professor had told him: "Just use the knowledge you have and you'll be alright."

On the day of the exam, he assured himself that what he had studied would get him through the exam. When he finished writing, he felt sure that he had passed it. His professor informed him that it would be some time before he got the results.

After spending the week in town and they had accomplished all they had set to do, they said goodbye to the family and headed home. On the drive back Daniel said, "I'm so grateful that you and the baby are all right. Maybe we should be thinking about moving back to town."

Kit gave him a smile and said, "The doctor said all is okay with me and the baby. Stop with your worrying, we'll be just fine."

By the time they arrived home they had agreed that they would continue to live at their mountain home for the summer. Charlie and his family were happy to see them and happy to hear that all was okay with Kit and the baby. When it was time for Charlie to return home, Daniel and Kit thanked them for coming and for all their help.

One afternoon, Kit was alone at the house when she heard a snort at the front door. She looked up and saw a massive brown bear sniffing at the screen door. Without any hesitation, she ran to the door and slammed it shut. Then she put the two by four in the slots on both sides of the door to bar it.

When she took a peek out of the window, she saw that the bear was off the deck and heading toward the barn. She went to the side window just in time to see the bear stand up on his hind legs and come down right on the chicken wire surrounding the pen. The frightened chickens scurried as fast as they could into their coop. Again, the bear reared up and came down on another section of the wire. This time the whole fence went down. The next thing she saw was Daniel driving up by the barn headings straight for the bear, honking the horn. When the bear saw the truck barrelling toward him, he took off down the driveway. Daniel kept going at it until the bear ran in the trees and could not be seen anymore.

When he returned home, Kit was waiting for him on the deck. She came running to the truck and said, "I'm sure glad you came when you did. The bear was right at the front door sniffing the air. I ran and I slammed the door shut on him." Kit explained. She didn't know whether to laugh or cry because she felt so frightened. Daniel noticed that she was shaking so he walked her to the house and they both went to sit on the couch.

"Kit, are you okay? I should have never left you alone," Daniel said.

"Just a little shaken, that's all. I have never seen such a big bear. He demolished the chicken pen. He must have been ten-feet tall when he stood up. He sure looked mean," Kit said, cozying up to Daniel.

"That was a grizzly bear. There must be something wrong with him. They don't usually attack like that. We should stay close to the house. He might be back," Daniel said.

In the following days, Daniel carried his rifle everywhere he went. He did not let on but he had a feeling this bear would be back. By the end of the week, the bear proved him right. Daniel was just finishing fixing the wire around the chicken pen when he saw the bear walk up the driveway. As he ran for his rifle, he yelled to Kit to stay in the house. The bear was by his truck. The next thing he saw was the bear standing up and coming down with both of his front paws right on top of the hood of the truck. Daniel could not believe what he saw.

"Hey, that's my truck!" he yelled at the bear and shot a bullet right above the bear's head. Instead of scaring the bear away, it only made him mad. He turned toward Daniel and stood there, shaking his huge head from side to side. Daniel stood his ground with the rifle aimed right at the bear. In a flash, the bear charged. Daniel fired two quick shots and the bear fell to the ground, just mere feet away from where he stood. Daniel did not take any chances that the bear was still alive, so he put another shot in his head, right between his eyes. Kit watched all this from the dining room window. She was so traumatised by what she saw, her knees buckled from under her and she slid to the floor. When Daniel came in the house, he found her sitting on the floor.

"Kit, what's wrong?" he said as he ran to her, picked her up and laid her on the couch.

"Daniel, that bear could have killed you." She sat up and threw her arms around his neck. "I don't think I have ever been so scared. You were so brave. How did you ever do that, Daniel? You just stood there when this massive bear ran at you. Weren't you scared?"

Daniel held her close and said, "I don't think I had time to be scared. I just did what I had to do to keep us safe. Are you okay, Kit? This can't be good for you or the baby."

"Danny, I'm a little shaken but I feel fine. I'll be okay. The bear is dead now. There wouldn't be two of them, right?"

"Yeah, it's dead. Now we have a huge, dead bear in the yard. What ever do you do with that?" Daniel asked. They sat together for a while. Then Daniel said, "I'm going to have to report I shot this bear. I'll go see if the game warden is at the lake. The campsite should be opening soon. He might just be there."

"Danny, can I come with you? I know that the bear is dead, but I don't want to stay here with it."

"Of course, you're coming with me. From now on, you are not leaving my side," Daniel said, giving her a kiss and helping her stand up. Her legs were still weak but she managed to follow Daniel outside.

Daniel just about cried when he saw the damage to his truck. The hood was practically flattened, and Daniel noticed that it would not latch. The truck could not be driven like this. He would have to somehow bring the hood back to shape so it could be latched. He put the hood up and hammered it somewhat back to shape until it would latch properly.

"That bear would have demolished the truck if you hadn't stopped him. What a crazy bear. Why would he do something like that?" Kit asked as they drove down to the lake.

"I don't know. He must be sick or very old. Maybe he lost his mind. Now I'll have to get the truck fixed. The hood will stay latched, but I can't leave it like that," Daniel said with disgust.

They got to the lake just as the warden was getting in his truck. Daniel parked by him and went to talk to him. He introduced himself to the warden and told him where he lived. Kit stayed in the truck.

The first thing the warden noticed was the hood and he asked, "What happened to your truck? Looks like a bear walked over it."

"Yes, and that bear is now dead in my yard," Daniel said with some satisfaction. He went on to tell him what the bear had done. The warden asked, "Was it a big grizzly?"

Daniel said, "Yeah, the biggest I've ever seen!"

The warden gave a chuckle and said, "You probably killed old grouch! He sure gave us trouble last summer. I trapped him last spring and tried to relocate him four hundred miles from here. He was back within two weeks. You should have seen when I let him out of the trap. He was so mad. Instead of running away, like most bears do, he attacked the cage. I got out of there so fast. When he came back, I tried to trap him again but he never took the bait. Instead, he attacked the trap and broke off one of the trap doors. I tell you that bear was vengeful. If you did something to him, he would come back and take his revenge any way he could. But I've never known him to go after any person."

Daniel agreed and said, "Well he certainly took his revenge on my truck. Now I have this huge bear lying dead in my yard. Can you help me get rid of it?"

"I'll have to get a bigger truck, then I'll take it away for you. Might take me a day or so."

"Good, the sooner the better," Daniel replied.

"Would you mind if I came to look at it today?" the warden asked.

"Sure, I'll meet you back at my place," Daniel said. He went back to his truck and drove back home.

Kit stood way back as the warden and Daniel went to take a closer look at the bear. The warden looked at the bear's paws and noticed that on one paw, there were some claws missing. When he looked in it's mouth, he noticed that most of the teeth were worn down and some were rotten.

"He looks to be a very old bear. He must have been in pain or something to make him act like he did," the warden said. Once they were finished examining the bear, Daniel invited the warden in for coffee. When they were in the house, Daniel introduce Kit to him. He in turn introduced himself as Wayne.

"When I took the job last summer, I was told about you. I had hoped to come by to see you but I never found the time," Wayne said. "They were expanding the campsite and my job was to oversee the work. Time just flew by."

"It's a nice place to camp by the lake. I stayed there my first night on the mountain. I guess more and more people will be coming now that the campsite is larger," Daniel remarked.

"Yes, but it's only for the summer months. There's a plan to put in a phone. That will help if there are any emergencies. It should be in sometimes in July," Wayne said. Daniel agreed that a phone would definitely be a good thing. Wayne finished his coffee and promised to come back to take the bear away.

That night, Kit had a terrifying dream that the bear was coming for her. She woke up with a scream, scaring Daniel awake. "What? What? Kit, you in pain?" He reached for her in the dark and brought her close to him.

Kit was still shaking but said, "I'm fine. No pain, just a nightmare of the bear. I'm going to be happy when I see it gone."

"Yes, I'm with you on that." Daniel tried to go back to sleep but his thoughts kept him awake. *I should take Kit back to town, what are we doing living here with a baby on the way. I'm going to talk to Kit in the morning.*

As they were having breakfast, he said, "Kit, maybe we should think about moving to town. It might be better for you and the baby."

"Danny, I'm fine, stop your worrying. The bear is dead now. We just put in the garden. I think we can stay for the summer," Kit replied.

"Yes, I worry about you and the baby. I want you to be safe. I don't want anything bad to happen to you," Daniel said, trying to convince her to move.

Kit looked at him and explained, "Danny, in town I always feel uneasy and agitated. Here I feel safe and at home. Isn't that better for the baby? Please, Danny, let's stay for the summer."

"Kit, okay, just for the summer. Once the phone is in at the campsite, I'll call the doctor for an appointment. Maybe Ted and Lilly can come up to care for the place when we go to town," Daniel said.

As the summer progressed, Daniel became very uneasy. He kept a close eye on Kit. He tried to do more of the work himself, to a point that Kit sometimes felt she was suffocating. Kit never said anything for she knew he was worried, and if she protested, he would say it was time to move to town.

Every weekend, Daniel would go check to see if the phone was working and on the last week of July, to his relief, the phone worked so he phoned his dad. When he came back home, he did not tell Kit that the phone was working. She did not ask, because if it did work, he would certainly tell her, she thought.

A few days later, on a cold, rainy day, Daniel and Kit were in the house when Daniel happened to look outside. He saw a car coming into the yard. "We have visitors," he said and went to the door. Kit followed.

"It's my dad. I called him the last time I went to see if the phone worked."

Kit was shocked and said, "The phone worked and you never told me?"

"Kit, honey, I wanted to surprise you," he said as he brought her close and kissed her. "Don't be upset."

"I'm not upset, just very surprised. Danny, you should have told me," Kit said, returning the kiss. Ken's car came to a stop beside the house and it was Daniel's turn to be surprised when he saw Lilly and Beth were with him.

"I didn't know you were coming," Daniel said as he gave his sister a hug.

"Surprise! I've been wanting to come for so long and when Dad said he was coming, I decided I had to come too," Lilly said. She turned to Kit and said, giving her a hug, "Kit, you look so wonderful. How are you doing?"

"I'm very well, Lilly. Come, let's go in the house. It's a bit cold out here," Kit said.

"I can't believe how beautiful it is up here. I can see why you would want to stay here, Kit," Lilly said as Daniel came in the house carrying Beth on his back.

"Lilly, what do you think? How do you like my place?" Daniel asked as he put Beth down.

"It's very rustic but I like it. Everything here looks so fresh— even the air smells different. Would you show me around?"

The rain had stopped so Daniel took their visitors outside and showed them around. Lilly was impressed with all the work Daniel had done on the barn, and when she saw the big garden, she said, "Daniel, what a lovely vegetable garden! I never knew you liked gardening."

Daniel smiled at her and replied, "It's not that I like to garden so much but that I like to eat."

Lilly snickered and said, "Yes, gardening is a lot of work. Garden vegetables are so much tastier."

Kit had made coffee and it was ready when they returned to the house. They sat around the kitchen table and visited for a while. When Daniel and Ken went outside to get the luggage and the supplies they had brought, Ken said, "Daniel, I have the law exam results. I thought it would be better to give this to you when we were alone." He reached in his inside coat pocket and handed Daniel an envelope.

Daniel looked at the envelope and said, "I've been wondering if you had them. Now that they're here, I don't know if I want to know."

"Well, son, go ahead and open it; unless you want to be alone to see the results?" Ken said.

"No, let's go back in the house. I'll open it with everyone there," Daniel replied.

Once they had brought all the things in the house, Daniel said, "Dad just handed me my results." As everyone looked on, Daniel slowly opened the envelope and saw the mark but did not say what it was.

"Danny what does it say?" Kit said.

Lilly chimed in and said, "Yeah, what does it say?"

Daniel looked up and said, "Well, it looks like I passed!" Everyone gathered around to congratulate him. "That is wonderful Daniel, that calls for a celebration!" Lilly said.

"Yes, you're right Lilly. That's why I brought some wine." Ken opened the bottle and they all toasted to Daniels achievement.

The next day, after showing his dad how to care for the animals and showing his sister around the kitchen, Daniel and Kit set off for town. When Daniel drove his truck out of the garage, Ken noticed the hood and asked, "What in the world happened to your truck?"

"We had a close encounter with a grizzly," Daniel said but did not give anymore details.

"Where is this bear now?" Ken asked. "He's not going to show up when your gone, right?"

"No, relax, I killed it. He attacked my truck so I put three bullets in him." He went on to explain what had happened and how the game warden had taken it away.

Ken was astonished and said, "You faced a charging grizzly and shot him down? You make it sound like it's an everyday thing. Daniel that took a lot of courage. I don't think I could have done that."

"Dad, it's surprising what you can do when it comes to protecting the ones you love," Daniel said as Kit came to the truck with Lilly and Beth. Daniel helped her in the truck and said, "Dad don't worry. We haven't seen any wild animals for a while now. You'll be okay. Once we're finished at the doctor's, we'll come right back."

Beth was standing by him so Daniel picked her up and said, "Beth, make sure you listen to Mommy and Grandpa. I might even bring you back something." He put Beth down and before Lilly could ask him about his truck, he said goodbye to everyone, got in the truck and drove off.

As they drove down the road, Kit sang along with the radio and at the end of the song, she said, "Beth is such a lovely little girl. I like it when she calls me Aunty Kit. She makes me feel so special."

"She sure is special. We'll have to get her something from town," Daniel said.

They were just in time for the doctor's appointment. After the doctor examined Kit and blood tests were done, Kit and the baby were declared in excellent health. Before heading back home, Daniel stopped at a dealership to see if he could get a new hood. The attendant at the dealership informed him that one would have to be brought in. After ordering a hood, they quickly went shopping and headed for home. It was very late when they arrived. Ken and Lilly were sleeping so they quietly went to bed.

In the morning, Daniel was up before the others. He went to tend to the animals and was entering the house when he met his dad. "Good morning, Dad. How did you sleep?"

"Good morning, son, I slept like a baby. I was just on my way to milk the cow but I see you already did."

"Yeah, how did it go yesterday?" Daniel said as he placed the pail of milk on the counter and took the eggs from out of his pocket.

"It went very well. It reminded me of my boyhood. Beth loved the chickens. I think she gave them all a name. That black rooster sure is mean, though. He attacked me the first time I went in the coop," Ken replied.

Daniel was alarmed by the rooster attack and said, "Did he hurt you? He's only nice to Kit."

"No, I saw him coming and got out of his way. He left Beth alone. I guess he does not like men," Ken said.

Daniel and Ken were having coffee when Lilly and Beth got up. Beth went to sit by Daniel. She wanted to ask him if he had brought her something but knew not to ask. Daniel finished his coffee and said, "Beth just wait here; I have something for you." Daniel quickly came back holding two boxes.

Beth's eyes grew bigger as she eyed the boxes. "What is it, Uncle?"

"Well, open the boxes and see," Daniel said as he placed the boxes on the table. Little Beth pulled the cover off one box and found toy furniture: a couch and a lounge chair. And in the other box was a table and four chairs. "Ah, this will fit in my doll house perfectly. Thank you so much, Uncle Daniel." She gave Daniel a hug.

"Give Kit a hug too, because it was her idea," Daniel said. Beth turned to Kit, gave her a hug and said, "Thank you, Aunty Kit."

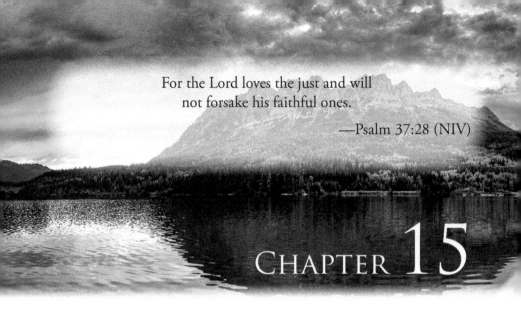

For the Lord loves the just and will
not forsake his faithful ones.

—Psalm 37:28 (NIV)

CHAPTER 15

One evening, as they sat on the front deck watching the sunset, Daniel said, "We should start to think about moving to town soon."

Kit gave him a smile. "I suppose, but why not stay 'til after your birthday? By then we will have most of the garden harvested."

Daniel shook his head and said, "We said at the end of summer. Why do you want to change it now?"

"Danny, I feel good and the doctor said I was in good shape. One more month will not hurt. Please, Danny, one more month," Kit said, using her sweetest voice. Daniel could not argue with her so he agreed to stay. They busied themselves with harvesting the garden, packing their belongings and preparing the property for when they would not be there. It wasn't until Daniel's birthday, that Kit realized the month had gone by.

"Where has the time gone?" she said as she served Daniel a piece of birthday cake.

"I don't know." Daniel answered, "Hard to believe it took us this long to prepare for the move. I just have a few things left to do, then we'll be ready."

A week after Daniel's birthday, they were set to move to town. All their personal possessions were packed. The canned goods were in boxes and vegetables in bins, ready to be put in the truck. Daniel went out to get the truck closer to the house. He turned the key but to his shock, the truck did not start. All he heard was a clicking sound. His heart sank. Now what were they going to do?

When he returned to the house, Kit saw the troubled look on his face and said, "Daniel what is the matter?"

"The truck won't start. I think the starter is gone," Daniel said disheartened.

"Oh, no, I'm so sorry. What are we going to do, Daniel? Is there any way you can fix it? You fixed the generator, maybe you can fix the starter," Kit said, worried that it was her fault.

"No, I don't know how to fix a starter. What I need is a new starter and that means I have to somehow get to town," Daniel said. He sat down and passed his hands through his hair and continued, "It will take days to get there on foot."

Kit began to get very worried. Suddenly, the remoteness of where they lived became real to her. "Oh Daniel, there has to be something we can do," she said as she looked to Daniel for reassurance. He went to put his arm around her. As he did, he felt that Kit was shaking. He led her to the couch. They sat holding each other for a while not saying anything. Then Daniel said, "Well I could take my old bike and go to the campsite to call Charlie."

He got up and ran to the garage. The bike had been hanging on the inside wall of the garage since he had moved there. He took it down and noticed the chain was a little rusty and that the tires needed air. He oiled the chain and pumped air in the tires, and rode it around the yard.

"It should get me where I want to go," he said, getting off the bike. With a packed lunch and water bottle, Daniel set off for the campsite. He gave Kit a goodbye kiss and said, "I should be back before supper. You just rest. Bye, Sweetheart."

The ride down to the campsite was easy enough, mostly down hill. When he got to the gate to the campsite, he found it closed. He walked to where the phone booth was. His heart sank when he saw that the phone was missing from the booth. "Oh, what in the world am I suppose to do now?" he said aloud. He felt so beaten and frustrated.

As he walked back to his bike, he kicked at rocks in front of him. He had only one mission now: to somehow get to town. When he had ridden back to the main road, he took the road toward town. *There's no sense going back home*, he thought.

By mid-afternoon, he came to the rest stop by the side of the road, and to his astonishment, he saw a vehicle there. He rode to it but did not see anyone around. "Hello, is anyone here?" he yelled as he checked the jeep. He tried the driver's door and to his surprise, it opened. He looked inside and found the keys were in the ignition. *Why would anyone leave his vehicle here with the keys in it?* Daniel wondered. He pressed on the horn a few times and waited. He went and sat in the jeep, and waited some more to see if anyone had heard the horn. *What if I took the jeep and drove to where I find a phone signal. I could call Charlie. I could be back before they ever knew I took their jeep*, he thought.

He got out of the jeep and yelled again. Then he went to honk the horn again. After waiting over a half-hour more and no one appeared, he got in the jeep and drove away.

Meanwhile, Rodney, the owner of the jeep, and his girl friend, Emma, were hiking down the foot trail that led from the rest stop to the far side of the lake. Rodney was an amateur photography buff and he wanted to get pictures of the lake with the mountains in the background. Rodney worked as an EMT and had met Emma when he had brought in a patient to the emergency room where she worked as a nurse.

That morning, the sun was just over the horizon when Rodney stopped to pick up Emma. She had packed all the necessary things for a picnic.

As they drove, Rodney's spirit lifted. He was looking forward to spending the day with Emma, hiking and taking pictures. "We finally get to do this. Looks like it's going to be a beautiful day," he said.

"Yes, I think so too. I can't believe we finally have days off together. We've been planning this hike all summer," Emma said, enjoying the scenery.

It was mid-morning when they arrived at the rest stop. They stepped out of the jeep and as they were putting on their packs,

Rodney said, "I think I'll leave the keys in the jeep. I'd hate to lose them on the hike."

"You sure you want to do that?" Emma asked.

"There's no one around. If they got here, they'd have their own vehicle. Why would they take mine?" Rodney replied as he went to read the information sign at the head of the trail.

"Says it's a three-hour hike. We should have a lot of time for pictures and be back here before the sun goes down," he said, following Emma to the head of the trail.

As they walked, Rodney would stop to take pictures, mostly of Emma by a large tree or Emma sitting on a big rock. When they got to the lake, Emma said, "I think it took us more time to get here than the sign says. I'm starving. Why don't we eat now?"

They found a sandy beach and set up the blanket Emma had brought. As they both sat eating their lunch, they heard some Canada Geese honking. A few minutes later, they saw the geese fly toward them in a perfect V-formation. Rodney took out his camera and quickly took pictures of the birds flying overhead. "I've never seen them so close," Rodney exclaimed as he put the camera down. "These are just perfect! They'll make for very lovely pictures."

When they finished eating, Emma packed up what was left from their picnic and Rodney went off to take more pictures. This place was very scenic, providing Rodney with many beautiful shots, making him lose his sense of time. It wasn't until Emma told him the time that he realized the afternoon had flew by. It was time to head back to the jeep.

The hike back was mostly uphill, making it more difficult. It took them more time than they had anticipated. When they got to the parking lot, the sun was setting. Emma was the first to notice the jeep was gone and said, "Rodney are you sure we are at the right place? Where is your jeep?"

It took a moment for Rodney to react. *How could the jeep be gone?* he thought, looking around to make sure they were where they had parked the jeep.

"No, we're in the right place," he said. With that, Emma became very frightened and cried, "We're going to die. Rodney we're miles from nowhere! There're wild animals here! They'll eat us up! We can't walk back to town. It's too far!"

Rodney quickly went to her, and as he held her, said, "Emma, we have to stay calm. Calm down!"

Emma looked at him and said, "What are we going to do?"

Still holding onto her, he said, "First, we'll see if we can find some type of shelter." He looked around and saw a dirt bank across the road that had been cut out when the road was put in.

"There!" He pointed to the bank. "That should cut the wind. Okay, before it gets too dark, we have to collect as much wood as we can. We have about an hour before it gets dark. Emma, do you think you can get wood?" Emma nodded so he let her go and they both went to gather some wood.

Once they had a pile of wood stacked up beside the bank, Rodney found some rocks and put them in a circle to make a fire pit. He saw Emma was shivering so he said, "Emma, why don't you get your blanket and wrap it around yourself. I'll start the fire." With the blanket around her shoulders, Emma watched Rodney start a fire. She found a rock, sat down on it, and waited for the fire to give off heat. Once the fire was well established, he went to join Emma.

"How are you doing? Still cold? Here, let's move you closer to the fire," he said as he helped her get closer to the warmth of the flames. They sat by the fire, cuddled together with the picnic blanket around them.

"Rodney, I think I'm more scared than cold. It's so dark. I can't even see one star up there," Emma said in a trembling voice.

Rodney brought her closer to him and said, "Yeah, it sure is dark. It must have clouded over. Emma, try to relax. We have a fire, we'll be okay."

"Oh, I hope it doesn't start to rain. That would be the worse. I'm so cold already," she said as she tried to get even closer to Rodney. They sat huddled together for a while. Emma stood up to put some more wood on the fire and as she turned to go sit by Rodney, she said, "Rodney I see a light." But when Rodney looked, there was no light. "My eyes must be playing tricks on me," Emma said as she cuddled back up close to Rodney. Although she questioned what she had seen, she kept looking in the direction she had seen the light.

A while later, as Rodney was putting wood on the fire, Emma stood up and with some hesitation, said, "Rodney, there's the light. Look! Look!" This time the light did not disappear but kept getting bigger. Emma could not contain herself. "We're saved Rodney, there's a car coming! We're not going to spend the night in the woods," she said, dancing around Rodney and giving him a hug. They watched as the lights came closer to them and then came to a stop in front of them.

"Thank you for stopping, man, you're a lifesaver," Rodney cried as he ran to the vehicle. He abruptly stopped when he got closer to the vehicle. Daniel recognized him and said to himself, "It's Rodney, the EMT."

He got out of the jeep just as Rodney came to a stop in front of him. "That's my jeep! Why did you go and take my jeep? I ought to knock your head off!" Rodney said angrily.

Daniel, not wanting to be hit, went to his knees and with his hands up, pleaded, "I'm so sorry, Rodney, I have an emergency. Please forgive me." Rodney was not listening. He did not want to hear any excuses from this thief.

"Do you know what you did? You stranded us here in the middle of nowhere," he continued.

Emma could not stand it any longer and said, "Rodney, listen, this guy knows you." But Rodney still did not listen. So, Emma continued, "I'm too cold to stand out here anymore, I'm getting in the jeep. Come on, let's go, Rodney."

This brought Rodney back to reality. "Get in the jeep, I'm driving you straight to the police," he said to Daniel, grabbing him by the shoulder.

As they were getting in the jeep, Daniel tried to protest. "Please, Rodney, we have to go get my wife. We can't leave her alone. Please, Rodney, drive me to my house."

"Now he wants a favor from me! All I'm doing for you, mister, is driving you to the police," Rodney said, still very angry.

Daniel became very desperate and said, "Please, drive to my house and get my wife. Please, Please."

Emma heard the anxiety in his voice and said, "Rodney, let's go get his wife. We can't strand anyone up here," She turned to Daniel and asked, "How far is your house from here?"

"It's about forty minutes up the road. Please, go get my wife," Daniel pleaded.

Rodney shook his head and in an angry voice said, "Okay, then I'm driving you to the cops."

No one said anything on the drive to the house except for Daniel who gave the directions. Once they got there, Daniel got out and ran to the door. He tried the door and found it locked, so he shouted, "Kit! Kit! It's me, open the door!"

A few seconds later, he saw a light go on in the house and the door opened. "Daniel, I'm so glad you're finally home!" Kit cried as she put her arms up to give him a hug. Before he could say anything, Kit let go of him and doubled over in pain.

"Kit, what's wrong?" Daniel asked.

Emma, not wanting to stay in the jeep with an angry Rodney, followed Daniel to the house. She saw the woman double over in pain and answered the question Daniel had asked. "Well, I think it's obvious. I think your wife is in labor." When Daniel heard that from behind him, he turned to see Emma.

As the pain subsided, Kit looked up and saw Emma. She asked, "Who is that lady, Danny? Why did you bring a lady here?"

"Kit, this is Emma. They brought me home," Daniel said, holding Kit close to him.

Emma came closer to them and asked, "How do you know my name? Who are you?"

Daniel gave her a big smile and said, "I'm Daniel Erickson and this is my wife Kit. You probably don't recognize me because of the beard." Emma was about to reply when Kit suddenly started to moan.

"Daniel, get Kit to lay down and I'll go get Rodney," Emma said as she turned to go back outside.

When she got to the jeep, Rodney was sitting there, still fuming. He said, "What's taking so long? We have a long drive back, you know."

"Well, Rodney, I don't think we will be going back to town tonight," Emma said in her softest voice.

This made Rodney even more furious. "And why not?" he shouted.

"Rodney, you have to calm down. Turns out that we know this guy. Remember Daniel Erickson? The cop who quit his job and went to live in the bush? That's him Rodney. And his wife is in labor."

When Emma told him that, she saw his demeanor change. "What a cheese head. Who would live here with a pregnant wife?" With a sigh and a shake of his head he said, "I'll get my medical bag."

As Emma returned to the house with Rodney, they heard Kit crying, "Danny, this is not supposed to be happening now. It's too soon for the baby to be born." When Kit saw Rodney come in carrying a medical bag, she asked Daniel, "Who is that? A doctor?"

Emma ran to her and said, "Kit, this is Rodney, he's an EMT and he can help you deliver your baby. Come, Kit, let's find you a place so you can lay down."

Daniel showed them to the bedroom and helped Emma put Kit to bed. Rodney followed them to the bedroom. When Kit was comfortable in bed, he said to her, "Kit, I'm not a doctor. I know you don't know me, but I promise you that I can take care of you and deliver your baby."

Kit looked at Daniel for assurance, so Daniel said, "Kit, listen to what he says. He's delivered babies before." With Daniel's acceptance of Rodney, Kit agreed to do what Rodney asked of her. More pain gripped her so Rodney waited for it to stop. Then he asked if he could check how she was doing and listen to the baby's heart. Kit nodded so Rodney proceeded with the examinations.

"Kit, everything looks really good. The baby's heart sounds very strong," Rodney said once he had done his examination.

Although Kit heard Rodney's reassurance, she was still very worried and said, "The baby is not due for another three weeks."

Rodney took her hand and said, "Babies can be unpredictable sometimes. I guess this one is in a rush to be born." He turned to Daniel and said, "Is there a way we could have more light in here?"

"Yes, I'll go start the generator. Kit, I'll be right back," Daniel said as he rushed out of the room. In a few minutes, the light in the room got brighter, and when Daniel returned, Rodney said, "That's much better. This place is off the grid, I take it?"

Daniel was not in any mood to discuss the workings of the house so he said, "Yes, we run on mostly solar. How is Kit doing?" Rodney gave him a smile, and told him that his wife was fine.

As the labor progressed, Daniel and Emma took turns holding Kit's hand and offering encouragement. The pains were becoming more intense and closer together in their intervals. Within an hour of Daniel's return, their little baby son was born. After Daniel cut the cord, the baby was placed in Kits arms. When Kit saw her son, she was overwhelmed by emotions and she said to Daniel, "Oh my, he is so small but he sure has a loud cry." As she looked him over to see if he had all his little fingers, she started to cry.

Daniel sat on the edge of the bed and gave a little laugh. "Kit, why are you crying?" He reached over and took a closer look at his boy, and said, "He's just perfect. He's beautiful, Kit, just like his mom."

He turned to Kit, gave her a kiss and said, "I love you, Kit." This brought more tears to her eyes.

"Daniel, I love you too. These are happy tears. I never thought I could be so happy!"

They sat together watching as Emma cleaned the baby and put a diaper on him from Rodney's medical bag. Then Emma said, "Daniel, why don't you take the baby while I clean Kit up?"

Daniel very gingerly took the baby from Emma, telling Kit he was going to the living room. As he sat down in his big chair, Rodney came to sit on the couch opposite him and said, "That sure is a beautiful boy you have there, Daniel."

Daniel was a little surprised by what Rodney said. "Thank you. I'm so grateful for what you did for us tonight," Daniel said looking down at the baby, and he continued to say, "There are no words I can express to say how sorry I am for taking your jeep. I hope you can forgive me."

Rodney gave him a smile and said, "Well, I'm sorry too. I have a very short temper and I let it get the best of me. Sometimes things happen that are out of our control." Rodney was silent for a while, then continued. "I forgive you. Come to think of it, I would probably do the same thing if I was in your situation."

Emma came to the living room to tell Daniel that Kit wanted to see him. When Daniel returned to the bedroom, Kit was sitting in bed wanting to hold the baby. He handed her the baby and he asked, "Is there anything I could get you?"

"Yes, Danny, I'm so thirsty. A glass of cold water would be so nice. And I'm a bit hungry. Maybe Rodney and Emma would like something to eat too," Kit replied, looking down at the baby.

"Yes, of course, why didn't I think of that? I'll take care of it right away." He leaned over and gave her a quick kiss. A short time later, Daniel returned with a slice of sourdough bread with a thick layer of raspberry jam on top, and a glass of cold water.

"Thank you so much, Danny," Kit said as she took the bread. Once she had finished eating, she said, "That was so good. Thank you, Danny."

Daniel gave her a smile and said, "I have a little surprise for you, Kit."

"What have you done now, Danny? What is it?" Kit inquired.

"Just wait a minute, I'll get it." Daniel went out of the room and quickly returned holding a baby cradle. "I made this for our baby. What do you think?" Kit gasped as she looked at the cradle Daniel was holding.

It looked like one of those old-fashioned cradles with a high, rounded headboard. The side boards and backboard were half the height of that of the headboard. The cradle was held up by two wooden rockers.

"Well, what do you think? I made it out of those boards that were in the odds and ends shed. Took a while to get the rockers the same, but I think it rocks okay now. I sanded the boards and painted them white. See, I even tried to paint in some flowers on it," he said as he pointed to the yellow bits of paint on the headboard.

Kit was so surprised. "Daniel it's just beautiful. When did you find the time to do this?"

"I worked on it when I had time. What do you think? Should we have the baby sleep in it?" Daniel asked. Kit loved having the baby by her side but let Daniel lay the baby in the cradle. He folded up a towel and placed it at the bottom of the cradle. Then he picked up the baby and carefully placed him in the cradle. Daniel made sure the baby was well covered up so he would keep warm. He returned to Kit and said, "I think you should get some sleep now. Good 'night, my sweet wife." He gave her a kiss. "You did so very well today. The baby is perfect."

When he returned to the kitchen, Rodney and Emma were sitting at the table finishing the snack Daniel had offered them. They looked like they could use a good night's sleep also. "Kit is going to sleep. You two must be exhausted too. There're two beds you can have. One in the loft and one is the couch; turns into a bed," Daniel offered.

"I think we'll take the bed in the loft. If that is okay with you, Emma?" Rodney replied.

"That is just fine. I'm so tired I could sleep on the floor," Emma said. Daniel showed them the bathroom facilities and brought them up to the loft. After saying goodnight to them, he returned downstairs to join Kit and went to sleep.

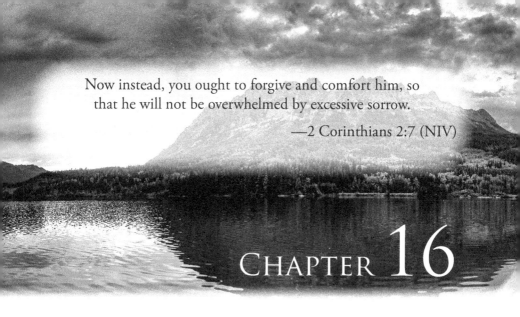

Now instead, you ought to forgive and comfort him, so
that he will not be overwhelmed by excessive sorrow.

—2 Corinthians 2:7 (NIV)

CHAPTER 16

I t was dark when Daniel was awakened by a strange sound. It took him a few seconds to realize that the sound was that of a baby crying. Kit was sitting up in bed searching for the lamp.

"Kit, it's okay, I'll get him." He switched on the headlight he kept by his pillow and went to pick up his little son. "There, there, little one, what is the matter?" He brought the baby up to his face, pretending to listen to what the baby was saying, and said, "You want your mommy? Of course, you're just little. I think mommy wants you too." He placed the baby in Kit's arms saying, "Here mommy, this little guy might be hungry." Once he had handed the baby to Kit he turned on the lamp.

"Ah, about that Danny, I'm a little apprehensive about nursing the baby. I have never been around a little one before. What if I can't nurse him?"

Daniel gave her a smile and said, "Kit, just try it. Relax and let nature take over." She held the baby to her breast, and just like that, the baby latched on and started to nurse.

"Look at that! He must be hungry. You're a natural, Kit. I'll go rustle up the fire and warm up the house. I'll be right back." When he returned, he saw that the baby was not nursing, so he asked, "Is something wrong? He did not nurse very long?"

Kit looked at the baby, rubbed his little head and said, "He fell asleep and stopped nursing. I guess he's more tired than hungry. Can you take him? I think I'll get up. It's a little cold in here, I don't want the baby to get cold." With a little kiss on his cheek, she handed the baby to Daniel.

"Okay, it's warmer in the living room," Daniel said as he took the baby and went to sit on the couch. A few minutes later, Kit joined them on the couch. Daniel handed her the baby, took a blanket and wrapped them both up snugly. "Coffee is just about ready, would you like a cup?"

"That would be very nice, Danny, thank you," Kit replied. As they sat having their coffee, Daniel told her how Rodney and Emma happened to bring him home. Kit was shocked by the story and said, "Daniel, all of that is my fault. I should have listened to you when you said we should move to town earlier this summer. I caused two wonderful people pain. Daniel, I'm so sorry. How am I going to repay them for all their kindness?" Big tears rolled down her face.

Daniel brought her close and said, "Kit, it's not anyone's fault. You didn't break the truck. Now relax, don't get so emotional. Everything turned out right, didn't it?"

Daniel wiped her tears and said, "We have to give this little guy a name, Kit. Is there a name you prefer?"

Kit looked down at her baby. She took his little hand and played with his little fingers. She looked up at Daniel and said, "Daniel, what if we name him Rodney? Would that be alright with you?"

Daniel gave her a big hug and said, "That is what I was thinking, Kit. Rodney will be his name."

"Did I hear my name?" came a voice from behind them. They both turned toward the stairs and saw Rodney coming down. "I slept so hard. How is the little tyke doing this morning?" He came to sit on the big chair opposite the couch.

"He's doing very well. He sleeps a lot. Rodney, I want to thank you from the bottom of my heart for all you did for us yesterday. Daniel told me what he did and how you got to come here. Don't blame Daniel for taking your jeep because it's all my fault," Kit said. "I'm so sorry for what happened. If I would have listened to Daniel, it would have never happened."

"Kit, don't worry about it. Daniel and I have already settled that," Rodney said. Emma joined them as he finished speaking.

"There's some coffee on the stove. Would you like a cup?" Daniel asked. Both said yes, so Daniel got up and went to get them some coffee. When Daniel returned with the coffee, Rodney and Emma were sitting by Kit on the couch.

Kit gave Daniel a smile and said to him, "Do you want to tell Rodney?"

Everyone looked at Daniel so he sat down and said, "Rodney, we decided to name the baby after you. We're so thankful for all you did. I'm so sorry for putting you through all the trouble."

"Yes, both the baby and I thank you," Kit added.

This surprised Rodney and he asked Kit if he could hold the baby. He brought the baby close and said, "Hi, there, little Rodney. It's a big name for such a little boy but my guess is you'll grow into it." As he handed the baby back to Kit, he said, "I have never had anyone name their baby after me before. Little Rodney will always be special to me."

It was then that he noticed Kit's disfigured face. The look in his face changed. Kit saw the change and out of habit tried to cover her face with her hair.

"Kit, please forgive me for staring, may I ask what happened to your face?" Throughout all this, Emma kept looking at Kit.

"Rodney, don't be sorry. I've gotten a lot of stares in my life. It doesn't bother me so much anymore. I was in a bad housefire." She turned to Daniel and said, "Daniel I think it's time we started breakfast."

"Yes, mommy, I'll get on it right away," Daniel replied. Rodney followed Daniel to the kitchen leaving Kit and Emma sitting on the couch, caring for the baby.

As they ate the sourdough pancakes and fresh eggs Daniel had made, Daniel told Rodney and Emma about the events of yesterday's morning. How they intended to move back to town and when his truck did not start, how he set off on his bike to make a phone call. He told them about the missing phone and how he got to be at the rest stop.

"When I saw that jeep, I thought it was the only way I had to get to a place with a phone signal. I'm so sorry I did that," he said and ended by saying, "I finally got a phone signal just at the edge of town. I called my cousin Charlie and asked him to bring a new starter. He should be here this afternoon." He looked at Rodney and Emma and added, "I didn't think I'd be gone that long. I thought I would be back before it got dark. I'm sorry for stranding you and Emma."

"I forgave you the minute you came to a stop," Emma replied. "It's like someone orchestrated all this."

"Someone sure did a good job of it too!" Daniel agreed.

Once breakfast was over, Rodney stood up from the table and said, "Daniel, will you give me a look around your place? I'd like to take a few pictures. Would you mind?"

Daniel agreed to show Rodney the place, so they went outside leaving Kit and Emma with the clean up duties. Kit placed the baby in his little cradle and went to help Emma with the dishes. As they worked, Emma said, "When I was young, I had a good friend named Kitty. She used to be the best skipper in our school."

When Kit heard this, she dropped the plate she was drying and gasped. She put both hands over her face. Afraid if she said a word that Emma would disappear, she slowly said, "I used to like to skip, and I used to have a friend named Emma. Are you my Emma?" She took a closer looked at Emma. Recognizing it was her, she exclaimed, "Oh my, you are her!"

"Yes, Kitty. Last night, when I first saw you and when I heard your voice, I knew it was you. I never thought I'd see you again. Oh, my Kit!" she said as she looked at Kit who was shaking and had big tears rolling down her face. They hugged each other and both started to cry uncontrollably.

At the same time, the guys came back in the house and became alarmed when they heard both women and a baby crying. Daniel ran to see to Kit and Emma, while Rodney ran to pick up the baby. "What is the matter? What happened? Kit, are you alright?" Daniel asked.

"Danny, all is fine, we're crying happy tears. I just found my best friend. Emma is my childhood friend I told you about," Kit said, wiping the tears from her face.

Emma wiped her tears and said, "The last time I saw Kit was the day before we were to start grade three. When she wasn't at school, I went to her house and her dad told me she had gone to live with her Aunt and not to bother him again." She looked at Kit. "Kit what happened to you?" When Emma saw the horrified look on Kit's face, she said, "Kit, why are you looking at me like that? What happened to you?"

Kit got the baby from Rodney and went to sit on the couch. Daniel joined her, putting an arm around her shoulder. He knew how much she hated to remember her past. After a short while, Kit said, "Emma, I'll tell you. When I told my story to Danny, I thought I'd never have to tell anyone else. I have always thought of you as my very close friend, so I'll tell you. I'll start with the last time we saw each other." Kit went on to tell her all of what had happened to her and ended with how she came to live with Daniel. Rodney and Emma were both in tears when she ended her story.

"Kit, that is so awful! I'm so sorry to hear that happened to you. When your dad told me you had gone to live with your aunt, I believed him. He even offered to show me your room, but I was too scared to be alone in the house with him. I should have asked him for your new address. He was a very scary man. I never went back to your house. I'm so sorry. I should have gone back," Emma said.

Kit gave her a smile. "Emma, you did not know, you were just a little girl. There was nothing you could have done. You were with me in my dreams, playing with our dolls." She paused, looked at her baby boy, and said, "It's in the past and I don't live in the past. I live in the present now, for my husband and our little boy." Emma reached over and they hugged for a long time.

"Kit, I never stopped thinking of you. I have missed you. Every time I walked by your house when I went to school, I felt so sad. My best friend was gone and I had never said goodbye to her. We were like sisters. You will always be my best friend," Emma said as she held Kit.

"Yes, we were sisters. I have missed you too. There is so much we missed, but now we have found each other. Let's make sure we make the best of our time together," Kit replied, holding onto Emma.

Emma saw that Rodney was looking at them and said, "Rodney I know you want to get back to town. But we just found each other, I can't leave now. Can we stay? Would it be alright?"

"Oh! No. You can't go. I won't let you. Please stay." Kit pleaded.

"Of course, we'll stay. Besides I want to take more pictures of this place. We're not in any rush," Rodney replied.

Later that afternoon, Charlie came driving up the driveway. Daniel and Rodney were outside. Daniel greeted him with a warm handshake and a manly hug. "Hey there, Daniel, I see you have company," Charlie said, looking at Rodney. Daniel introduced Rodney then asked if he had the part to fix the truck.

"Sure do. It shouldn't take too long to get it fixed," Charlie said reaching in his truck to get the part. They walked to the garage, and when Daniel opened the garage doors, both Charlie and Rodney's mouths dropped when they saw the damage on the hood of Daniel's truck.

"What in the world happened to your truck?" Charlie asked.

"Looks like something big stepped on it," Rodney added.

Daniel gave them a big smile. "Yeah, something did step on it. This grizzly bear took his anger out on it, but I got the best of that bear."

"What did you do, Daniel?" Charlie asked.

Daniel did not want to get into the story, so he said, "I'll tell you another time. Right now, I just want to fix the truck. Let's push it out of the garage so we can have more light." Once the truck was out of the garage, Daniel raised the hood and began taking the old starter out. With Charlie and Rodney's help, the new starter was put in place in no time. Daniel went in the truck to start it. He was so relieved when he heard it fire up.

As Daniel was putting away the tools, Charlie asked Rodney, "Have you been friends with Daniel for long? What brings you here?" Charlie was a little puzzled why Daniel had called him to bring him the starter, when he could have gotten a ride to town with Rodney.

"No, were not good friends, but we've known each other for a while. I think I'll let Daniel tell you how I got here," Rodney replied.

Charlie was now very curious and said, "Daniel, what's going on? Is there something you're not telling me? Rodney makes it sound very mysterious."

"Charlie, let's go in the house. Kit will want to see you," Daniel said, giving him the biggest smile.

This made Charlie wonder even more, so he said, "Daniel stop being so secretive and tell me."

"Just wait, you'll see," Daniel replied as they all walked up the deck.

When they entered the house, the two women were sitting on the couch. "Hey, Kit look who's here," Daniel said.

Kit turned to see Charlie walking in, and as she got up to meet him, she said, "Charlie, it's so nice to see you."

When Charlie saw she was carrying a baby, he said in shock, "You had the baby!"

"Charlie, our son was born last night, or I should say, early this morning," Daniel said, beaming with pride.

"Congratulations! Why didn't you say anything, Daniel? May I hold him?" Kit handed him the baby and when Charlie had a closer look at him, he said, "He looks just like you, Daniel."

Daniel gave him a sheepish look and said, "I'm sorry, I should have told you before, but I knew if I told you, the truck would never get fixed."

"Daniel, sometimes I could just…"

But before he could finish his sentence, Kit said, "Charlie, I'd like you to meet my good friend Emma. She and Rodney helped with the delivery."

Charlie handed the baby back to Kit and greeted Emma. Once the introductions were done, Daniel said, "Charlie, come and sit. Let's have coffee and I'll tell you what happened."

Daniel went to get coffee for everyone. They all sat at the kitchen table and recounted the previous night's happenings to Charlie. Charlie sat in disbelief. The story sounded like someone had taken the pains to organize it.

"Carol would say it's supernatural. There were too many things that fell into place for it to be just a coincidence. Someone was certainly taking care of the two of you," Charlie said, finishing off his coffee.

"Charlie, I think we all agree with that," Daniel said. He looked at the time and said, "This day calls for a celebration. If we are going to have something to eat, I have to get things going."

Kit knew what Daniel meant and did not want to be around, so she asked, "Daniel, would it be okay if I go lie down?"

"Of course, Kit, you go have a nap. We'll take care of the baby." He took the baby from her and gave her a kiss.

"Okay, what are you planning to do?" Charlie asked. Daniel headed outside so Charlie, and Rodney followed, leaving Emma with a sleeping baby.

A short time later, she heard the guys at the backdoor and went to see what they were doing. She gasped as she saw Daniel and Charlie each plucking the feathers off the chickens.

"What have you done?" she cried. Daniel looked at her and said, "These are going to be for our supper. Is Kit still asleep?" When Emma nodded, he continued saying, "Good. She never liked it when I slaughtered a chicken. It's good that she's still sleeping. I'm sorry if this bothers you."

Although it did bother her that the chickens were dead, she was curious about what Daniel would do to prepare the chicken for dinner. Being a city girl, she had never thought much about how food was processed. Daniel was a little astonished when she asked, "Is there anything I can do to help?"

"You want to help? For real?" Daniel inquired. "There is one job I just hate doing—gutting the chicken. Do you want to do that?" Daniel asked, a little apprehensive.

"Oh, I think I could do that. I used to work in a lab, we dissected all kinds of things. This could be interesting," Emma said, surprising the three guys. "Rodney, would you keep an eye on the baby so I can help Daniel?" Rodney agreed to care for the baby so Emma could join Daniel outside.

When it came time to gut the chickens, Daniel instructed Emma how to go about it. Daniel watched her take the entrails out of the chicken and inspect them like she was some type of forensic scientist.

"You really don't mind doing this, do you?" Daniel asked her.

She looked at Daniel and replied, "Well, the internal working of a body has always interested me. Do you think that's strange?"

"Oh, don't ask me. There're a lot of things I like to do that people think are a little strange. Tell me, if you like lab work so much, why are you in nursing?" Daniel asked.

"It was hard getting full time work in the lab so I went into nursing. Besides, it pays much more," Emma said as she finished cleaning the second chicken.

When Kit got up from her nap, the scent of roasting chicken filled the house. She found Daniel and their guests sitting at the kitchen table. Daniel was the first to see her. "Hey, honey, you're up. Had a nice nap?" he asked as he got up to pull a chair for Kit to sit.

"Yes, I can't believe I slept for so long. How is the baby?" she asked, looking at Emma who was holding him.

"He's starting to fuss a bit. He might want his mommy," Emma replied with a smile. Kit went to get the baby and invited Emma to join her on the couch. As Emma watched Kit nurse the baby she said, "Kit, you're a natural at this."

Kit gave her a smile and said, "Emma, I still can't believe that this is really happening. It's like a wonderful dream."

"Yes, I feel like that too. I'm so sorry for what happened to you. If only I had been braver," Emma replied.

Kit put her hand on Emma's and said, "Emma, it was not your fault. You are not the one to blame."

"Yes, but there were some red flags. We moved away at the end of the school year, and I wrote you a letter telling you where we had moved to. I even put the letter in your mailbox. I should have known there was something wrong when you did not reply to it. We were very close friends and I never understood why you never replied."

Kit shook her head and said, "Oh, Emma, I never got any letters. You were so young, it was not your fault. I don't want you to feel guilty about this. You could not have known. Please, Emma, let's talk about something else. Tell me about yourself."

"Well, Kit, there is not much to tell. My family moved to Toronto. I did not like it there, it's so big. So, after I graduated from nursing school, I learned that there was a position at the hospital here. I moved back west just six months ago. I work as an emergency nurse."

"Is that where you met Rodney?" Kit asked.

Emma gave her a smile and said, "Yes, but we have just started to date. I don't know if we are that compatible though. He likes the great outdoors. I'm more of the city type."

"But you like him, don't you?" Kit, the romantic asked.

Just as Emma was going to reply, Daniel approached the couch and asked, "What are you two whispering about?"

"Oh, we're just talking," Kit replied, giving him a mysterious smile.

"Well, supper is ready. Would you two ladies please join us at the table?" he said, helping Kit up to her feet. He took the baby and placed him in the little cradle. When Emma got to the table, she was surprised by the amount of food on it. Beside the heaping platter of chicken and dressing, there was a big bowl of mashed potatoes, peas and carrots, squash, sliced bread, pickled beets and butter.

"This looks so delicious," she said. "You even have butter. Where did the butter come from?"

Kit smiled and said, "I churned it yesterday when I was waiting for Daniel. Most of the food you see on the table was grown here. Come, sit. Let's eat."

Emma could not believe what Kit had just told her. "You made the butter? But how?" Kit laughed and went on to explain how the butter was made. When Kit had finished explaining, Emma said, "I have always lived in a big city. My food comes from the supermarket, ready to eat. It's a lot more convenient. I don't think I would like to live like this all the time. It's like living in the past."

"Yes, it is, but we like it," Daniel replied.

When Kit agreed with Daniel, Emma responded, "Well, I guess it's what you get used to. I've never experienced living like this before. I'm not much of an outdoors person."

When they had finished eating the main course, Daniel said, "Is everyone ready for dessert?" He went to the stove, and when he returned to the table, he said, "We have apple crisp from apples grown here." He placed the pan on the table and said, "Just wait, I'll get the topping for it."

He returned with a jar. "This is yoghurt, sweetened by wild honey. Any takers?" Everyone were more then willing to have dessert.

As they ate their dessert, Charlie asked, "Where and how did you get wild honey?" Daniel explained how Zeb had showed him where and how to get the honey, and how he had to get it before the bear did.

"Speaking of bears, you never told us how your truck was damaged," Charlie said.

"That's a day I would like to forget," Kit replied, looking at Daniel.

"Yes, it was one frightening day. One I hope to never experience again."

"What happened?" Emma asked, a little uneasy.

Daniel told them the story, and when he finished, he noticed that Emma's face was very pale. "Emma, are you okay?"

"What's the matter, Emma, are you feeling sick?" Rodney asked, very concerned.

"I'm okay, Rodney. It's just that I suddenly realized that we were in the woods all of yesterday. We could have been attacked and eaten up by some wild animal, and no one would have known what happened to us," Emma said in a shaky voice.

Rodney could not help but laugh. He said, "Emma, most animals would rather run away than to come near a human. It's very unusual for a bear to attack like that. Come on, relax. All worked out didn't it?" Emma nodded, but was still very worried about being in the wilderness.

"Yeah, Rodney is right. Daniel and I have gone on many walks, and every time we saw an animal, it would run away from us. Some were curious and would come to see what we were about, but they ran away once they knew," Kit said, trying to reassure Emma.

"Kit, I know what you are telling me, but I heard about others who were not so lucky," Emma said.

"Well, Emma, you don't stop driving a car because someone had an accident. So, you should not stop enjoying hiking in the bush just because you heard of something bad happening to someone else," Rodney added.

Emma did not reply for a while. Then she said, "Rodney, you're right. I'm going to have to get used to it. I like it here, the beauty and the freshness are lovely."

Later that evening, as Kit nursed her little son, she recalled all the happy memories of the past years. When Daniel came into the room, she said, "Danny, I was just thinking about when you brought me here. I was just like a little girl. I knew nothing. Even though you did not want me to stay here, you let me. You were so kind and generous to me. You know, not many people would do what you did for me. Thank you, Daniel."

Daniel came to sit by her and replied, "Kit, I should thank you too. You added all that is worthwhile in my life. I must tell you a little secret, Kit."

"What secret, Danny?" Kit asked, a little curious. Daniel smiled and said, "Well, Kit, I must confess that I was pleased when you insisted on staying here when you first came. I somehow knew you belonged here."

Kit was very surprised by Daniel's confession and said, "Really, you thought that? But I did insist I was not going back. And here we are now."

"Yes, here we are. Who would have known we would find love here of all places?" Daniel said.

"Danny, I will miss this place. It's the place I grew up in. I wish we did not have to move to town but the baby must come first. I want him to grow up having many friends and to learn all that there is to know," Kit said.

"I do agree." Daniel gave her a kiss on the cheek and said, "Yes, now that we have the baby, we have to put him first. There'll be a lot of time to come here when he's older. I think he'll love it here. After all, it is the place where he was born. We'll come back next spring and plant the garden. We'll still have good times here, you'll see."

"Yes, I know. It won't be the same, but we'll make many new happy memories," Kit agreed. "We better get some sleep. Tomorrow will be a big day," Daniel said as he cozied up to his wife.

Restore us to yourself, Lord, that we may
return; renew our days as of old.

—Lamentations 5:21(NIV)

CHAPTER 17

I n the morning, Daniel was awakened by the baby crying. Kit
was sitting on the bed, changing the baby.

"What time is it, Kit?" he asked.

"It's just about seven. It's a good thing we're going back to town
today. I only have one more diaper left. I'm sorry he woke you. I was
trying to change him without making him cry," Kit said.

"It's alright. I should get up. There's lots to do before we can
leave," Daniel said as he got out of bed.

Kit wrapped up the baby in a towel and said, "Poor little guy
doesn't have any clothes." She brought him up to her face and gave
him a kiss. "We'll get you some as soon as we get to town. Now you
can cuddle with mama 'til your daddy gets the house warmed up."

She lay down and as Daniel covered her and the baby up, he
said with a big smile, "Yes, it's not very warm in here. Get some rest,
honey."

When he got to the kitchen, Charlie had already started the
stove and the coffee was just starting to percolate. "You're up early.
Did the baby wake you?" Daniel asked when he saw Charlie.

"No, I was up before he cried. I want to get home before it get's
dark. Daniel, tell me what you want done and I'll get it done."

"I think the first thing will be to milk the cow and feed the chickens. Once that's done, we can have breakfast and start loading up the stuff. Does that sound like a plan?" Daniel said. He went to the stove to see if it needed more wood. After putting in more wood, they both went outside to tend to the animals. A short time later they were back with a pail of milk and some eggs.

"This will be along day; if I make a big breakfast, it will take us through the day. How about we start with some porridge then we can have pancakes and eggs. What do you say Charlie?"

"Sounds great, let's get started," Charlie said as he went to get more wood for the stove.

The porridge was ready when Rodney and Emma emerged from upstairs. "It sure smells good, what's for breakfast?" Rodney asked. When they were offered some porridge, they both hungrily accepted it.

As they ate Emma asked, "Is Kit up yet?"

"She was up earlier but I told her to get some rest. I'm sure the baby will wake her up soon. We also have pancakes and eggs, by the way." Rodney accepted Daniel's offer of pancakes and eggs but Emma took only an egg.

Everyone was finishing their coffee when Kit got up. "Why didn't you wake me? I did not want anyone to wait for me," she scolded Daniel.

"You needed your rest, Kit. I know you were up half of the night with the baby. Now do you want to start with porridge or pancakes?" Daniel asked, giving her a big smile.

But Kit did not return the smile. She was a little annoyed with him for not waking her up. "Danny, here, take the baby. I'll fix myself some breakfast." She handed the baby over to Daniel and went to get herself some pancakes and the last of the eggs. She went to sit by Emma.

"How are you feeling today, Kit? You sound a little down," Emma said.

"I'm feeling okay, I guess. Just sad to be leaving my home," Kit replied.

"You might be experiencing some mother's blues, Kit. Having a baby is a big life-changing event. Top it off with moving and that can be very traumatic. Try to relax. Rodney and I will stay 'til you are ready to leave," Emma assured her.

"Oh, thank you, Emma, that is so nice, but you don't have to do that. You've been here a whole day already because of me. I don't want to take more of your time."

"Kit, we just found each other and I want to help. Rodney and I don't have to be back at work 'til tomorrow. And besides, I think Rodney really likes this place. I heard him ask Daniel if he could come spend some time here."

Kit gave her a smile. She loved it that someone cared about her. She realized Daniel cared for her too and she had treated him badly. As she finished eating, she looked at Daniel holding their son. "Danny I'm sorry for being so grumpy. You have been nothing but loving and kind to me. I should have been nicer."

"Kit, there's nothing to be sorry for. We all love you. All new mothers get emotional." Daniel got up and gently laid the baby in the cradle, and started to clear the table.

"Danny, I'll do that. You go load up. Emma and I can clean this up," Kit said. "I'm sure our guests want to get going."

"Are you sure you feel up to it?" When Kit nodded, he said, "Okay, I'll leave the clean-up to you two ladies." He gave Kit a kiss and left to join the other men outside.

Kit helped Emma clear the table and was just about set to wash the dishes when the baby started to fuss.

"Go get your baby," Emma said, "I've got this."

As soon as Kit picked him up, the baby calmed down and went back to sleep. She placed him back in the cradle, but two minutes later, he was crying again. After a few times of doing this, Emma showed Kit how to make a shoulder sling so Kit could carry the baby while she worked. "I think he knows there's something strange happening and he can probably feel that your upset," Emma said.

By early afternoon they were ready to set off. The animals were loaded in the trailer Charlie had brought. Daniel's truck was full of boxes and containers. The house was cleaned and winterized, the water tanks emptied, and the windows were covered by the shutters Daniel had built. Everything was ready except for locking up the house.

"You make sure you call me the minute you get settled. Don't lose my number," Emma said to Kit as they hugged. "Now that we have found each other, you'll see a lot of me."

"Yes, we will, Emma, thank you so much for all the help. I don't know if I want to let you go. You might disappear again," Kit said, holding onto her.

At the same time, Daniel and Rodney were also saying goodbye. "Remember what I told you. You can come up here any time you want. Just let me know when you want to come," Daniel said.

"I remember. I'll keep in touch," Rodney said as he shook hands with Daniel then went to say goodbye to Kit.

"Kit, take care of yourself and that little boy," he said, giving her a hug. "I'll be coming to visit you and little Rodney. Bye for now."

"Thank you, Rodney, for all you have done. You have been so kind. You will always be special to both of us," Kit replied.

Once Rodney and Emma had left, Daniel said to Charlie, "I think everything is ready. I'll go lock the house, then we can be off." After helping Kit and the baby onto the truck, Daniel got in and followed Charlie down the drive. As they drove away, Kit looked back to see the last of the house.

"Bye, house, see you next spring!" she said, as big tears rolled down her cheek.

When Daniel saw the tears, he said, "Kit, we'll be back. It'll be okay to live in town." Daniel stopped at the gate to lock it and placed a Keep Out, Private Property sign on it.

They drove in silence for a while. Little Rodney lay asleep on the seat between the two of them.

"Looks like he likes truck rides. When we were cleaning the house, he would not let me put him down. It was like he did not want us to move away," Kit said.

"He can probably feel that you're unhappy. We'll all be back. No one else can say that they were born here. He's part of this place. He's our little bush baby," Daniel said fondly.

210

As they drove, Kit paid special attention to the scenic beauty of the mountains and the lake. She would miss living here but knew they had to move because of the baby. The thought of the night the baby was born came to mind, and she remembered what Charlie had said, that it was "supernatural."

"Danny, do you think there is such a thing as supernatural?" she asked.

"What do you mean? Are you asking if I think there is a God?" Daniel replied.

"Yeah, I guess so. When I was little, my mom brought me to Sunday school. They taught me that God made everything and that He cared for us. When I was locked up, I use to ask God to help. One night, I had this dream. It was so real. I was in what I thought were my mother's arms and she spoke to me. She promised me that I would have my family back one day. Then she promised me that I would also have my special friend back too. But when the fire happened, I knew it had only been a dream and that God did not care. I stopped believing in God and in dreams. Danny what do you believe?"

"Well, I went to church and Sunday school too, but stopped going when my mother died. I did not understand why my mother had to die. I just stopped believing in God. But now, after what happened on the day Rodney was born, I'm not so sure. I'm sure there had to be a divine hand in it," Daniel said.

"Yes, and the promises have come true. I have my family and I have my special friend, Emma, back. I now know that promise was from God. He never stopped caring for us even when we stopped believing in Him," Kit replied.

Daniel gave her a smile and said, "When I first came up here I was so depressed. Everything was dark. In my work, all I saw was ugliness, conflicts, and selfishness. There wasn't a day that went by without seeing that, so I moved up here. This place healed me. I found peace and patience. Every morning, when I saw those mountains, I was thankful for another day. But it was a hard way to live. I had to have self-control and faith in the work I had to do to survive. Living here brought me you, my love. Kit, you brought joy and goodness in my life. Because of you, I learned kindness and gentleness. I always thought I was doing it all on my own but I think God was with me all along."

"Daniel, thanks for saying those kind words. I think we should learn more about God. Do you know of anyone who could teach us?" Kit asked.

"I think Barry and his wife go to church. I'll ask him the next time we see him," Daniel replied. With that said, Kit sat back and closed her eyes. Daniel was left with his thoughts. He was so thankful for the care they had received the night his son was born and as he reflected on it, he felt an embrace of peace surround him. He now understood that he had never been all alone. God had given him the strength and the wisdom to live in this remote place. He always thought that he did not need anyone, that he was his own man and was self-sufficient, but that wasn't the case. He had relied on Charlie when it came to food and to care for his place when he had to be away. He now appreciated the fact that what he did mattered to others. He was part of a wonderful group of people that cared for him and loved him. It was now time for him to show that he too cared and loved them in return.

From the first time he came to live in his mountain home, he had felt a hand guiding him. Now he knew that it was the hand of God. He thanked God for all the many blessings he had received.

ABOUT THE AUTHOR

Cecile Czobitko lives with her husband and their two dogs—Duke, the Jack Russel and Zeva, the black German shepherd. They have lived in Jasper Alberta in the beautiful Jasper National Park for forty years. They have three grown children and six grandchildren. After working as a banker for twenty-five years, she retired and now works as a casual librarian. She passes her leisure time reading and with her new endeavor in writing books. This is her first time publishing one of her books.